WEAVING WATER

Other books by the author:
A Silent Life
Death in the Family

WEAVING WATER

RYHAAN SHAH

Cutting
Edge
Press

A Cutting Edge Press Paperback Original

Published in 2013 by Cutting Edge Press

www.cuttingedgepress.co.uk

Copyright © Ryhaan Shah

Ryhaan Shah has asserted her moral right to be identified as the author of this work under the terms of the 1988 Copyright Design and Patents Act.

This book is sold subject to the conditions that it shall not, by way of trade or otherwise, be lent, resold, hired out or otherwise circulated without the publisher's prior consent in any form of binding or cover other than that in which it is published, and without a similar condition, including this condition, being imposed on the subsequent purchaser.

The characters appearing in this book are fictitious, any resemblance to real persons, living or dead, is purely coincidental.

All rights reserved
Printed and bound in Great Britain by CPI Group (UK) Ltd, Croydon, CR0 4YY

PB ISBN: 978-1-908122-38-4
E-PUB ISBN: 978-1-908122-45-2

All rights are reserved to the author and publishers.
Reproduction in any form currently known or yet to be invented, or the use of any extract is only permitted with the written approval of the publishers.

For my daughters
as magical a tale as has ever been told

'....myths are always true. By their very nature, myths inhere both legitimacy and credibility.'
REZA ASLAN, *NO GOD BUT GOD*

PART ONE
RAMPAT

A leap into the unknown is a leap into water.
GASTON BACHELARD, *WATER AND DREAMS*

Waiting for Neela • Falling in Love • Crossing the Kala Pani
A Home in the New World • Cutting Cane • Meeting Billa
Rampat's Secret • Georgetown • Settling In
Billa and Sampson Fight • The First Rage* Reverend Davies
Sampson • Politics • Neela Returns

RAMPAT EASED HIS EYES into the darkness outside. The full moon had brought pitching rain and it now slipped in and out of clouds that threatened more. He moved through the crisp night air and out the back gate that led to the canal where the water was big and full, and brimming nearly to the top of the dam. It would be after midnight judging from where the moon hung. It was her usual time: when the night was shut tight, when the stillness was solid and only the moon was a witness. The whisper of her feet over the floorboards had broken through his sleep and woken him, and at the water's edge he looked for the familiar figure, the figure that would be crouched on the bank of the canal, crouched with her feet in the water, stirring the black wetness of it before slipping in; or maybe she was already in. If she were, he would pick up the soft ripples by the light of the watery moon. They would mark her smooth progress, the moonlit pleats of water that would curl away and disappear moments after she swam past. He always marvelled at her easy grace, would even feel the proud father as he stood on the bank, stood near enough to a tree or a bush to mask his presence. He did not question any more for what was there to question? He might as well ask: why the moon, the grass, the sun, anything at all, and he was not a man who worried his head about things he could not understand.

He shifted his eyes from the shiny blackness of the water to the neat lines of the sideline dams but he could see, could see clearly that there was no movement other than the sluggish drag of the silted canal that was moving to empty itself into the sea a mile and more away. She was already in, had already gone, and he found himself a grassy patch under a spreading tree and settled down to wait.

The water was more sweet than brackish there by his house and the children liked to jump in and play in it almost every day but, even when she was very small, she always stood on the top of the dam and watched them, would watch them and shake her head when they called her in. She would shake her head and her hair would swing from side to side down her back, would swing and sway like tall grass in a wind, and she always waited for the sky to darken and the water to lay still before she slipped into it, alone. Rampat sighed and shook his head. Perhaps, it was all of that that helped to start the talk about her, her standing apart and aloof like that and just watching everything that went on around her. In their little village where lives mixed and mingled freely with comings and goings, where conversations were picked up on a breeze and carried to every open door and window, her separate, still figure was an invitation to the whispering talk that was held in by cupped hands and poured from ear to ear. But he knew what they said, and even the children who used to laugh and play with her when she was very small, even they grew up to be suspicious, even afraid, and Rampat shook his head again and made a promise to himself that he would always be there to keep her safe, that he would never allow anyone, anyone at all to ever lay a hand on her.

His eyes skimmed the water again looking for any rippling movement, any movement that would show that she was moving through it, gliding through it. He knew that he had to look closely, to look carefully for she never made any sound, no splashing or thrashing sound, and would leave the water behind her barely disturbed. But no matter how closely he looked, Rampat could see nothing but the smoothness of the water for the canal slept with the rest of the night and only the mirrored moon sailed over it. As he faced the moon, he told himself that on this very night he was going to stay right there and watch her come out of the water. He was not going to run back to the house and pretend sleep. He thought that she might see him and choose to ignore him, look around him, or even act as if it was nothing extraordinary at all, or she might joke and make light of it. Or, she might say something to him, something explaining for he always believed that she felt the air stir with even his slightest movement, felt it like a high wind, and that she always knew just where he hid even though he was crouched low in his own shadow. His heart became tight, became fearful at the thought of all that she might say to him, all that she might say to make him understand, but he knew that whatever it was that he was ready.

It was years before when he first heard her feet stealing away into the night, heard them whispering across the rough floorboards of their plantation hut. She was barely running around on her baby legs when the tiny noise woke him, and he looked and saw at once that her cot was empty. Without waking Parvati, he followed her, followed her white nightgown which danced before him in the dark. He hurried after her, his bare feet scrabbling over the dry earth of the narrow lane that led from the plantation's bound yard, from the huddle of poor huts and barracks built for the indentured labourers like himself and Parvati, led from the bound yard to the sideline dam and the canal. He hurried, thinking to save her from falling in, from falling into the canal, and he was about to call out to her, Neela, Neela, when he stopped, and his mouth closed silently over her name for she was standing at the water's edge, was standing very still, and was looking into the deep blackness of the canal as if waiting for something – a sign, a movement – or waiting to catch some sound, some music that she was expecting to hear. She looked older than her baby year.

He watched her that first time, watched her from behind a big bush, and saw how she looked up the canal, looked northward to where the sea crashed onto a narrow beach that was choked with crab grass and broken shells and he remembered how he had felt his first hesitation, his first uncertainty. He had put it all away, all his unease as he had watched her grow, had seen her cheeks round out as full as moons and her fine hair lengthen to curl around her face. She was his princess, his heart's ease and the months had filled out with so many sunblessed days — never mind the slave work of cutting sugar cane — that he had let go of his disquiet, had let go of it gladly. But when he saw her that first time at the water's edge, watched as she lifted her dimpled hands and beckoned to the sea, his skin prickled and he remembered how he had searched her tiny face so carefully when Parvati first handed him the baby and said, 'Our baby girl, Ram. Doctor Sahib said it will be alright.'

He had searched her face and looked at her fingers and toes and squeezed them gently, checking for he knew not what but checking all the same to kill the whisperings he had heard among his *jahaji* brothers, his shipmates on that journey out of India. They had all sat huddled outside the door of the small cabin during the night, listening to the sounds inside and shifting about on their haunches. The women had gone in and out of the cabin carrying basins and pails and heaps of clean, white cotton. They had never looked their way but had stepped past them wrapped tight in their female mystery and each time the cabin door was opened, the men had heard the screams, the terrible screams before the stout door was shut back quickly in their faces. Their eyes had slid guiltily from each other, and Rampat and his *jahajis* had preferred to look, instead, at the deck or out toward the wide sea, and that was when the whispers had started, there as they had sat shifting about on their haunches outside the cabin door.

'The sailors saw them,' was how the whispering began.
'Dancing like waves.'
'The whole sea was swelled up big.'
'And was frothing up with waves that touched the sky.'
'And the wind was howling out a long belly pain.'
'With bringing in a new one.'
The whispers had come to him through the still night air, when

the sea had lain itself down all smooth and calm all around him and was stretched out to the horizon as smoothly as a freshmade bed. Only the mighty could behave so, could behave as if nothing had ever happened, Rampat had thought. Only the mighty could change itself over so completely and pretend that just hours before it had not lashed out at them with fury, had not tried to topple their ship, and had not raised screams of terror, and prayers to every heavenly god for safe-keeping. The ship itself had thrashed about like a birthing woman, his *jahajis* had said while they sat and waited there outside the cabin door, waited for the birth of the child. They had known already that the baby would be a girl and that she would take her mother. They had known it all, even that the waves would lay themselves down, and that the wild storm they had met coming around the bottom of Africa would still itself, would become spent and weary as the moment of the birth approached, at the precise moment when the girl would start to make her way into the world. And so it was, so it came to be, but Rampat had shaken off all the whispers he had heard when he held the baby close and looked at her face, for she was beautiful. That was all that he could think. He had thought that, and that his *jahaji* brothers knew nothing, nothing at all, because a baby so beautiful could be nothing but a blessing to the world.

Oceans met there at the bottom of the world, at the bottom of Africa, he had told himself, and the Indian and the Atlantic – they fought there for supremacy. Their battle had nothing to do with the birthing of a child, of a beautiful baby girl. Theirs was a battle that was older than life itself, an epic struggle between East and West, and the ship had heaved and crashed like every other that had ever dared to come through those straits. It was clearly not a place for mortals and he had crouched low and held Parvati close and they had prayed aloud for their lives along with their *jahajis* and *jahajins* as the ship had been lifted on waves as tall as mountains only to be hurled back, down to the very bottom of the sea. They had all prayed that the ship would not drown, and that their lives would not roll away to settle on the ocean bed.

'It's the *Ganges*,' Rampat had shouted, pitching his voice high above the sea's wildness. 'She will not drown us.'

The very name of the ship, the *S.S. Ganges*, had been a comfort, an omen even. To sail in her would be like travelling in the arms of Ganga Mai herself. They would be safe and the *Ganges* would bear them to a rich and fruitful life. He had told all that to his wife, to Parvati, had told it to her wanting to ease her fears of the journey, of whatever it was that awaited them on the other side of the world. But she had not been so easy to convince. She had not wanted to come for she had become accustomed to the abuse, had toughened herself against the daily name-calling in his home where she wore a blank face and moved about on quiet feet as she helped to prepare the meals and sweep the rooms, and help her sisters-in-law with their many children.

'A barren woman is worse than mud,' his big brother's wife had said.

'Even a tree would grow in mud,' his second brother's wife had said.

'And bear fruit,' his little brother's wife had said.

The taunts had come from behind their hands, at first, but they had become more open and brazen when they saw that Parvati never quickened her steps to escape them but chose to endure them instead. His father would toss his upper cloth onto his shoulder and walk away, and his mother would put a hand to her mouth as if to stop her tongue from flying off with its own curses. They had given him no comfort, nor had his brothers, for he had married Parvati against their wishes, against their explicit wishes so his misfortunes were his alone to bear. He had married the smooth-skinned, brown girl with the deeply dimpled cheeks and the doe eyes rimmed with kohl who helped her father sell sweetmeats in the bazaar. It was a schoolboy love that grew up with him, grew up with him as he got taller, bigger, and even then, grown as he was into a man, his heart still filled out in his chest whenever she walked into a room and smiled. She always brought the sun with her and never knew how dark his world had been just moments before. It was like that from the very first time he saw her, when he saw her look back at him and smile then titter behind her hands, and saw how, as the years passed, she grew bolder and looked at him openly with wide laughing eyes. She became part of his every day, like the sun itself, even as his parents dismissed her as a boyish infatuation. They believed he would grow out of her like he did his clothes and they even indulged him with the sweetmeats he bought from her each day. They laughed as he munched on the sugary pastries as much as to say that the bazaar girl was nothing, nothing but a plaything that he would tire of soon enough for they were sure that he knew better than to entertain any serious thoughts about her. For his part, it was not that Rampat had a rebellious spirit or was setting out to defy conventions but that he simply could not conceive of a life lived without her, without Parvati, and it was that quiet certainty that had made him bold.

'If you turn the world upside down, son, you'll only find yourself at the very bottom,' his father had told him. He had laughed when he said it but Rampat had never discounted the warning in the words.

His father owned twenty acres of rice lands, a smallholding, and he was not about to let his foot slip for any reason. He leased the land out to small farmers for a quota of their crop and did nothing when they complained that the drains were choked or the dams breached. 'You think it's easy for me to make a living from what you bring me? The skinny paddy you bring me? You think it's easy for me to sell that to pay back for the land – my land – that you are using to make yourselves fat on? I hardly make anything and you want me to spend money to clear drains? Clear it yourself!' His father would talk like that then turn his back on the farmers and return to the cool interior of his home where he would settle down to chew his betel leaves. The matter had been dismissed, taken care of, and he would not return to it; and that was how he had treated Rampat's talk of marrying the sweet vendor's daughter: he would settle himself on his cushions and make a dismissive flick with his fingers.

'Cha, *bayto*!' he would say, turning away from the whole idea and even chuckling to himself. 'You don't worry your head about a wife, my boy. We'll find you one, a rich one, a pretty one, one with the moon in her smile, no?' He would laugh then. 'Cha, *bayto*! A bazaar girl you will marry? *Nahi, nahi.*'

So, when Rampat had brought Parvati home and presented her to them as his wife, both still wearing the garlands from their wedding ritual, their bold *jaimaal* wedding where they had exchanged the marriage vows between themselves, when he had presented Parvati to them with the *sindoor* still fresh in her hair, the whole house had screamed. Shut windows had flown open under the force, and curses and fevered laughter had chased each other head to tail, tail to head around each room, and the noise had rumbled in the rafters and whistled under doorways like a beast of a storm. Everyone had rushed from room to room, pushing the commotion before them, spreading the quarrel into every corner as if every lintel, every cupboard space must bear witness. Such things were said that made Rampat retreat to his quarters where he had held Parvati and let her cry, let her cry endlessly into her bridal sari. It would have been useless to tell her to stop so he had just held her close and let her body quiver and beat against his, and he had held her like that and waited for the storm to pass. It had taken days but the voices had eventually grown tired and, one by one, like a choral work winding down to its final breath, they had dropped away, spent and exhausted. Calm was restored, but it came with a deadly silence that was only broken before company when Parvati would be summoned and introduced to friends, and Rampat's parents would laugh and talk of their son's romantic impetuousness.

'Brought us a bride,' his father would say, snapping his fingers, 'just like that! They went to the *mandir* and married themselves, a *jaimaal* wedding. My boy! A head full of romance, he has.'

'No time even for a wedding party,' his mother would say, laughing, before dismissing Parvati, before sending her back to her many tasks, and saying, 'A dutiful girl, a blessing, really.'

Rampat always saw how the friends would nod and smile and he knew that they only went away to whisper in each other's ear, and that they cared little that their words would escape to fly about the town, their words that Rampat had brought home a bazaar bride. He saw Parvati's spirit grow dim, and watched her lose her laughter and turn herself into a shadow that slinked along walls and over floors, a shadow that moved about the house, too afraid to make a sound. It made Rampat's heart ache and his head spin with all kinds of ideas and he came to understand that they would have to leave and make a life for themselves somewhere far away. They could move to the city, to Calcutta, or journey across to Bombay, and he would find a job and they would settle there. But he had seen the destitute in the streets of Calcutta, people who had fled their small towns and villages and ended up with only a patch of dirt-packed street to call home, ended up beggars, and he knew that he could not do that to Parvati. He had even thought that children, that the children born to them would soften his family's faces, and that their hands flung wide to embrace grandchildren, and nieces and nephews, would also gather in him and Parvati. But as each year passed and Parvati showed no signs of bearing any, the very air turned hard and hostile and eventually slammed shut. And it was then, when he felt that he had no place to turn, when he felt that every door was closed to him, that Rampat heard the *arkati* speaking in the market about the Demerara, about the golden sugar lands in the new world, and how good men and women were needed to help to *chaley cheeny*.

'That's all you would have to do, *bhaiya*,' the recruiter said, 'just turn around the sweet sugar, just *chaley cheeny*. Such easy work, a child could do it. No hard work, no sweat. And you'll get good pay and live in nice quarters. Sun and sweet sugar. Just for five years and then you sail back home rich as maharajahs! Bring your women, too. There's work for them. Easy work. Such sweet, sweet work in the Demerara sugar lands. And we take care of everything, the boat crossing and everything then we bring you back when your work is done. Come tomorrow, right here, and we go to Calcutta to board the *S.S. Ganges*.'

The words were magic. The recruiter spoke as if he had been there and seen it all himself, had sat in the Demerara sun and sucked on the sweet sugar cane. The fat promises had danced about in the marketplace hung with hot dust and more rumours of battles, and Rampat went home and whispered all the words the *arkati* had spoken into Parvati's ear. He talked for hours, telling her that the English sahibs in the Demerara were good men, that they were not like the *rawans* the king had sent to India to make war and steal their country from under them, *rawans* they now had to fight to take back their land. They could escape all the troubles and come back to a free India; and the work in the sugar lands would be easy, he told her, tacking on his own open-eyed dreams about the nice house they would build when they returned with the sweet sugar money. He spread his arms out wide to show the bigness of the rooms they would live in, and his voice jingled with the richness of the bangles and anklets she would wear but Parvati only turned her back on all his words, turned her back and fell asleep and Rampat gave up on pressing the journey on her. But the music of his words must have crept into her dreams with all their dancing notes for she woke up well before sun-up and shook him awake then crept about on silent feet to pack a small bundle of clothes for the journey. They stole away under a lightening sky, their hurrying figures becoming part of the shifting morning mist, and by the time they reached the marketplace, a big, yellow sun stood on the edge of the world, ready to push itself high into the sky. Rampat saw it as a mark of their new life, their new beginning, saw it as a good omen for their journey. There were about twenty others waiting about in the marketplace, and Parvati was among only a few women.

They had all shifted about restlessly until the recruiter had bustled up, had bustled up busily with plans and orders and had led them then on a long walk to the courthouse where other groups like theirs were sitting in the shade or shifting about in the dusty yard and Rampat remembered how impatient he was to get going. He had wanted to board the train to Calcutta right then and sail off on the

S.S. Ganges. Instead, he too had to stand about kicking his heels in the dust and wait to stand before the magistrate to get registered as an emigrant. And when that finally happened, when they stood beneath the high ceiling of the courthouse, he did not even look at them when he asked them whether they were willing to emigrate and whether they knew where they were going. He sang the words like a mantra. They were easy, familiar. They needed no thought. And all around Rampat had heard shouts of *acha, acha* and it was only then, after the busy stamping of many papers, that they were all hustled back into the yard to begin the journey.

The trickery of the thing, Rampat thought, laughing at the moon. He had boarded the ship thinking he was such a big man, a big man setting off to his own Benares, but as the *Ganges* had ploughed on through days then weeks, with only more sea before them and with the horizon forever shifting away to drown itself at the far edge of the world, he had trembled. The world could not be that big, he had thought, as he had watched the sun die each day in a blood-red sky as if on a field of battle, and he had trembled again when he realized that the journey was taking them to the very heart of the unknown. They were crossing the *kala pani*, the world's dark waters. They would break with their karma forever. Their fates would be changed. Standing at the bow of the ship, and with his feet planted apart to keep him steady, he had looked hard at the horizon and had watched it move away as the *Ganges* approached, had watched it move away like a lure, a temptation. Earth and sky had touched all around him, all around the ship, and it was then that he came to know the true vastness of the world and the true depth of the water beneath his feet. It had surged and ebbed, had swelled up from the very centre of the earth. It was big and heavy and as he had rocked up and down, up and down, he had known with every certainty that the horizon would shift away forever, that the journey would never end. They would never arrive, never reach land. They would lose family, homeland, everything, and would sail forever in that circle of sea and sky. There was no escape, he had thought, and he had panicked then. His heart beat faster at the memory, and he remembered how Parvati had come up behind him and put a hand on his shoulder and how he had turned towards her and laughed, and had flung his hands out to the horizon and claimed all the sea as theirs. 'Look! So much room, so much sky. So much! So much! It goes on forever.' She had laughed with him and he had looked away from the drowned horizon into the softness of her eyes and it had steadied him. Rampat remembered it, remembered that softness, and how it had drawn him back to safe ground.

Overhead the moon glowed as softly, reminding him of the moment. Hours earlier it would have shone over his family in India, over their little town, a sprawling village really and, in his quiet moments, he still wondered what they had thought when they had woken up that morning and found them gone. Had they cried at all, or had they thought it best and gone about their day, walking past the empty rooms hurriedly as if their vacancy was no more than a hole in the wall that they would fill when they had a spare moment? Perhaps, the bigger boys had moved in and sprawled themselves all over the bed and chairs, had made themselves comfortable and paid no heed to the warmth that still lingered among the bedclothes and the quiet corners of the rooms. He tried to see their faces but the pictures shifted, shifted like the horizon once did. The lines were blurred, the edges vague, the colours all faded. Nothing stayed still enough to be pinned down, to become a focus for any memories and, perhaps, any thoughts of him and Parvati had long since faded under the Indian moon.

They never talked of returning any more. He never brought it up and he did not know whether Parvati in her quiet moments thought of her family, of the busy bazaar and the friends she had left behind. Perhaps not, since her days were full, were busy. There were batters to mix, pastry to fold over, and dough to knead to make the *methai, gulgullas, gulab jamuns, laddooes, jilebies, prasad,* and *payras* for her many customers. Everyone had found out, found out soon after they arrived that she could make the sweetest sweets and she was soon busy on most weekends filling orders for wedding houses, for big prayer meetings, and every kind of celebration and festival that the villagers held. She turned it into a thriving business as soon as her indentureship was completed, and she employed two young women to help beat, knead and fry the various pastries and batters in large pans that straddled the kitchen fires. All day the kitchen bustled with their chat and laughter, with the hiss of hot oil, and the busy beating of batter. Parvati was happy and her business thrived and Rampat did not think she had thoughts of home, or the bazaar, of ever going back.

It was her savings that helped to pay for the house they had built in Coverton, built in the village near the sugar estate. It was a nice house that sat high on stilts, sat high up from the ground with windows to catch the light and air, and with a little verandah for Parvati to breeze out on in the afternoons. She would sit there after she washed her hair and she would run her fingers through it and let it dry in the warm evening air. He would sometimes hear her and Neela laughing and talking softly to each other, hear their voices carrying on the breeze then Neela would fetch the big blue comb from the dressing table in their room and comb her mother's hair while it dried. She would sing as she combed Parvati's hair. The songs were always sweet and full of pathos, like the *biraha* songs he remembered from his youth, songs about love, about lost love, and the pain of parting. The words were much too grownup for a child but she sang them with such innocence that Rampat never asked questions about it and, now that she had grown into the songs and was old enough to understand their meaning, Parvati was beginning to talk about marriage plans for the girl. Rampat sat up and pushed the thought away and scanned the canal again. He thought he heard a phrase from one of her songs drifting in from the sea and it raised all kinds of worry in his head, all kinds of questions, but he pushed them away as well and laid himself back on the grass, shutting his eyes tightly against the light of the moon. Those were the times when he told himself that he was a simple man who wanted nothing but a good and simple life with his Parvati and his Neela, and that it was not his task in life, not his task at all to pry and question things of the world that he would never understand. He had already come to know that in life there was much that required nothing more than faith, simple faith and belief, from a man. And Rampat knew that he was such a man, a man who knew when it was best to leave things be, when turning away from a worry was the best way to deal with it. That night was no different and when he opened his eyes again to the moon he was ready to turn his thoughts to his paddy fields and the crop that was ready to be harvested, was ready to go over all the work that would have to be done.

He had ten acres under cultivation and was planning to add more the following year. He had started with half that acreage, bargaining hard for two acres from the new estate manager, a stout, tall man named Blanchard, who wanted him to stay and continue to work as a cane-cutter alright but had tried his level best to keep him from getting any land in exchange for the return passage to India, the return passage that was part of the indentureship agreement. It was his good friend and *jahaji* brother, Billa, who had gone with him time and time again to the manager's office to help him make his petition for the land. He had experience in the thing, he had told Rampat, for just a year before he had got himself a nice house lot, had been granted the patch of land without too much trouble. But Rampat wanted more, wanted a good acre or two and he knew that that would not be so easily granted even though Billa had waved his hand about and dismissed his fears. 'They owe you more than two acres, brother. To take you back to India would cost them more, plenty more, so you go and stand up in front of him and make your claim like you already own the two acres of land because, my brother, you do,' he had said, and Billa had gone with him to Blanchard's office and stood by his side and bristled and made himself fierce. He had looked straight into the manager's eyes without flinching, without once looking away, and when the man relented, when he gave in, Rampat knew it was only because he had become tired of seeing them on his doorstep day after day, for just a day or two before he had heard the man curse them under his breath, curse them, the coolies, and their confounded patience.

They had simply worn him down, he and Billa, and they had allowed him to laugh and fling his arms out wide when he gave them his decision, when he acted as if the land, the land which was once used for sugar cane crops but which was sucked dry and abandoned, was a gift, a reward to be granted only because of his great benevolence. Gratitude was expected and Rampat had brought his palms together and bowed and said *shukria, shukria* and had made Blanchard feel like the big and important man he thought he was. It was a small price to pay for the independence and the good life that the land was going to bring him and his family.

The two acres were part of a large plot of unused estate land, land left fallow as more fertile fields were used for the crops, and Rampat had already eyed the large plot with the idea that if he were granted an acre or two he could buy another couple of acres and put them under rice cultivation. He had thought it through and felt that a five-acre plot would be a good start, that he would be able to handle most of the work by himself since he knew enough about planting and reaping paddy, knew all the stages of the growing: that the seedlings had to be planted with the big rains in January and June, and harvested months later when the grains ripened. But the land would take all their savings and there were all the perils of bugs and water weevils, of rains falling out of turn, and of finding smut and blast on the stalks before the grains had a chance to ripen. Whole crops could disappear if he missed a sign, if he were not watchful, and they could lose everything, all their savings. He had trembled at the risk and he knew that were it not for Parvati's swift decision he might never have done it, might never have ventured beyond jobbing for the meager wages of cutting cane on the estate for there was safety in the fixed sum even if it was little. But when he had taken her to look at the land, at the two acres he was granted and the three acres that they could buy to extend the plot to a good-sized paddy field, she had looked out across the bushy, rutted land and had noted at once all that would have to be done: that the holes in the access dam would have to be filled, that the plot would have to be fenced, and drains dug, and she had said, 'You have to bargain with the estate and get a good price, Ram.'

She was like that, sharp in money matters, and she ran her sweet-making business with the same kind of quickness, the same kind of keenness. It was because of all the years spent in the bazaar and Rampat had seen before how she could calculate risks and factor in profit margins with a shrewdness that would be the envy of the biggest city merchants. Just then, her swift decision had helped him to ease his trembling and he had spread his hands wide to take in the entire plot and fill it to the very horizon with a field of gold, with grains that were fat and heavy and swaying in the wind, and Parvati had laughed at his pretty picture and reminded him of all the work that he would have to do before he could harvest any of that gold.

She had been right about that for it was back-breaking work to get the bush cleared, and the field ploughed and prepared for the first seedlings but friends and neighbours had helped, especially with the task of fixing each of the paddy sprouts to the earth, of stooping and pressing them firmly into the black mud with their thumb. A crescent of clay settled and hardened under Rampat's nail from that particular task and he wore it as a badge of honour, and there was no feeling, no satisfaction in the world like the one he had when he bagged his first crop of paddy and readied it for the mill. It was then, when he had planted it and it had rewarded him for his labour, that he truly felt attached to the new earth. He and Parvati held a *jhandi*, a prayer service, to give thanks to Mahalakshmi for her bountiful blessings, and when the pandit blew the conch shell, blew the curled shell during the thanksgiving prayers, it was then that Rampat felt truly at home. They were blessed. He milled a good hundred bags of paddy in the big crop, a good yield, and he and Parvati and Neela were comfortable; they wanted for nothing. And how Parvati had bloomed!

Rampat had taken note of it, taken note that there was no more slipping and sliding about silent as a shadow. She bustled about everywhere with quick footsteps, and threw big laughter before her, cast it out like a net to draw in friends, acquaintances, even those she was meeting for the first time. She was popular, well liked. He had noted the change in her even while they were aboard the *Ganges*, had noted how she had become more like the girl he had always known and loved. It was a sea change, he had thought, when he saw how she talked easily with her *jahajins*, and even joined in in the drumming and singing when the late afternoon sun threw long shadows on the deck. That was how she had become so close to Taijnie, to the shy, tiny girl who had crouched down low and pressed herself into small corners, trying to disappear and to invite no attention. But that had been difficult since she was heavily pregnant, and Parvati had felt sorry for her and would always find her, pull her up and walk her around the deck, letting Taijnie lean on her arm to steady herself.

'She's had a hard time, Ram,' Parvati had said to Rampat once, after one of their walks. 'She doesn't say much but I can tell.'

'Where's the father?' he had asked.

Parvati had shaken her head from side to side. 'I can't get anything from her. She's just a child really. She says she went to the river to bathe one day and that the water frothed up all around her and gave her a baby.'

Rampat had laughed a little and Parvati had shaken her head again. 'She's only a little girl. She knows nothing, poor thing. She told me how the water bubbled up all over her skin and how warm and nice it felt running down all over her. Who knows what really happened? And imagine the trouble when her family found out! They would have chased her out the house for being a badwoman, a loose woman.' Parvati had hesitated then continued. 'Ram, when we get to the sugarfield place, I want Taijnie and her baby to come and live with us. She has nobody, Ram. She's just a baby herself and we can help both of them.'

Rampat had not answered. He had only shaken his head from side to side and said something noncommittal like, 'We'll see.' That was fifteen years ago: the sailing across the *kala pani*, the coming to British Guiana to work on the sugar plantations, and he thought again: the trickery of the thing, but he did not laugh that time. Five years of indentured labour in the cane fields and another five cutting cane to earn enough to pool with Parvati's earnings in order to build their little house and to buy their first bit of rice land – he still tasted the bitterness of it in his mouth. There had been no easy riches, no sweet sugar money.

Most of their *jahaji* group had been assigned to other plantations but he and Parvati and a few others were bound to Coverton Estate and had been put to work as soon as they arrived. They were in time to cut the year's first crop, and Rampat's memory still screamed with the pain of it, the pain that would surely follow him into his next life for it was too much for one lifetime to bear. A blunt cutlass had been shoved into his hands and he had sat outside his *logie*, outside his small square of living space in the estate barracks, had sat and filed and filed, and had rubbed oil onto the hot metal from time to time, and had honed the blade until it had turned into a glistening thread of silver, a whip-sharp thread that would slice through the bony bark of the cane with one clean stroke. It was the bound yard's evening music, the grinding, teeth-edging sound of metal on metal as the cane-cutters readied their blades for the next day's task. On his first day, he had joined the gang, not knowing what to expect. He had fallen into step with them, everyone moving as one and walking like jumbies in the dark morning time, walking a mile or more along a deeply rutted dam, their feet slipping into every hole and crack, and promising to break with every fall. They had moved along in silence, not disturbing the darkness with any talk. It was as if they were steeling themselves for what lay ahead, were conserving all their energy to lift and crash their silver-edged blade deep into the bone of the sugar cane bark.

Rampat could only have guessed at what it would take to lift and chop, lift and chop with the sun chasing him on with its early morning heat then boiling over on his back when it burned a hole in the middle of the day. None of his guesses ever got close to the reality of the thing, the reality of sweating and choking and spitting dry spittle because his body was drained, of feeling how his muscles stretched and broke then re-knitted themselves, and men, men bigger than him smoked ganja, or drank cheap rum to numb the worst of the pain and to stretch themselves far beyond what was possible.

'The *backras* don't care if we live or die.'

'They're just going to ship us back anyway.'

'And if some of us die then…'

'Less to ship back!'

'More savings for them.'

That was the kind of talk that went around among the men. Some were bitter, some were angry, but most of them, like Rampat, were resigned to their fate for anyone who ran was eventually caught and fined, or jailed, then brought back to the fields, and any rebellion or strike was dealt with swiftly: with gunshots and a counting of the dead. Soon after he arrived in nineteen hundred and seventeen, Rampat heard of one at an estate called Rose Hall that had occurred just a couple years before. Fifteen *jahajis* were killed in that one. Rampat never had thoughts of running or rebellion for he did not consider himself a fighting man and he had Parvati and Neela to consider. He was a practical man. He had taken the journey and made the contract and he took each new experience as it came and he always remembered how he had looked at the cutlass when it was shoved into his hand, had looked at it stupidly and turned it this way and that, inspecting the blunt blade, and how he had cut the air with it to feel how it weighted in his hand. Flashes of glory had gone through his head and he had seen himself fighting on a field of battle, of using the blade, once sharpened, to cut and kill an enemy horde for that was how he would have played with a cutlass that was put into his hands back home in his family's fields in India. He would have slashed and cut the air before handing it back to a field hand and laughing and noting to the man how comfortably the handle rested on the palm, and how well he would complete his day's work with a cutlass like that once the blade was well honed and sharpened to a silver streak.

But there was never any time to dwell on the turn of fortune that had placed the cutlass in his hand and had made the palm of his right hand all tough and thickened, and he still picked up a cutlass now and then just to whip it through the air, and to feel how the cushions of skin fit snugly against the handle. At first, even with the sharpened blade, he used to chop and chop again to fell one stalk, and he had felt every muscle stretch and ache, had felt his heart race and his breath sputter and threaten to die. It had taken him a day and more to learn how to hold the tall stalk of cane and fell it with one clean chop at the base then lift the cutlass in a clean, upward sweep to cut the bush at the top. The movement had rhythm, the momentum of a dance that swept him up the line of tall cane, and carried him on as he threw a downed stalk aside and brought the cutlass to the base of the next until a whole army of cane lay ready to be bundled and punted off to the factory. Learning the movements of the dance eased the worst of the aches but the daily tasks set by the estate manager could still stretch even the biggest men to breaking point for even they were not as big as the African slaves who had set the measure of a day's work centuries before. Still, with the daily bending, chopping and throwing, Rampat's arms became muscled, and his stomach flat, and he had understood then why his friend Billa bristled with such fighting energy for the physicality alone gave him a swagger, and even made him believe that he, too, could be a fighting man if he wanted. But the very idea made him laugh, the idea of being a fighter. That was Billa's calling, was his calling entirely, and Rampat could never understand how he had read him so wrongly when he first saw him at the depot in Calcutta.

He first saw him, the dark little man with the big muscles at the depot by the Hooghly River, and he knew him immediately for a South Indian, a Tamil most likely. He had hair that was curled close to his head, wore rings in his ears, and had muscles that were packed down tightly into powerful arms and shoulders. He walked with his feet apart as if he was constantly laying down a challenge, as if he was always ready to pounce, and his muscles moved and bristled even when he stood still. He had the easy tongue and big laugh of those who were sure of their might, and it was his laugh that first drew Rampat to him because sitting around at the depot compound, waiting for the ship, waiting to start their journey to the Demerara made the hours drag and Billa's big laughter always held the promise of entertainment. He told stories of his escapades, which always involved a fight, and he would recreate the steps, the lunges, the locks and holds, and the thrusts of his powerful arms that had brought his opponents down. Rampat always watched from the edges of the crowd that would gather around the man and had noted the scar right off, the inch or two of rough, shiny skin that extended above the waist of Billa's new pants, the pyjamas that were part of the bundle of new clothes that were given to them when they arrived at the depot. He knew from the width of the gash that it must go a good way down his abdomen and he had wondered then whether Billa had been slashed defending his honour or seeking revenge, some rough justice. Perhaps he had been slashed first, and Rampat felt sure that if he had, Billa would have fought boldly and would have dispatched his aggressor with ease, and would have probably inflicted a deeper, perhaps even mortal wound on him. Maybe that was how he had ended up so far from his home, why he had travelled so far north to Calcutta. Perhaps it was to escape. Whatever it was, he had learned Hindi along the way and Rampat guessed that his urge to brag, to tell the stories of his fights would have been incentive enough. He was going to board ship with them and continue his adventure, or make good his escape, whichever it was that had driven him from his home and his family in Tamil Nadu, and when Rampat watched Billa swing and dodge a phantom fighter, watched his feet kick up puffs of dust, he had trembled, had trembled at the fight that was packed down tight in his squat build. He was not a fighting man himself and he made a promise to himself to keep out of Billa's way.

But the fighter turned out to be one of his *jahaji* group on board the *S.S. Ganges*. They were going to make the journey together as shipmates, and were to look out for each other and help each other through the long days and the rough waters ahead and, aboard the ship, the man continued to entertain everyone with his stories and Rampat continued to skirt the edges of the gatherings, always listening to the tales from a safe distance. He imagined that any touch from Billa would be rough, even savage. He never imagined that the man's hammer fists could ever be gentle, so when he had felt a touch on his shoulder, a touch so soft that it was almost not there, like a petal falling or a cloud skimming by, he had turned away from the ship's rail, expecting anyone, anyone but Billa, and Rampat had stood there with his mouth hanging open, too surprised to speak. It was Billa who had smiled and said, 'It'll be okay, brother. She'll grow up to be good and beautiful. Don't worry your head with what these *jahaji* brothers are saying. I heard many stories when I was a boy – of real demons, of *rawans* breathing fire, of the *naga* serpents and their rich palaces below the waters – but Mother Ganga, a fish maiden in Lord Shiva's hair…' Billa had stopped then and smiled. 'She's a gift to the earth, you'll see.'

Billa had joined him then at the ship's rail and they had looked out at the sea's black waters and Rampat believed that it was the grand stretch of the sea, the sea that seemed to go on forever like a flood upon the earth that made Billa recount then the story of the goddess Ganga and how she was first brought to the earth. Rampat knew the story well. His mother had told it to them, to him and his brothers when they were small, and he had heard it recounted by pandits at the temple, and had read it for himself in different books that told the stories of the creation of the deities, of how God came to earth in all His many forms to destroy evil, to protect the good, and to cleanse and purify the earth. The story of Ganga Mai was a favourite story of everyone, and Rampat had noted straight away that the tone that Billa used to tell the story was not his usual one, the one he used when he was recounting the tales of his fights and escapades. He was not aiming for distraction or entertainment. Instead, there was a reverence in his voice, a reverence that Rampat had never heard before, and the story of Ganga's creation being told as they had cut through the *kala pani* made the story live and gave it meaning.

Billa had recounted the story from the Puranas, had told how the prayers of the sage, Bhagiratha, brought Ganga to earth from the toe of Lord Vishnu, brought her from the heavens in a full flood to purify the earth of the ashes of the sixty thousand sons of King Sangara who had been destroyed by the angry glance of the sage, Kapila. The force of Ganga's fall, Billa had said, was broken by Lord Shiva who caught her in his thick hair, caught her so that she would flow gently from his brow in ribbons of water, flow out in seven streams. When he had finished his recounting, Billa had paused and told Rampat again not to listen to the whisperings of their *jahajis*. 'They talk of evil and omens because they do not know God. If they did, they would know that the goddess Ganga always comes to earth for a reason, for good reason.'

His words had helped to lessen his unease and when Billa was there again to put a hand on his shoulder to steady him during their first days in the cane fields when he had flayed at a stalk with his cutlass and had been unable to make anything but tiny baby cuts in the bark, he remembered thinking then that Billa's stories of his fights and escapades were probably nothing but a lot of swagger and showing off, were probably just a small man's way of protecting himself from bullies for Rampat found that the man was nothing if not good natured and easy-going. He had caught the rhythm of the cane-cutting task easily, perhaps because he had a fighter's ease with his hands and feet, had a natural coordination and rhythm, and it was he who had shielded Rampat in those early days from the whip by keeping an eye out for the driver, a large African called Sampson, a son of slaves who delighted in pushing and shoving and whipping the Indian indentures for anything, anything at all. Even with his tightly packed muscles, Billa, the only fighting man Rampat ever knew up close, was puny next to Sampson. The man towered and terrorized, and had a way of standing with his feet apart and laughing at them with his head thrown back and roaring at the sky.

'Little coolies trying to do big-man work. I could cut this whole cane field by midday, man; me alone.' He would beat on his chest, thump it like a drum, then raise his whip and laugh. 'I can make you dance,' he would say and he would bring the whip down to the ground with a snap. It would whistle and strike, whistle and strike, and raise little dust clouds from the dry earth, and Rampat saw how Sampson played with the whip like a child with a toy, like a child who liked the sound and thrust of it, liked to catch its tail after each strike then let it go again, let it flick through the air in a graceful arc. It was beautiful to watch, and Rampat had wondered once whether Sampson had ever been whipped for anything, but he had thought not. That would have been his foreparents' lot, the lot of his grandfather and great-grandfather for it was obvious that Sampson had grown his muscles and oiled them to a high gleam to win his master's approval, not to challenge him. His black body shone unmarked and pristine. The muscles rippled under his skin, moved about with a life of their own, and whenever the manager rode up on his horse, he would smile and nod at Sampson and talk to him quietly from atop his horse, would even lean down a little to Sampson's ear. They would talk and laugh, and Sampson would always promise to make sure the coolies completed their task for the day. He would raise his whip and grin up at the manager. 'Don't worry, Massa,' Sampson would say, 'the whip and me are good friends and I know how to use it.' Sampson would roar again and turn back to look at them in the fields and, as the manager rode off, he would flick the whip, the long length of leather, polished and dark and gleaming like a snake, and laugh as he swished it through the air.

But as much as he pushed them around and threatened harm

with the whip, Rampat noted that Sampson stayed clear of Billa and he thought that it was because he recognized him as a fighting man, someone who might even dare to challenge him. He did not approach Billa but Rampat saw how he circled around him and watched him work and he guessed that the giant was probably sizing Billa up against the day when they might pit their strengths against each other. He kept his pushing and shoving for the weaker men and for the women. He shoved them about for nothing, nothing at all, and he liked to come up behind the smallest men and watch them work then laugh and flick the whip over their heads threateningly then laugh again when they flinched. Rampat was always grateful for Billa's light hand on his shoulder. It kept him steady during those early days when he felt that his body would simply collapse in the cane fields, and that as it lay there it would be swallowed up by a black shadow, and that a thunderous laugh would break over his back, readying it for the lightning crack of the leather falling, flaying, cutting into. But Billa's hand was always there to hold him, to prop him up just when he felt that he would let go, would just let go and fall flat onto the earth and surrender himself to the darkness.

The South Indian became his greatest friend, his true brother, his *jahaji bhai*. He knew that he could count on Billa, could depend on him, and he did not care how his own northern Hindu people looked at the Indians from the south, and how they saw their devotion to their strange gods, gods who demanded sacrifices from them, animal sacrifices. They saw the South Indians, the Madrasis as they were called, as primitive, even savage people, and would hurry past their hut temple in the village, which was filled with *murtis* of all the deities including the blackfaced goddess from their Tamil villages. They had shaped the deities in every detail from memory, shaped their features from the heavy, black clay that they dug up from the canals and trenches. They were called Madrasis because they had been shipped, most of them, out of the port of Madras but there were not many of them because the English overseers found them difficult to manage. They liked to argue and fight and they ran away often. Because they had too much of a rebellious spirit, the *arkatis* were instructed to concentrate their efforts in the northern parts of India, to gather labourers from Bihar and Uttar Pradesh for the ships that sailed out of Calcutta, so most of the people Rampat met when he arrived in the colony were Hindus like himself, Hindus who had the same rituals and beliefs and were strictly vegetarians and did not like being thrown together in villages with the Madrasis who ate meat, even pork, and with the Muslims who ate the flesh of the sacred cow.

There were many reasons for division and discord but, in the end, they tried to pull together because they were all too far from home and too broken down by the hard labour in the fields to go about looking for more worries, for more trouble. The white master saw them all as coolies, anyway, and treated them no differently from each other, so they kept their different customs and beliefs for their private moments, for the lives they led within the walls of their homes, and lived together side by side even as Rampat and Billa did, lived together in friendship and as *jahajis* who had taken the journey out of India together.

Rampat had only managed to smile at the short, dark man when he had first come up to him at the ship's rail and promised him that the baby would grow up to be good and beautiful, and it was later, much later, when the sun had lain long shadows across the deck, when Taijnie's poor body had been wrapped up, her soul prayed for and she had been slipped into the sea, that he had come up to Billa at the rails again and started up a conversation. He could not remember what they had talked about but he smiled at the moon at the memory of it. He needed a friend just then and Billa was there without him even asking. It was his words, his easy assurance that had given Rampat the confidence to go below deck and check on Parvati who was busy fussing over the baby, over Neela. She had named the child Neela because the waters had churned blue, she said. She saw it herself, she said, how the whole sea turned as blue as the sky when Taijnie had cried out with her first pain. 'Neela, yes, Neela.

Blue and crystal clear like the sea and the sky,' she said, singing the name into the baby's ear over and over again.

She felt sorry for Taijnie. 'Poor, poor child. The doctor sahib said her little body just couldn't take it and her life just bled away.' She trembled. 'I heard the women say that the sea had to take her, that it was a life for a life,' Parvati said, then stopped and looked at the baby. Her hair was a soft fuzz and her eyes gleamed darkly in her fair skin. Taijnie was dark, was all that Rampat could think, but Parvati was already pushing ahead with her soft sentiments. 'She's so sweet, Ram. Look! How could our *jahajis* think that she is a stranger to the earth? Look how sweet, Ram. I hope they'll let us keep her.' Rampat watched how she nestled the baby close to her breast and rocked her, and it was then that he had gone back on deck and found Billa and struck up a conversation about anything, anything at all, because he had wanted to push away all thoughts of the birthing and the death, and the baby born out of the belly of the sea.

He had never seen Parvati as happy as she was then. It was as if some inner light had been turned on and Rampat marvelled at how Parvati became a busy, bustling mother overnight. She took charge of Neela as if she had nursed and mothered babies all her life, and when they arrived at the British Guiana port of Georgetown, and passed through the red earthen streets lined with low wooden buildings, in a long horse-drawn cart, and seen, for the first time, African people with their matted hair, seen the town built on a bank of the Demerara River, then turned up the coastline and seen the sea surging behind a stout wall, and rode until they came to Coverton sugar estate and the low *logie* barracks, the small squares of living spaces – close, cramped and dirty – it was Parvati who set to sweeping and cleaning to make the place livable. There had been no fuss about them taking the baby. The authorities wanted the matter resolved with a minimum of fuss so Parvati holding the baby close and answering all the questions put to her with *acha, acha* was a godsend and the baby was issued with a birth certificate marked: 'Father Unknown' and 'Born at Sea'. The adoption papers would follow they were told but none ever came. She was theirs as much as if Parvati had birthed her herself.

Neela knew nothing about the sea storm or Taijnie, had never seen her birth certificate, and sometimes Rampat wondered if it was not time to tell her. He propped himself up on his elbows and looked out over the canal but it was still lying calmly under the moon. Hours had passed and she had still not returned. It would be sun-up soon, and she would come home, she always did, Rampat thought, and he settled back on to the grass.

She was a gift, good and beautiful, just as Billa had said. An old woman who everyone called Ajee, who was everybody's grandmother, looked after Neela while they worked in the fields. They started out for the fields long before sun-up and returned in the afternoon when the day still held some light, and it seemed that they had watched her grow up in spurts, leaving her a baby and coming home to see her walk, talk, run. Somehow, Parvati always found the energy to play with her, tired as she was from stooping to weed beds, throw dung, fetch cane, to do whatever task was required of the women. And he, too, would swoop Neela high into the air and make her laugh then carry her around the bound yard with his chest pushed out a little and showing off his pretty child, his pretty baby girl. The women made clucking sounds and gave her sweets and the men smiled when the dying sun picked out flecks of gold in her red brown hair. Rampat opened his eyes and smiled at her prettiness. She filled the sky, his pretty, smiling child. She filled his life and he would be lost, would be completely lost without her.

How he used to love to swing her back and forth in the hammock slung between two posts in the little covered space in front of their *logie*, when she was just a little thing. He would swing her up and down in the cool of the afternoon and tell her stories about everything, about when he was a boy, about the journey out of India, about jumbies and fairies and princesses with crowns. It was all the same to her and she would giggle and laugh and tell him to go higher, faster, dada. But she was all grown up and taking on womanly curves, and Parvati was starting to talk about her marriage and was already offering up some of the neighbourhood boys for inspection. That was her evening verandah talk those days and Rampat would smile and indulge her while he smoked a cigarette and flicked the ash over the rail for the talk was safe, it rambled and promised no action and he would take long drags on his cigarette and make an occasional nod of his head, and listen to all of Parvati's plans.

Suresh, he was a quiet, hard-working boy, but Parvati had heard that he was a hard drinker already. 'His rum bottle comes first and no good will come of that,' she would say, dismissing him. 'Navin's boy is good. He helps his father cook even, now that his mother is dead. But he's so short and so dark. No, he won't be a nice match for our Neela. She must have a prince, a rajah!' She would sigh then and speak of Dolly's son, Parvesh. Dolly was her closest friend and her son had played with Neela when they were children and the boy had taken to hanging around outside the yard under the big tamarind tree to catch glimpses of her as she helped in the kitchen to mix and fry the sweet batters all day. Neela always ignored him. She looked around him, over him, even through him, with a straight, even face. She was by far the prettiest girl around but only Parvesh dared to show his heart. The other boys watched her from a distance and were called away by their mothers if they were caught. '*Bayto*, you come here,' the mothers would say and mutter prayers to heaven. 'Come, come inside quick! That one there is not for you.'

Rampat frowned at the lightening sky. He pushed away all thoughts of the talk, the whispers, the slammed doors and hastily shut windows that followed his daughter about. Many times he felt he should say something to her, something comforting, profound, even, if he could manage it, except that he noticed that none of it ever seemed to bother her. She always walked past it all, undisturbed and calm. She was a remarkable child to be able to do that, to not run and hide and cry, but then she was like no other, Rampat thought, feeling the proud father, feeling his chest swell out a little in a secret boast. It was only Dolly who never listened to any of the talk. She was too good a friend to Parvati to let it bother her, and they were too busy, anyway, with their business deals and business expansions, to listen to gossip and village stupidness. Rampat chuckled. To hear them talk you would think they managed a huge manufacturing concern that employed hundreds. But it was only a cake shop that Dolly ran by the main road and she sold most of the sweetmeats that Parvati turned out in a day. It was a profitable arrangement for both of them, and it was Dolly who helped Parvati to get started in her sweet-making business, it was she who had said that Parvati should turn her hand to making a business out of it after she had tasted some of Parvati's *methai* at a wedding house. It was the best, the sweetest, the lightest she had ever tasted, she had said, and she had sought out Parvati and put it to her that she could sell everything that Parvati could turn out in a day. That was the start of it, the start that turned Parvati into a bustling businesswoman, and gave her her closest friend, and, if Parvesh and Neela were to marry, it would be their happiest moment but the boy was no prince, no rajah, and Rampat always heard it in Parvati's voice, heard her disappointment whenever she brought up the boy's name. But she would sigh and count the boy's many good qualities, say that he was nice and quiet and that he was learning to be a good motor mechanic, and that it was his father, Lakhram, who was teaching the boy the work.

Lakhram worked as a mechanic at the sugar factory and fixed cars and lorries on weekends but he was always promising to quit the factory work and open a proper mechanic shop where he would tinker and fix carburettors and exhaust pipes all day, and whenever Rampat went past their house and their shop, Dolly's shop on the main road, Lakhram always had time for a chat about the boy, about Parvesh.

'He's a good boy, Ram, the best. Just the other day, Suchit brought in his truck to fix and Parvesh just listened to the engine and knew right off that it was the timing chain gone bad. And he fixed it, too! Learned from just watching me. Quick as a whip, my boy.' Rampat always recognized the boasting for what it was and would say nothing, and Lakhram took that as encouragement and would show off his son for Rampat's benefit, would tell him how Parvesh knew how to fix any engine of any model of car or truck, and would always tell him that as soon as the boy was married, they were going to make him a proper mechanic shop. At that point, Lakhram would sweep his hands out to take in the spacious yard and show Rampat just where the shop would be built, there between the spread of the mango tree and the hibiscus bushes in the front yard, right there beside Dolly's cake shop. 'It would be a very lucky girl who would win our Parvesh, eh Ram?'

Rampat always smiled whenever Lakhram talked like that because he knew what it was like to be the proud father even though, try as he did, he could never place Parvesh's face besides Neela's, beside her pretty, smiling face. They simply did not fit together. He had heard it said that no suitor was ever good enough for your daughter and he thought back to his parents and the quarrel over his marriage to Parvati. They did not think she was good enough for their son, either, a bazaar girl, a sweet vendor's daughter. But what would they make of their life now, he wondered, of Parvati the businesswoman, and Neela their pretty child, and their five acres of paddy fields, and their nice home built high to catch the breeze? And he was looking to buy himself a motor car. It was one of the reasons he was going around to see Lakhram recently. He planned to ask Lakhram to teach him to drive and that was why he humoured him whenever he boasted up his son. He would ask him about makes and models, about which one had the best engine and which was the best value. He had already gone to Georgetown, to the city, and had looked in at the showrooms at Ferreira and Gomes, at Bookers and Central Garage and Geddes Grant. He liked to stand back and look at the cars, liked their shiny gunmetal look, and he would imagine himself at the wheel of one of them with Parvati beside him and Neela sitting up in the back and looking out like a princess at the passing scenery of green fields and golden sugar cane and bougainvillea run wild over fences.

He planned to buy a car and drive it home. It was to be a surprise. He wanted to catch the delight on Parvati's face, to watch her pick up a corner of her apron and shine up the silvery chromium trim to make it even more sparkling then watch her open the doors to sniff the leather interior. She would be no different from Neela in running around the car and clapping her hands, and laughing, and neither of them would care one bit about the make and model, about the number of cylinders and the engine's horsepower, but that did not stop Rampat from standing about at the car dealerships and weighing up the possibilities and smiling to himself about the big surprise.

He would take them on long drives once he had the car. That was his plan, that he would drive Parvati and Neela into the city regularly to shop for fine clothes and bright jewellery. They would like that, would like bustling about the bright stores. And he would stand about outside the windows and wait on them, would stand beside his automobile and smoke a cigarette and put his foot up on the fender and take in the scenery for he liked the city, the country's capital, liked the feel of the place even though the first time he had passed through it on that horse-drawn cart, fresh from his journey aboard the *Ganges*, it had been too strange, too different for him to grasp. He had only known the streets and bazaar of his little town in India, and what he had seen of the busy Calcutta streets as they had made their way through that teeming city to the ship's depot by the Hooghly River. Those were all that he had had to measure the city by, so the first time he saw Georgetown with its redbrick streets and its low wooden buildings and the few people walking about, he had panicked. The small city, a township really, sprawled in the crook of a river and the sea, was nothing like Calcutta, was nothing like home. It was too small, too sparse to hold any promise of riches, and he had panicked and thought then that the whole thing was a mistake, that the *arkati* had lied, and that they were sure to return to India as poor as they had come. It had taken time, had taken years to give up that first impression, for him to start to like the little city by the Demerara River, the very river that the *arkati* had spoken about. It was a big river, and deep, and busy with ships, and if he stood on its bank and looked out toward its wide mouth he saw clearly how it flowed out to the sea, and how the waters swirled and swirled all the way back to the Hooghly from where he had travelled. It was all connected and that comforted him, made him feel easy, and he grew then to like the city and its neat crisscross of streets

He knew every new shop that went up and, like all the townspeople, paid little attention to the Atlantic which pounded and pounded against the sea wall to the north each time the tide was high and the sea ran over the narrow beach. Everyone had faith in the strip of wall, the stout wall of brick and stone the Dutch had built when the colony was theirs in order to keep the sea away from the drowned port, the port which was not built on solid ground but on mudflats that were below the level of the sea, was built as a fortress by the earliest conquistadors against marauding invaders. It was never meant to be a city, at all, but it had grown, had sprawled and become a busy port and it was probably because of the wall that kept the Atlantic from washing over it and taking back its natural shoreline that created a feeling of safety and gave it room to grow. He would bring Parvati and Neela for afternoon drives, bring them to take the evening air and to stroll along the top the wall along with the townspeople, and while they strolled, dressed in their finest, he would tell them all about its history. He would tell them that the Dutch had built it, and he would spread his arms wide to measure its length, its breadth, then point to show how it curved along the shore, how it hugged it in order to keep the city safe. It was the Dutch, too, who had created the neat little city, who had mapped out its streets which cut each other at right angles.

It was a transient place, as impermanent and fragile as life itself, and

Rampat liked that, liked its vulnerability, its need for protection. All of it, all of its orderliness, its canals which flowered with pink and white lotus blossoms, and its wide avenues which were shaded by spreading flamboyants that flamed red when they flowered, could disappear, could be swallowed up by the sea within minutes and whenever he walked through the city streets and entered its buildings, he felt that he was continuing a tradition of guardianship, of protection that had started with its first inhabitants, the earliest conquerors who had come – the French, the Dutch, and the English – looking for the gold of El Dorado. That was the lure. They battled for the chance to become rich, to become heroes, and when the dream proved elusive, false, and was uncovered as a mere phantasm fashioned for a new and exotic land, another breed of men followed. They grew riches from the land, created plantations of sugar cane, and they, too, sought heroism through long guns, guns that were pointed at the people they brought as slaves and labourers, people to be used then discarded once their work was done, once they were no longer useful. They were as transient, as vulnerable as the city itself and Rampat felt that he, too, could survive, could survive everything just as the city did. It was his greatest triumph that he was able to put it all behind him, put behind him the brutal field work, the humiliation, and the threatening whip and see, instead, that the place could give them a fresh start and a nice future. Neela and her children would live on in the colony. That alone was a grand enough future, something to look forward to, and he chuckled at the moon when he saw her riding across the night sky, riding across the sky seated in the back of his sleek new car in full bridal finery.

She wore a glittering sari of red and gold, and the *sindoor* was fresh on her forehead. There was a young man beside her dressed in a silk *kurtha* and a *maur*, the bridegroom's splendid headdress hung with strings of flowers that danced before his face, and Rampat pushed himself up on his elbows to shake off the picture. Behind the dancing flowers, the groom had no face and Parvesh's long, solemn one still did not fit, never mind all his father's boasting. He was too quiet, that boy, Rampat thought. He had no gusto, no fight. He would never take a chance on a dream, an adventure, would never set foot aboard a ship to test the edges of the world. He was glad that Neela showed no interest in him, or any of the boys in the neighbourhood, and Parvati would not force a match on her, Rampat was sure of that. She was too much of a romantic, his Parvati, so he shook his head, shook the pictures from his head.

There was time for all that yet, he thought, for Neela was only fifteen and, even though she was grown nearly as tall as him, she was still the baby girl he had held close and rocked to sleep on fretful nights, the child he still watched over to keep safe.

He was glad that Parvati did not know of all the nights he spent by the canal waiting for Neela to come home, waiting to let out a deep breath and to laugh a little at all the worry he had allowed to creep into his head. His chest would expand and make more room for his heart whenever he saw the water part and her head appear above its surface. Everything always became right with the world again, and he always convinced himself as he hurried home that he knew she would return, that there was never any reason to doubt and Rampat scanned the canal again but it was still, and he asked himself: what if she did not return this time? What if the rising sun overtook the moon, faded it away from the sky and she still did not come? But she always did, she always did, he thought, and he placed a hand over his heart and lay back on the grass. Yes, it was good that Parvati was spared all this, he thought.

If she knew, she would only worry the air with questions, with demands and fears, and she might even drag poor Taijnie up from the bottom of the sea to answer for herself and her child. It was better this way, that Parvati planned and prattled, running on even to count their many grandchildren, naming them Rajendra and Saira and Dharmendra in turn, and remaining blissfully unaware of the mysteries ancient and deep that he kept watch over. He believed that it was his watching that kept the worst of all fates from happening, though, were he pressed, he would never have owned to what that fate was for he knew that once a thing was named, once it was out in the open it took shape, so he skirted the heavy thoughts that weighed on his mind and hoped that they would disappear one day, that a time would come when he would wait night after night and he would not hear Neela slip away quietly from her bed to creep down the stairs and head for the door. Most nights he lay tense by Parvati's side, listening to her quiet snores, hoping against hope that the time had come, that the dark silence would not be broken by the whispering of feet across the floorboards, by the light-as-air footsteps that went down the stairs. Two nights might pass without a sound then on the next he would sigh and leave his bed to follow her again, to follow Neela and become resigned to start hoping all over again. It was the only thing he kept from Parvati. They had no secrets except for that and he knew that he was doing the right thing to protect her from the worry.

As it was, she explained every harsh word, every slammed door as envy, pure and simple, as people being jealous of everything they were unblessed with. 'Look at our Neela. You would be jealous, too, if she were somebody else's jewel, eh?' she would say, and she would turn back to her dough and batters and leave Rampat to wonder whether he did indeed worry too much. As if hearing his thoughts, Parvati would often add, 'It's your duty to worry your head about your daughter, Ram.' She would say that then chuckle and he was often convinced enough by her lightheartedness to put away his fears for a while.

Neela's quietness and even temper made it easy for him to do that. She never gave them reason to worry. There were never any tantrums, or willfulness, or childish squabbles with friends. He had seen her back away from drunken brawls that erupted in the streets, and move away from the children playing by the canal if they started to yell and fight. Even when he and Parvati quarrelled sometimes over godknowswhat, Neela would sit quietly aloof and wait for peace to return. Once, after a squabble with Parvati, he found her sitting on the verandah singing softly to herself and combing her hair. Her hair had shone and so had the comb she was using. It was ornate and golden. It was the first time he had seen it and he wanted to say something, ask something, but he had chosen to turn away instead for he did not ever want to know about things he could not understand. It made for easy acceptance.

Rampat settled himself more comfortably. The morning was still and the air cool. He had a long day ahead of him. The rice was nearly ready for harvesting, the second crop of the year. He would have to pass by Billa's place and arrange the hiring of his truck to take the paddy to the mill. Billa was doing well for himself, had become an important man with a busy trucking business. In the harvesting season, it was Billa's truck that fetched everyone's paddy to the mills, and their rice to the markets or to the export depot in the city where the grains were poured into the bellies of large ships and taken to the West Indies, to dinner tables throughout the islands. Rampat liked that link with the outside world, liked the idea of his rice being cooked and eaten by people he would never meet. It took know-how to grow rice that good, and he had it. Billa had tried his hand at planting rice himself but had given it up soon enough. He did not have the patience, the patience it took to wait for the shoots to grow out of the flooded plains then watch as they slowly, slowly rose up to meet the sun. He much preferred to delve into the mysteries of the inner workings of the truck he had bought secondhand. It had been in a ramshackle state at the back of the rice miller's yard, had been thrown aside as junk, but Billa had seen its possibilities and had fixed it up and nursed it back to life. 'Tip-top shape, tip-top shape,' he said to everyone who came by to hire his truck, and he would pat its fender as if it were the flank of a prized beast. The truck still rumbled and hissed with enough noises to keep Billa interested in its engine and underbelly and Rampat swore that it was the tinkering about rather than the delivery business that Billa liked best.

He was married and had two boys though that did not settle him into a quiet life. It just brought on bigger ideas, and one day he tacked up a sign over his gate that read: Billa Kotiah & Sons Trucking Service Co. Ltd. and his wife, Savo, had come out to inspect the sign, and had tut-tutted and fretted about the need for it. 'Everybody knows is who business this is so why we need a fancy-shmancy sign, eh?' she had asked, but everyone had seen how she had blushed and given the sign a little shine-up with the corner of her apron.

Billa had laughed. 'Ah, Savo girl,' he had said to her, 'when we get old, our boys will take over the business. There'll be a truck for each one of them, eh? And we will just lie back in our hammocks and ease ourselves into a nice old age while our boys take over and do all the work.'

Rampat remembered that and thought about how much had changed in just fifteen years, how much had happened since that journey out of India, and from the time they first set foot in British Guiana. The plan then was that they would complete their indentureship and return home with stories of gold, and of all the strange peoples they had seen on the other side of the world. They were not going to return and tell about their slave labour, of the whip and cutlass, and the rotting *logies* in which they had lived. Such pain and humiliation were best put away, were best packed away, and laid over by plans for a bright future, so they were going to ride back in triumph as adventurers with pockets laden with gold, and tongues full of tales of splendour. Everyone would gather around to hear their stories, and everything would be forgiven, and when he and Parvati appeared with Neela, his family would rush to greet them and they would pinch the child's cheeks and marvel at her red brown hair that glinted with gold. Rampat sighed. Life, the day-to-day plans of what must be done tomorrow and the next day and the next had drawn out the years until fifteen had passed, and that distant life in India was a memory that was like a treasure, a treasure that was only taken out occasionally to be marvelled at. The hurt had long been forgiven and were he to see his parents again, he would touch their feet with a *namaskar*, and they would smile into his face and *arti* it, circle it with the sacred flame to welcome home their son and his family. It was a nice picture, and he had played it over in his head often and filled it in with many loving details of what his parents would say, and how welcoming they would be. It was all just a journey away and like all things certain, it could wait.

The ship on which they had travelled out of India, the *S.S. Ganges*, turned out to be the last one to cross the *kala pani* to British Guiana, and that year, nineteen hundred and seventeen, and their ship, even they themselves, became part of history. It was recorded in books everywhere as an ending of the way things were for nearly a hundred years, as the year when the last of the indentured labourers came to the Demerara sugar lands. Many good people fought to bring about the end, as so many had done before for slavery. The *logies*, the ranges of poor huts that the contract labourers lived in, the harsh working conditions for the most meagre wages – they were unjust, criminal. A young lawyer in India named Mohandas Gandhi talked about it, about the conditions for Indian contract labourers in South Africa where he himself had worked. They were the same ones that existed everywhere else in the colonial empire, Gandhi noted, everywhere where the colonial masters worked their plantations for good profits and exploited people, used them as nothing more than expendable tools. Even though some of the words were new to Rampat's ear, he knew exactly what Gandhi was talking about because he had lived it, had lived out the words like all the *jahajis* and *jahajins* who had made the crossing. But as much as the *S.S. Ganges* closed a chapter in the history books, for Rampat and Billa, and for everyone else who chose to stay, it marked a beginning of a life in the west.

Rampat could not remember clearly when the talk of returning home to India stopped and got overtaken by plans to build a house and to buy paddy fields, for the new life had settled in around them without any conscious thought or planning, and Rampat marvelled at how easily life slipped by, how the sun-up to sundown circumstances moved in, took over and set new patterns in train when you were not even looking. They had no complaints, he and

Billa, and Billa, too, stopped talking about India as going home when he got married to Savo. He had built his own little house by then, a house to bring his bride to, and he had a big wedding with a proper *maro*, the traditional wedding tent, which was decorated with flowers and streams of crepe paper. How handsome he looked when he brought Savo home through the gate, which was arched over with coconut branches and dressed with lotus blossoms and shiny mango leaves. She was draped in the brightest red sari and Billa walked beside her, straight and proud, in his bejewelled *maur* and yellow satin *kurtha*, and with golden rings in his ears and on his toes. His *jahaji* brother looked like a true Tamil prince on his wedding day, and Sampson was the good friend that was there at Billa's side to help with all the wedding preparations. It was Sampson who had shoved the bamboo stakes into the ground with a single thrust to support the canvas for the *maro*, and it was he and Billa who had stayed up to drink and dance all night to the South Indian *tapoo* drums all through the week before the wedding. They were bonded together forever those two, Rampat thought, and he thought how strange it was that it was a fight, that it was pitting their strengths against each other that cleared the way for their friendship.

The fight between the two broke out after years of them circling and watching each other from a distance in the cane fields, and it was an almighty roar that brought everyone rushing to the spot that day to see Sampson towering high against the noonday sky. The cane was nearly all cut and everyone was dawdling, taking a long lunch break, and Billa must have dozed off; he must have taken a sip of rum and dozed off, Rampat remembered thinking, and Sampson had found him, had closed in on him, at last. The giant stood over Billa and roared, and Billa woke up, startled, and scrambled to his feet to find that the whip was already raised, was raised and ready to come down on him. And it was then that Billa put up his fists, and Sampson looked at him and laughed then roared again, 'Oh, so you want a fight, eh? Lil coolie! You think you can beat Sampson, eh?' Sampson looked down at Billa, looked down at all of them from his great height then threw the whip off to one side, threw it among the cane stumps and put up his fists as well, readying himself for a fight.

Rampat closed his eyes against the early morning sky there on the bank of the canal, closed them like he had done that day when he had not wanted to see how Billa would be knocked flat onto the dry earth. He would fall and his life would ebb away into the dust, would bloom red then dry up fast in the noonday heat. He was his *jahaji bhai*, closer even than his own brothers. They had crossed the *kala pani* together holding fast to nothing but each other and in a faith in the unknown, and, with only each other to lean up against in the new world, their *jahaji* bond was stronger than blood itself. Rampat was not a man to dwell on death and dying but, that day, he was sure that he smelled death among the cane stumps and heard it in the indrawn breath of the crowd that stood around the two men. Muscles were all for show, Billa told him once. They were just there to scare your opponent, he had said, and Rampat, not a fighting man himself, had appreciated Billa's knowledge of such things, of what he could do with his fists and his footwork and his lunges – the battles he could win. But Sampson was another matter. His muscles bulged. They were not there to be challenged and definitely not by someone as puny as Billa, and Rampat saw how Sampson planted his feet wide apart, how he stood like a colossus and waited for Billa to make the first move.

Rampat was sure that his brother would die there in the cane fields that day and that they would have to place his broken body in a hole in the new earth. The English did not allow the Hindus their sacred and ancient ways of cremation so Billa's body would not be laid out on a *dholi*, a funeral berth strewn with fresh flowers and ready for the flames. His ashes would not be returned to the Ganges. He would never see India again and all of the strange, new world would walk over his bones forever. Rampat had mourned for Billa with his eyes shut tight, waiting to hear the crack of bone, to hear the thud of his friend's body hitting the ground. Only then would he open his eyes and, then, only to weep. He remembered how tense he became and how, when he heard a cheer go up from the crowd, instead, he opened his eyes to see Billa dancing. His *jahaji bhai* was dancing, was dancing around the giant, and Sampson, his movements heavy and cumbrous, found his opponent twinkling away behind him again and again as he struggled to swing his body around to face him. Sampson swayed and swatted the air. He turned and turned again, his large feet proving a clumsy pivot, his bulk and weight proving a disadvantage against the nimble footwork of Billa, of Billa the dancer. The giant became angry, and he grunted and lunged, charged and jabbed, but he came up against empty air each time, and this unsteadied him, threatened to make him fall, but Rampat knew that it would only take one punch to bring Billa down, and he felt sure that Billa would tire long before Sampson did.

Maybe the giant would play for time then take him down, Rampat thought and he had no sooner thought that, that Sampson let out another almighty roar and put his whole weight into a punch that would have cracked Billa clean in two had it landed. Except that Billa leapt out of the way at the same moment that the punch was thrown, had gauged its direction from the time Sampson unleashed it. Billa leapt and his feet actually left the ground in a quick sideways move and, for a moment, he hung suspended like a god lifted by fair winds and being carried to safety. But, for Sampson, it was over. He had put his whole enormous weight into the punch, and he was down! The whole length of him thundered onto the dry earth and raised up a dust cloud that many still swore darkened the sun that day, and Rampat stood there with all his *jahajis*, all their breaths drawn, all their hearts racing. They waited for the giant to rise up from the earth and strike Billa dead. But Sampson stayed down and breathed hard. The fall had stunned him and before he had the chance to push himself up from the ground they all roared and swung Billa high onto their shoulders, and paraded him between the cane stumps as on a battlefield spread with glory. Everyone sang and clapped, and the women lifted their skirts from around their ankles and danced, and the men perched one hand on their hip and held the other high in the air and swirled and twirled and danced around the women. The children who had come to the fields for the last day of the crop ran everywhere, laughing and cheering, and Billa strutted among them with his hands on his hips and his head held high. He had felled the giant. He was their hero.

He still was, even though he took his rum at times and would become boisterous and argumentative. Parvati kept on at Billa about his drinking, but he always had an answer, an excuse. 'You think we could have cut all that cane, sister, without a lil sip now and then to put some iron in our backs?'

'Well, you're not cutting cane any more,' Parvati would say to him.

'Ah, but the lil sip eases up the remembering and speeds up the forgetting,' Billa would say. He would laugh and take another sip from the quarter bottle, the flattie that he kept in the back pocket of his trousers. The truth was that no one minded much that he drank. He was indulged. His triumph over Sampson brought him eternal forgiveness, and he drank and played dominoes and cards when he was not working his truck, or tinkering about with it. He led the Coverton dominoes team against the neighbouring Paradise players and he often triumphed there too.

Rum always flowed during the matches which were noisy, boisterous affairs. Sampson was always there with his village team and much of the banter between the men centred on the legendary fight between Sampson and Billa, and Sampson would throw cuffs into the air to show how he had taken Billa down, and the men would wait for Billa to suck his teeth and say, 'I knocked you down flat, man.' At that, everyone would whistle and stamp their feet and shout, 'Tell it! Tell it!' between the hard slams of the dominoes against the makeshift table set up beneath the wide spread of the mango tree which fronted the houses at Coverton. Rum and talk would flow in equal measure, and Sampson always went first, reliving the fight for the men, reliving every lunge he made, every cuff that fell. 'I was only down for a second when his people carried him off. They carried him off to save him!' he would say, and he would slap his knee and laugh.

'You were down and out, man. Out like a light!' Billa would say and he would start off on his story about the fight, how he dove into the belly of the giant and knocked him clean off his feet. They were inseparable after the fight, Sampson and Billa, and it hardly mattered who had won and who lost, although everyone who worked in the fields noted how the fight changed Sampson. Where before he used to harass the women, used to prod at them with his whip, he started to help them steady the bundles of cane stalks on their heads, and to fetch their baskets of weeds. Nothing was said of the fight for a long time until the day that Billa handed Sampson a drink, a sip from his flattie, right there in the fields, and the two had slapped each other on the back and recounted the tale of the fight, each with his own version. That was the start of their friendship. It was a matter of respect, Billa said. It was a matter of standing up for yourself, he told Rampat.

The story of the fight grew with each telling. The fight became hours long, lasted until sunset, then on into the night, and the crowd grew to thousands and covered the entire cane field. The victor was always a matter of who was telling the tale but the men became legends in their own villages and friends to each other and everyone who hung around the dominoes games between the teams knew the story well and knew how the victory swung from one to the other. They knew when each punch was thrown, how Sampson lunged and how Billa jabbed the air. They knew it all so well that no one ever thought that a stranger could come out of nowhere, could come among them and stop the storytelling dead in its tracks because of what he heard, or thought he heard because he did not know the whole of it.

But it happened, and it took months for the games and the storytelling to resume and, even then, the players would look over their shoulders, would look out to the edges of the crowd to see if anyone unknown had come to stand among them, for no one could forget that afternoon when a rage, a surging rage rolled in from there, from the very edge of the crowd and disrupted the story that Billa was telling. It was like a natural force, like high winds and a storm the way it rolled in and cut everything dead, and the words that drove it were hurled at Billa as he was telling how he had thrown Sampson and pinned him down, and he was showing how he had stood over the fallen giant when the voice came from the edge of the crowd, a new voice, the voice of a stranger. It cut into the tale and the man pushed his way to the front of the small crowd, pushed his way up to the dominoes table where Billa was standing. He was a young African and he was smartly dressed in what looked to be new clothes for they still showed the creases of neat folds.

'You lil coolie man could ever beat Sampson? That's a lie! You could ever beat Sampson, eh? Eh?' the stranger asked.

The thing happened so suddenly and was so odd, so out of place with the usual good humour of the afternoon games that no one was able to shift their thoughts quickly enough to respond, and their silence gave the stranger room, gave him permission to continue. He shook his finger in Billa's face. He pulled himself up to his full height. He looked around at all of them, at all the Indians who were standing around watching the game, he looked at all of them then spat on the ground. 'You lil coolies come here and think that you're better than everybody else, eh? You build your lil houses and your lil shops and make your lil money and you think that that makes you better than us, eh? You know how long we've been here and what we went through to make a life here? It's we who cleared the bush and dug the drains and made cane fields out of the jungle with our bare hands. We sweated and we bled for this earth, and you, you came here just the other day and think you're better, that you can come here and beat us up, eh? Eh?'

The man advanced and the Indians in the crowd stepped back from him, and Rampat remembered how he too had moved away from the young man and his rage, and he remembered that it was then, when they had all drawn themselves back, that he heard Sampson calling out to the stranger, calling out to him by his name. It turned out that Sampson knew him but, even then, when Sampson called out to him, the man did not stop. He did not stop until Sampson drew himself up and planted his feet on the earth and bellowed at the sky. It was years since Rampat had heard that roar but it still made him tremble and he was pulling himself back to the farthest edges of the crowd and was making ready to turn around and leave when he heard Sampson shout, 'Martin! Son!' and that was what stopped the young man and his rage, what finally shut it down. 'Martin, stop your stupidness, boy,' Sampson said. 'This man here is my buddy friend.'

They had all watched Sampson step up to the man, to the man called Martin and lead him away and it was much later that Rampat learned that he was one of Sampson's sons, that he lived in the city where he was a teacher at one of the big schools and that he had come to see his father, had come to pay him a surprise visit. Rampat did not believe that that happened too often since none of the Paradise villagers had recognised him, and Rampat, too, had never seen him before. In truth, he had never met any of Sampson's children even though Sampson liked to boast them up at times, liked to tell everyone how well they were doing, his son the teacher, another one, a policeman, and two girls who clerked in government offices in the city. They were never going to work in the fields, were never going to do the slave work that he had done and his father had done before him. 'No, sir!' Sampson would say, 'no more slaving for us' and when Rampat saw him again days later, met up with him as he was walking along a village lane he told Rampat that he was not to worry with all that Martin had said, and said that the boy was picking up too much stupidness in the city, that it was just city talk and that it meant nothing, nothing at all. But the disruption had ended the afternoon's game, and the Paradise team and their supporters had left, had packed away their dominoes and left without saying a word, without saying anything to Billa, or to anyone else, and Rampat had walked home slowly and had gone over the young man's words, had gone over the accusations in his head, and was even looking closely at himself to see if he could be found guilty of having picked up biggity ways, of thinking that he was better than everybody else.

All he knew was that he was making a nice life, a nice little life for himself and Parvati and Neela, that he had built a nice house and was making himself independent by taking a risk with his paddy fields. He knew of no other way to live other than that, that you built a life, shaped it, and gave it meaning. He had learned that much from his father, and he was just beginning to wonder whether he would be expected to change himself in the new world, to make himself over and become unrecognizable even to himself when the Reverend Andrew Davies fell into step beside him, and that made him think that they might all have to become Christians and give up their gods, for that was the man's work, teaching the Indians in all the villages around about Jesus Christ and converting them to Christian beliefs. Rampat had seen him standing about at the edge of the crowd that afternoon because he was a man like that – he liked to be a part of whatever was happening in the villages. That was how he found his converts, by being friendly and accessible, but when he fell into step beside Rampat, Rampat found that he was only looking for someone to talk to, to talk to about what had happened that afternoon for Rampat was one of the few good friends that he had in the villages.

Rampat had no quarrel with the man and even came to like him despite his conversion business because he saw the good that he did among the poorer Indians, among the people who lived in the mud-daubed huts at the fringes of the village. Rampat even felt ashamed that he and his neighbours who had done well for themselves, who had made nice homes and built up nice little businesses had neglected them, had neglected those people who were mostly the children and grandchildren of the first shiploads of indentured labourers, the first Indians who came out to the new world to take the place of the freed slaves in the cane fields over a hundred years before. They had faced the brunt of the hardships: the long voyage out of India on sailing ships, the harshest cruelties of the plantations, all the strangeness of a new world, and the diseases that had taken their heaviest toll among them, among those earliest arrivals. It was only because they had survived, had clung stubbornly to the new earth and scratched out a living, had stayed and shaped little huts from the very mud they walked on, had survived and put down the first roots; it was only because of the communities they had created, the little patches of India that fluttered with *jhandi* flags or rounded out the sky with minarets, that danced to the *dolak* or *tappoo* drums, and shone with the brightest silks and satins of saris and *shalwars* and *kurthas* that Rampat and Parvati and Neela and Billa had all come to an easier life when they arrived.

But they had paid them no attention until the reverend came all young and eager and fresh-faced out from Canada, came with all his good intentions and worked among them, and cared about them. He brought them to his church, his church which was nothing more than a small hut with a wooden cross on its roof that was named the Canadian Presbyterian Church. It was not until the young reverend came and did that that everyone kicked up a fuss and paid any attention to those poor villagers and said that he was stealing away the very souls of the Hindus and Muslims, and that he was teaching them to turn away from everything they knew to be true about themselves. They called him a thief and a devil and even Rampat had to put away his kindlier feelings towards the man when the new Christian converts started to speak ill of their old beliefs, started to curse Shiva and Vishnu and Hanuman as nothing more than figures in fairy stories, and started, even, to tell their neighbours that they were heathens who were all going to burn in Hell. It was too much, too much, and it was then that Rampat came right up to the reverend one day outside his church and told him right there and then that his religion was not better than anyone else's, and that it taught nothing new at all because there was nothing new about telling people to be good and honest and Godly.

'Everything in the world is a part of God,' Rampat told him, standing eye to eye, shoulder to shoulder with him right there beneath his wooden cross. 'We believe that to be so. We believe that good and bad, darkness and light, peace and war are all part of the infinite, the absolute and the everlasting, and that one cannot exist without the other. How have the day if there is no night to make it so? Heaven and Hell are not separate but twinned states and because our human mind is finite, because it cannot stretch itself out to even begin to understand the infinite, we give our gods form and face and functions. It is a very human thing to do, to shape the world as we understand it, and we believe that your Christ is also part of the one supreme God, that he is another form of Lord Krishna and we can very well place a *murti* of your Christ on our altar in the *mandir* and worship Him alongside Lords Vishnu and Shiva and every other deity. Lord Jesus! Born of a virgin mother and raised from death to the eternal Heaven. That story would fit very well with all the stories of our gods.'

Rampat chuckled to himself whenever he remembered the conversation, remembered how the words had come from him in waves, had come from him inspired, and how the young reverend had listened to him, his long, white face reddening in the sun all the while. He said nothing until Rampat was finished, and Rampat stood there and expected the man to take offence, expected him to turn away, and he was ready to stand his ground, to argue with him to the end when the reverend smiled and clapped him on the back and said that he was glad of the instruction. 'To know the other point of view is good for the soul. It keeps us humble,' he said, and Rampat felt that he was being humoured, even patronized, but, in truth, the young man did seek him out from time to time to talk, and to listen to anything that Rampat had to say. Perhaps it made him better at his work, Rampat thought, to understand the people he worked among. Or, perhaps, he just had need of a friend in what must have been, for him, a strange and hostile place, so he indulged him whenever he dropped by to chat, dropped by to sit with him in his bottom-house, the square of packed earth which fronted the kitchen that was built between the stilts, the stilts on which the house sat high up from the ground to catch the breeze. The bottom-house was hung with hammocks and put away with chairs and benches that were always ready to receive company, to receive anyone who was passing by and wanted to stop and chat, and the reverend took to doing that, to dropping by and pulling up a chair and talking about everything, about everything in the world, and that was how Rampat came to know that he was a reasonable young man and that he had a good head on his shoulders. But it was because of that, because he thought that the man was so reasonable and so sensible, that made Rampat become frightened when he heard all that he had to say about the incident, the incident of shouting and finger-pointing at the dominoes match that afternoon.

When the reverend fell into step beside him as he was walking home, Rampat expected him to make a few comments about the sins of temper, of vexation and fury, and he was prepared to agree with him, but the reverend stopped, instead, stopped in the middle of the lane that led to his house, and turned to him and said, 'It is going to erupt. It will not hold. The Africans feel entitled to this land. They feel that you're taking it away from them. If things remain evenly balanced then, maybe, it could hold. There is tolerance and good neighbourliness on both sides. I see that every day. But if the Africans begin to feel that they've lost the advantage of having come here first and of having suffered the worst then it will not hold. If they feel that they're being overtaken and are being disadvantaged because of your settling here, I fear there will be violence.'

'Violence?' Rampat said. 'What do you mean? I want no trouble with anyone. I want no fight with anyone. I just want to make a nice life for my family and to live here peacefully.'

'I know. I understand. We must have hope that the leaders who rise up will know that they'll have to tread carefully and will have to understand the needs and sensitivities of both sides. Or else, I'm afraid that all will be lost.'

The reverend walked on with him as far as his gate and left him there, and Rampat sat for a long time in his bottom-house turning the man's words over and over in his head. But, in the end, he dismissed them. They made no sense. The man was overreacting. He was an outsider, after all, and had never shared in their common experiences, and did not know the bond that existed between them. They had all worked the same fields, dug the same ditches, shared the same master, and the experiences were not that much different for any of them, and Rampat remembered thinking that then pulling himself back from the thought for he knew that it was not true. He and his *jahajis* were never bought and sold in the marketplace like goods as the Africans were. Rampat always knew that it was a horrible thing and that he could never know what that would do to a man's soul. He trembled whenever he heard the stories that were told, stories of pregnant slaves being whipped under their master's instructions, being whipped until the blood flew. 'Give it to them until the blood flies,' was how the master's words went in one of the stories he heard. Children born to those mothers were often seized and sold for profit. There were no families, no close relationships, and Rampat did not know what that could mean, to not have family for he had never lived without one, even without the family he had left behind in India, and he knew that without his Parvati and Neela, and even Billa, his *jahaji bhai*, that life would be without meaning for a man needed such bolstering to make his way in the world much like a tree needed roots and branches if it was to live and grow and be productive. But he also knew that Sampson and many of the villagers in Paradise lived like that, lived with that brokenness which had been handed down, handed down from father to son. Sampson lived alone, lived without any family around him, and all that Rampat ever heard him talk about were his mammie and grandmammie.

His father was only a vague figure in his memory and it was only once that Sampson ever spoke of him, and then it was only to say that he had drifted away from the home one day when he was still a small boy, that his father had just upped and left, and that he had never seen him again. 'He, too, never knew his daddy, his daddy who the master used to call "boy". It was too dangerous, you see, for his daddy to ever know that he was a man, a whole, big man, so they called him "boy" to let him know his place.' Sampson said that then fell silent, fell silent for a long while before he put his hat on his head and got up from the bench in the bottom-house, got up and left, and Rampat had never felt close enough to him to ask him more, to ask about his mother and grandmother even, the two women who had brought him up then left, and who, so Sampson said, were going to return for him one day.

Rampat had heard the story many times since Sampson liked to tell it over and over again, and he even told it to Neela a few years before when they went to his house with Billa for a visit one day because Sampson was sick, was sick with a cold and Billa was taking him some hot soup. The house was small and ramshackle with rickety steps and a low front door, and Sampson had to bend to get through it when he invited them in from the front stoop. He filled up the small living area with his considerable bulk, and Rampat perched himself on a small chair and pulled Neela up to sit on his knees. The furniture was sparse and the room was darkened by thick curtains, which were drawn across every window. Rampat remembered that the curtains had bold yellow flowers, and he remembered thinking that they were intended to brighten up the room. One of the women in the village had probably told him that, had probably recommended the curtains and told Sampson that they would brighten up the room. There was a woman's touch about them, and they were the only attempt at decoration besides the picture tacked up in the middle of a wall, a picture of Jesus Christ in a blue robe that was opened to show his bleeding heart.

They were all Christians, all the villagers in Paradise, and they were comfortable in the English schools where the day began with prayers to Jesus. Sampson's children, like Martin, got an education and got jobs in the government service for you had to be a Christian to get that kind of work and there was little chance of that ever happening for Neela or Parvesh or most of the children in Coverton. Rampat and Parvati had even kept Neela away from school once she was no longer a little girl and her hands clasped in prayer to a Christ spread on a cross could no longer be explained away as a childhood game. If she had ever asked why *murtis* of Jesus and Mary were not among the others of the gods and goddesses at the *mandir*, what would they have said? He and Parvati had talked about it and decided to take her out of school, the Anglican school that sat next to the church which fronted the estate's sugar factory, and the headmaster, a quiet African named Mr Wharton, had found his way to their home when Neela had missed school for a week. He came and sat in the bottom-house with his hat on his knee and tried to convince them to keep the child in school because, he said, she was bright and she could go far. Rampat never said anything to him, never said that they already knew that for Neela could already read the 'Bhagavad Gita', the whole of it, in Hindi, and knew all the stories of the deities, and she sang all the *bhajans* and *chalisas* at the *mandir* in the most beautiful voice, and that she knew all of those songs of praise by heart. He could have even told the man how everyone said that the girl was a *devi* with a voice so pure, so sweet, so rich, but he did not think that that would have satisfied Mr Wharton for he was talking of books of literature, of English stories and poetry, and books of mathematics that she could grow up to study if she were to keep up with her schooling. In the end, Rampat and Parvati had stayed quiet, and the man had given up, and sighed and left, and Rampat never knew what it was that made him do that. He thought that it was their silence or it was probably the singing that he heard, Neela's singing. She was sitting on the verandah right above them and she would have been combing and combing her long hair with the golden comb, would have been pulling the comb through it slowly while she sang one of those plaintive love songs that she liked for it was then, when he heard the singing, that the man had put on his hat and left. He would have heard, and must have listened to all the stories that had grown up around the girl and, perhaps, it was that that made him leave, that he himself was not willing to press on, to know too much about the truth of the matter. Rampat did not fault him for even the people at the *mandir*, the very ones who said that the girl sang like a *devi*, like a goddess, would pull away from her once the prayer service was over, would pull away from what they saw as her strangeness, and Rampat never regretted letting the girl stay close to home, to him and to Parvati and the people they knew well, people like Billa and Sampson who would drop by, would drop by with stories about everything in the world, stories about fights and fairies and dragons that were as big as the world.

They made her laugh, made her clap her hands and laugh, and it was they, Billa and Sampson, who had rushed in and rescued her from the children once when she had gone for a swim in the punt trench. It was the last day of the crop and the children had come with their parents to the cane fields to help bail out the leaky punts that were to carry the last of the cut cane to the factory but when they had tired of that, they had run off to play among the cane stumps, and Neela must have slipped off then, slipped off into the trench for a swim, and the children must have heard her soft splashing, must have heard her moving quietly through the water and they had gathered on the bank to watch. And they were standing around like that, just watching her, when one of the boys said something about a tail and the screaming and shouting had started.

'Look, look! The water mama's tail.'

'Look at her tail.'

'She's gone under the water.'

'She's swimming around under the water.'

'Like a fish.'

'She is a water mama fish!'

'She'll pull us in and drown us.'

'And eat us.'

'My mother told me so.'
'Neela is a water mama.'
'Neela is a water mama.'
'Neela is a water mama.'

The children had started to throw pebbles and bricks, and one or two big rocks into the water when Billa had rushed up and stopped them. Then Sampson was there and it was the two of them who had helped Neela out of the water and had shooed the children away. Sampson had roared at them, had roared at them as fiercely as he used to when they first knew him. 'It's me that will come and eat you,' he had said and he had rushed at them, and the children had run off screaming, screaming still about Neela, about Neela being a water mama.

She was a small child at the time and Rampat sighed at the waning moon and remembered how she had cried, had cried that the children had thrown rocks at her and cried that they were frightened of her. He remembered it well because he had had nothing to say to her that could have made it better. He was her father and he had had nothing to say to her. It was Parvati who had rocked her and soothed her, and they had talked quietly then of telling her something of her birth, of her birth at sea. It might mean something to her, he had said, but Parvati had said no, not yet, that she was still a child, and was too small yet to understand any of it, and he had wondered then at how much Parvati understood but kept hidden from him.

Perhaps everybody had their secrets, Rampat thought. Billa had his past which had left him scarred, and Sampson was full of his stories about his mammie and grandmammie and how they had disappeared. He had called Neela over to look at a shelf lined with coloured bottles that day when they had gone with Billa to his house, had gone with Billa to visit him when he was sick. 'My mammie's things,' Sampson had said to the girl. He was trying to whisper, was trying to be secretive but his voice was too big and the room was too small and Rampat had sat with Billa and listened again to the whole story, the whole story of Sampson's mother and grandmother.

'My mammie would be gone for weeks sometimes,' Sampson had told Neela, 'and people used to come from all over to get her to fix up their lives for them. They wanted to find love, make babies, make somebody sick, make somebody well – all those things that they couldn't fix for themselves, they asked her to do. Even as a little boy, I used to see the see-far look in my mammie's eyes and I knew that one day I would wake up and she would be gone. Well, she must have seen the fear in my eyes because she used to tell me that she would never leave me, that she would always be watching over me no matter where she was. I was only twelve when she went away one night and didn't come back. People round here, the old people, swear that she went into the canal that night and swam away to be with her own kind, with her own people, the water people. Her own mammie had gone away like that, too, but I know my mammie well. She said she would never leave me and I know that one day she'll come back for me.' Sampson had paused there, and Rampat thought that he had seen Neela trying to pull away from him. His face was right up close to hers and Rampat had got up then and reached for her, and Billa had sucked his teeth and laughed.

'You're filling up the child's head with that stupidness, eh Sampson?' Billa had said.

'It's not stupidness. Children understand the things of the world better than we do. We know too much, eh Neela? It gets in the way of believing, eh? My mammie is going to come back and I'll know her right off, no matter what form or shape she takes. It's not stupidness, no sir! It was when she left that the manager took me in and grew me up like his own son. He even wanted to take me away with him to live in England and I had to tell him that, no, my mammie is going to come back for me. I think my lilboy face was so serious that he couldn't argue with that!' Sampson had slapped his knee and laughed and Rampat had taken Neela by the hand and held her close.

All the way home, he had held her hand tightly and listened to Billa suck his teeth and go on and on about Sampson's stupidness.

'Everybody knows that that woman drowned in the canal. And his grandmother, too. They never found their bodies so everybody turned them into water mamas. Stewps! Sampson likes to boast himself up to make himself important; his water-mama mammie and his *bakra* manager liking him like a son.'

Billa would go on like that about everybody else's stories, that they were pure lies and stupidness, but if anyone challenged the ones he told, he would pull himself up smartly and say they were all true, were all real, and that only those who lacked belief in the world could have doubts about the stories he told. He always found new bits to add, new plots to weave into his stories so that they appeared fresh each time he told them. To hear him tell it, he had battled dragons and *rawans* and every kind of monster on this earth; and he always came out the champion. But he was entertaining and Neela always giggled and laughed at his stories and the way he told them, the way he put grand gestures, and a whole theatreful of voices – now a growl, now a roar, now a whisper – into his stories to make them live. Even Parvati would grow quiet and listen. That was the best measure of his success – that he got Parvati to give up her quarrel with him, even for a moment, about his drinking and his bigmouth ways and get lost in his stories. And Billa had found new tales to tell in recent months, had taken to imitating the young politicians who had sprung up around the marketplace and street corners with their talk about better housing and better wages and better lives for everyone. They were lawyers and trade unionists, men from the city in slick suits and ties and hats, and they wanted the people, the labourers and field hands to stand with them to fight for better working conditions. They said that they were going to represent them in talks with the government, with the English governor and legislators, and Billa would swagger and strut and repeat their words then suck his teeth and say, 'They are nothing to do with me, these city men. They don't know me at all.' But Rampat did not see the men that way, as men to make fun of, and he had stood many times at the edge of the small crowds that would gather to hear the men talk.

He liked to hear them, liked to hear what they had to say. Workers in the business sector were striking a lot just then and the politicians were promising better wages and standards of living, better housing and schools and more hospitals, and jobs for everyone. There was unrest throughout the West Indies and, everywhere across the region, politicians were starting to talk about independence and home rule. That was the only liberation, the true liberation, they said. They were fighting for the vote, for everyone to have a say so that they could all pull together and become free men, they said. It was all new to Rampat, all that political talk. It sounded nice and it made him feel important that the men would come and stand around at their marketplace and talk to them, to talk to them as equals. And the story they told about a bright future was as good as any tale that Billa ever told and Rampat often laughed and thought that that was why Billa did not like the politicians: they were competition. He would laugh at that and listen to the promises of all the brightness ahead and liked how it all sounded because it contradicted all of Reverend Davies' predictions of violence especially since the politicians were of all races, were Africans and Portuguese, Creoles, and were even Indians, Christian Indians who had rounded out the broader vowels of their Hindu names and bore first names like Robert and Edward and Andrew. They stood together and spoke as one, spoke of the times ahead, and the struggles that would lead them all on the road to development and progress. The words shone and were nice-sounding and Rampat cheered them on at every meeting even as Billa continued to dismiss the politicians and their fancy speeches. They were nothing but *arkatis* selling the promised land, he said.

But Rampat found the politicians' words reassuring and was more than ready to believe them. He wanted to know that he was making a life in a place that had a future, a real future. He never told anyone of the reverend's predictions, of what he saw that day when Martin shook his finger in Billa's face. Rampat had kept it to himself because he was afraid that to even speak such words, to let them escape into the air would give them shape, make them live, and he did not want to be responsible for letting loose such a dreadful thing upon the earth. He had stayed in the bottom-house until late that afternoon turning over all that the reverend had said to him, had sat there until the sun had set and Parvati had come up to him and asked why he was sitting alone in the dark like that. Did he have worries, she wanted to know, and he was starting to tell her then about the reverend's predictions, about the violence that he saw, was starting to tell her about the young man, about Sampson's son who had shaken his finger in Billa's face, was starting to tell her the whole story when Parvati waved it aside. She sucked her teeth and waved it aside as soon as she heard him call Reverend Davies' name. She had her fixed opinion about the man and his busybody work among the villagers, and she told Rampat straight that he should never trust anything that that man said.

She was a straight talker, his Parvati. Everyone knew exactly where they stood with her and she was not ever afraid to hold her ground. He liked that about her, and that afternoon she had dismissed the reverend's talk as pure foolishness, had seen right through it as pure trickery, and had told him that Reverend Davies was just trying to scare him into finding a safe place in his Heaven. 'He wants your soul, Ram, that's all,' she had said and had gone on to fret with him, like she always did, about his friendship with the man, the man who, she said, was doing the devil's own work by turning people away from all that they knew about themselves, and Rampat had listened to her and laughed a little to himself and given it up, had given up all the reverend's talk as pure foolishness.

Parvati was like that. She would get to the heart of the matter and move on to busy herself with whatever else was at hand, and, right then, it was wedding plans that took up most of her time. It was her duty to see her daughter well married and Parvati was not one to ever shirk in her duties. The truth was that he wanted to see Neela married and settled as well, but he was not prepared to marry her off to just anyone, and Rampat thought that Parvati was being too hasty with all of her plans. She had just about decorated the whole house already in her head, and she had also decked out a *maro* with flowers and beads, and with mirrors hanging everywhere like little suns, and knew exactly how it looked and how everything sparkled. That was as far as her future went, as far as she was prepared to go just then, and only when Neela was well married would she be able to settle down comfortably into her old age and play with her many grandchildren. Rampat started to laugh a little at the picture of he and Parvati playing with grandchildren.

They would have to tell Neela something before she left their home, Rampat thought. Perhaps, they would have to tell her husband, too. He sat up and shook the idea from his head: a husband! His Neela, his little girl, on the arm of a stranger – not even all the talk and talk of weddings and wedding plans made him easy with that picture, and Neela, herself, always moved away whenever Parvati started to talk about it. He would often find her sitting somewhere singing softly to herself, singing one of those *biraha* songs while she combed her long, red brown hair. He would never force her to marry, Rampat said to himself. He would let Parvati make all her wedding plans if they pleased her but he would protect his Neela forever. There would be talk if she stayed at home, unmarried, but there was talk already, talk that she was something strange, a water mama, a *devi* even, so they could bear it.

Rampat sighed and watched the sky lighten even more. The canal remained still, unruffled, and he did not know what to think, whether to be frightened that she had not returned as yet, or to simply be patient. He sat up, and yawned and stretched. The grass was damp with early morning dew and soon the houses would stir with life. Oil lamps would be lit and the women would be up, cooking meals for their husbands to take with them to the fields. The first crop of cane had been cut on the estate and everyone was turning their hands to their farms or to fishing to fill in the months before the next crop was ready, so the men would set out before sun-up for their vegetable gardens or paddy fields, or to the pastures to milk the cows. Or they would go out with cast nets to catch sunfish and *houri* in the trenches and canals for the market. The fishing boats would also be pulling up soon on the foreshore, pulling up with their catch of snapper and trout from the sea.

Neela always returned before the village stirred to its morning life, returned before the first lamp was lit, and Rampat yawned again and remembered that the world had its own unfathomable order, and that if he were to ask questions, if he were to worry the air with demands and questions that he would not know what to do with the answers. He was a simple man, a trusting man, he told himself. He grew up with all the stories of the Hindu deities, of gods that flew through the air, of rivers that sprang from their toes, and of mountains that appeared or disappeared at their command. He had never thought to question their truth and he could think of no reason why the mysteries of the earth, of the sky and the sea should not give shape to themselves in the new land on the other side of the world. He rested his head on the dewy grass and watched the moon fade away, fade away slowly as the sun rose.

He had watched the moon do that many times, had watched full moons and half moons and slivers of quarterly moons, and he had peered through the darkness on moonless nights, always waiting to hear the water stir and to see her walk up to the bank of the canal. It would not be long now, he thought.

He must have dozed off for a few minutes or an hour – he was not sure how long. All he knew was that he had closed his eyes and that when he opened them again, it was to a song being sung very softly, so softly that it barely carried on the cool morning air, and that when he pushed himself up onto his elbows, he saw her sitting on a rock just beside the bank of the canal, combing her hair, combing it with her golden comb, which glistened and glinted in the first light of the sun. Rampat breathed out then, let out a deep sigh and felt his heart lift and his chest expand. He smiled. You worry yourself too much,

Rampat, he told himself. You always worry yourself too much and over nothing, over nothing at all, he said to himself, and he scrambled to his feet and hurried home, hurried home to where Parvati would still be asleep, blissfully unaware.

PART TWO
PARVATI

Faith so certain
Shall never be shaken
By heaviest sorrow.
BHAGAVAD GITA

Keeping Faith with the World • A Match for Neela
Parvati's Trembling • Marrying Rampat • Neela's Magic
The Marajes • Gulab Jamuns • Neela Leaves Home

BUT PARVATI ALWAYS KNEW. She knew since the time Taijnie told her about the warm river water playing all over her skin. You can say that she knew well before Neela was even born. She grew up knowing that there were things unseen that had their allotted space and time and she was never one to question the ways of the world. It made her feel that she lived in an enchanted place where every twist of fate, every good fortune were all there waiting for the right moment to reveal themselves and to take her on journeys she never thought imaginable, and that all that was asked of her was patience. That she had in abundance. Just like she waited out the night darkness knowing that the sky will brighten with another day, so, too, she waited for Neela to return whenever she left the house during the dead of night, left to step off the edge of the earth. Like the sun, she always came back, and when she reached the bank of the canal to sit and dry herself in the warming morning air, Parvati always hurried back to her bed and waited for Rampat's tiptoeing footsteps. He was always careful not to wake her, and she always obliged with eyes shut tight, pretending sleep. He thought to save her from the distress and fear that drove him like a whip; he thought to save her when it was he that needed saving.

There were so many times when she wanted to go up to him and sit beside him on the canal bank and say something to ease his worry, wanted to tell him that they had given Neela a good life and that she was a sensible child and that she would make the right choice, that she would choose to walk across the earth with sure footsteps no matter her birth from the belly of the sea and all the whispers that had come from their *jahajis*. A life for a life, they had said, muttering low into the wind, and promising that no good would come of a child born out of a troubled sea, a child whose navel string, whose navel cord was cast away on wild waters to circle the world forever without hope of ever being recovered, of ever being grounded in the earth. They had promised death and destruction and Rampat had kept watch ever since on each day, each moment of their lives, fearing ominous signs in every hoot of an owl, and in every moth that plunged itself into the flame of the oil lamp. She looked for signs, too, but signs of deliverance, looked for the day when Neela would stop her singing, and when her voice, which haunted the air long after her songs ended, would crack, would hesitate and lose its way and drop away into the deepest silence, and when her hair, which floated like fine silk around her head, would grow heavy and drop down her back like rope. Parvati would think like that then clasp her hands and say I am sorry, I am sorry, and beg forgiveness of all the deities for wanting a child who was not an exception to the earth when they had chosen in their divine wisdom to place in their care a remarkable child, a child like no other.

Neela was an answer to years and years of prayer, and she was not displeased, Parvati would assure them, as she circled the pictures of Mahalakshmi, and the Lords Hanuman and Vishnu with the sacred flame during her morning *pooja*. They had brought them safely to a nice life, had given them prosperity and much happiness, and Parvati knew that they would not test them with any distress bigger than they could bear. She knew that for sure and wanted to tell it all to Rampat but she was afraid that her words would get tangled up and that she would only end up adding to his fears. It was like that on the ship, on the *S.S. Ganges* when Rampat had looked out at the water that drowned the sky all around them and had flung out his hands and talked big to cover up his trembling. But she had seen the fear in his eyes, the fear that there was no land beyond the horizon, no land for them to ever arrive at, and all she had been able to do was to look at him and smile because she did not have the words to assure him that the water would find land where it would foam and lap and ebb as oceans do, that land was there, just below the sight of his eyes and that the ship would surely be drawn to it. She had stood dumb before him, dumb and smiling, and she had been relieved when he had put away his fears to return her smile and was thinking, no doubt, that she was the one that needed comforting and reassurance.

He was like that, a good and kind man who was careful to hide his distress and worry, and she knew that the fears that kept watch with him on the canal bank were heavier than he could bear and that it would take more than a smile and a promise to fetch them away. And what could she tell him, after all? That the ship had brought them safely to a good earth where they had built a nice life for themselves, and that since Neela was part of that life she was bound to, one day, put aside ways that were not connected to it? She could stretch out her arms and show Rampat the world as if for the first time, show him that it was flat and green and sprouted paddy fields and tall sugar cane, that it was edged by a brown ocean and cut through by rivers silted and heavy as the Ganges, and that their neighbours beat *tassa,* sang *bhajans* and hoisted *jhandi* flags on tall bamboo stalks in front of their houses, that fate had landed them there after a journey many moons wide, that they had had strength enough to voyage out to meet their destiny and that having done that, having been so brave, so daring, that nothing could disrupt it now. But in the end, what would it prove, she asked herself, other than that her faith blinded her to what her eyes saw so clearly. He would listen to her, even smile at her pretty pictures but in the end none of it would help him to put away what his heart knew to be true, and Parvati thought that she would just have to wait on the world, that it had its own time. She would think that then sigh and count her many blessings, and felt sure that the final one would reveal itself to her soon, that same day even for, in truth, she had little else to complain about.

They had a nice home, a small house with two bedrooms and a

nice drawing room with a big kitchen downstairs that opened up on the bottom-house that was hung with hammocks, the bottom-house where everyone dropped by during the course of the day to bring news and gossip and reports of everything that was going on in the world. They had worked hard, she and Rampat, to save and build the house and they planned to extend it after the next rice crop, to make it bigger. Then she would fill it with polished furniture and spread a carpet that bloomed with fat pink roses in the middle of the drawing-room floor. They would have a proper *shivala* built by the front gate, an altar with a *murti* of Mahalakshmi seated in the centre of a pink lotus. Parvati smiled. She was drying her hair on the verandah and watching the sun set among the coconut palms in the neighbouring Paradise Village and she only wished that her family could see her, could come to visit once they added more rooms. How they would crowd in and touch the furniture as if stroking pet animals! They would be hushed and silent, and would look at her with wondering eyes. How she had grown, and how far she had travelled they would say, and they would look at Neela with her silken, red-brown hair and beautiful face and tell her that the child was a *devi*, a goddess, that Lord Bhagwan had blessed her indeed by giving her a child such as that. Parvati smiled again.

So many times she had asked Rampat to write to their families but he would only mumble and nod and promise that he would when he had some time, but the time never came for the truth was that he did not know what to say to the family he had broken with to flee to the other side of the world. Maybe he just wanted this space to be their very own, where they could spread themselves out and make everything new, and where they would not be called on to explain themselves. Or he probably felt that speaking of their nice life would be like boasting, and he was not a boastful man, not her Rampat. He left that to his loudmouth friend, that Billa. You would hear him before you saw him, coming up the street, hollering and calling out to everyone on the way then coming through the gate, laughing, talking, his hands wheeling and cutting the air, and telling a story that was halfway done by the time he reached the bottom-house. But Rampat liked him and so did Neela. The girl thought he was funny and she liked his big voice and the stories he told. Billa was the starboy in all of them, downing whole armies with his bare fists, and Neela would laugh and clap her hands even now, grown up as she was, at the adventures that he made up to entertain her. She had few friends, poor child, so Parvati indulged Billa and his racy tales though she found him tiresome at times and knew for sure that he would go too far and get himself into big-big trouble because his big mouth would swallow him up whole one day. She tried to warn Rampat about that, about being careful around his friend, but he would only shrug and wave his hand and dismiss her misgivings. 'You just be careful that you don't get swallowed up too, is all I'm asking,' she would say, and she would let the matter rest there and not let it spill over into a quarrel because Billa was his *jahaji* brother, after all, and he was all that Rampat had on this side of the world to call family besides herself and Neela.

'Ram? Ram?' Parvati called, turning to the sound of footsteps on the inside stairs that led up from the kitchen. 'Oh, Neela! Come and comb out my hair. Where is your father?'

'He and Uncle Billa have gone to Paradise,' Neela said and she took the big-toothed comb from her mother and ran it through her long, damp hair.

'It's going to be dark soon,' said Parvati. 'Why have they gone over there?'

Neela shrugged. 'To visit Sampson. Uncle Billa says he's sick.'

Parvati sucked her teeth. 'Sampson! That man! That man used to whip us for nothing, nothing at all – just to make himself feel big. Billa beat him one day and he got shamed into being nice. But people don't ever change underneath their skin. You remember that, Neela. People always show you who they are first thing and you must believe them. Sampson!' She sucked her teeth again. 'And it's getting so dark already.'

'They'll be alright, Ma. Uncle Billa has many friends in Paradise.'

'Stewps! Friends to drink with and to play cards and dominoes with all night! It's a good thing your father knows better.'

'Alright, Ma.' Neela combed her mother's hair and hummed a slow melody to calm her.

'What's that song you sing, Neela? It always touches my heart so. It's so sad.'

'It's not sad, Ma. It's like your heartbeat and the sound of the sea, and the wind sweeping across the ocean to make a skyful of clouds to bring us rain. If you listen carefully you can hear the whole world spinning around in it.'

But Parvati brushed all that aside, brushed it aside and said, 'There's big happiness in the world, too, and it sounds like the *tassa* drums. Sing something happy for me.'

Neela laughed and left off the combing to hum and dance to a *tassa* beat. 'There! I always knew it,' Parvati said and she clapped her hands. Her daughter would dance across the earth, would stay firmly on the earth with feet that tapped and stepped and twirled to every kind of music. She had grown into a beautiful young woman, and it was time she was draped in a red sari with a *pallu* that was heavy with golden threads, and with beads that glittered like little suns. The bridegroom would be dressed in silk, and they would circle the sacred fire, he leading her, then she stepping carefully before him. That ancient ritual, that walking round and round the sacred fire into a new life would guide her daughter's footsteps forever after. Parvati knew it. She was sure of it. And the bridegroom would be a maharajah, nothing less! Parvati chuckled. He had appeared so many times before her eyes that she knew him, knew him well. He was brave and tender, and knew how to deal with all that the world held, things both seen and unseen. He had travelled over vast lands, climbed cool mountains, crossed green valleys and followed the trails of deep rivers, all in a glittering palace built high on the back of an elephant. And, most importantly, he was born with the confidence of kings. He would keep Neela safe. The whole picture always glittered in Parvati's eyes. It would be such a wedding, such a wedding! No detail would be left unplanned, nothing would be left to chance. It would be nothing like hers, she thought, nothing unexpected and sudden, and born at a moment's notice.

One day she had been living in the two rooms where her family cooked and bedded down, birthed children and died at regular intervals, a place choked with dust and discord where she had expected to live out her days much like her family, tearing at each other's throat over everything and anything to protect their patch of earth. One day she had been part of that swarming crowd living head to tail, and tail to head, with each day heaped on top of the other bringing no change and filled only with chores and quarrels that ran over into the next day and the next, joining the years together into a seamless despair that was comfortable only for being known, for holding no surprises. One day she had woken up with no expectation of change then on the very next, a day that began like any other and which showed no sign of good fortune, of portents or lucky stars, she had married, draped in a red sari of pure silk embroidered with gold. It was an intervention from the gods, and it was the first time Parvati saw how a destiny never expected or planned could become real in an instant. It had made her a believer, had given her a faith that made her both bold and patient: you waited for the right moment then all that was needed was that you take the step, part the waves and all would be discovered.

She was so lucky, Parvati thought. She could have ended up her days right there in the bazaar if Rampat had not stopped one day to buy her *methai*, her sweets. Who would argue that that was mere chance, not fated, when she had been so chosen, so blessed? Her pretty dimples, honey skin and doe eyes were good for business her family had agreed, so she was the one who sat among the heaped bowls and platters of *methai*, of *gulab jamuns* and *rasgullahs* and *jilebis*. Ever since she was little she had been placed there to smile at every potential customer who passed by. She was dressed in the best bits of clothes, in bright shawls with glittering mirrors, and in wide bordered skirts that danced around her ankles. She had bangles that jingled, fresh flowers to dress her hair, and the darkest kohl to rim her eyes. They had given her a taste for pretty things so whenever she saw Neela sitting before her mirror and combing and combing her hair until it shone, combing it with the golden, ornate comb she had picked out at the market one day, Parvati would laugh and remember her own youthful days.

'I used to pin my hair with fresh flowers every day,' she told Neela watching the comb glint as she passed it smoothly through her hair. It was decorated with shells and bits of coral, all gilded with gold and she had watched Neela turn it this way and that to catch the light at the market stall where she had found it among a bunch of gaudy plastic ones and Parvati had bought it for her and said, 'It's like a mermaid's comb' and had laughed.

All the years that passed had not chipped the cheap gilt even though Neela combed and combed her hair several times a day. Parvati would pass by her open bedroom door and see the comb lying on the small dressing table. It seemed to grow shinier each year, each day, and one day she had picked it up, had picked it up to look at it more closely, to look for any wearing away of the gilt, and had dropped it back quickly onto the dressing table and rushed out the room. She had gone downstairs to the kitchen and picked up a bowl of batter and beaten it and beaten it until it had become runny and threatened to spill all over the kitchen table, but she had kept beating it to keep the confusion out of her head for when she had picked up the comb, she had found that it was heavy, that it was not cheap plastic at all, and that it had only grown heavier and shinier and more solid where she had expected it to crack and chip, had expected its teeth to become broken and that Neela would have thrown it out without giving it a thought a long time ago. It was to be a sign. It was supposed to make everything she feared untrue.

Parvati shivered. 'Come inside, Ma. It's getting cool,' Neela said, putting her arms around her mother, and Parvati let Neela lead her into the house and down the inside stairway that led to the kitchen where they lit the lamps and heard Rampat and Billa coming through the gate. They were talking and laughing.

'Sampson is sick, a high fever. But his neighbour made him some bush tea and he's feeling better already,' Billa said when he reached the bottom-house and sat on a bench.

'Come inside and eat some dinner,' Parvati said, putting out plates on the kitchen table.

'Not for me,' Billa said, coming inside. 'If I don't go home and eat, Savo will be up quarrelling all night.'

'You give her good reason.'

'Oh, sister, you know that I treat that girl like a queen.'

'Drinking and smoking and cursing and…'

'Alright, Parvati, done now,' said Rampat.

Billa laughed. 'It's alright, Ram. My sister here needs to have somebody to quarrel with; you just don't give her enough trouble, eh?' He laughed again and looked over at Neela. 'And you too, girl. But you remember all those times I had to come and rescue you from all the stupidness people round here would say? To hear big men throwing talk about water mama and fair maids and so on – talking like that to a lil, lil girl, eh? They're nothing but bullies to pick on a child so. But they turned tail and ran from a real fight, eh Neela? You remember?' Billa punched the air and laughed, and Parvati's face softened: he had his moments.

There was that day in the backdam when Neela was still small when Billa had plunged into the punt trench and rescued her from the children. How cruel they were, taunting her and telling her she was a water mama. You would think children could stretch their heads out to hold all kinds of magic, would be curious and fascinated by things out of the ordinary, Parvati thought, but not those ones. They were their parents' children; they stayed herded within the familiar, and were afraid of anything unknown, anything that could not be explained by the few words they knew. How Neela used to cry, not knowing how to be different, or how to make them stop – the children, the men, the women who watched her from lowered eyes as if she were a sin. And Parvati remembered that she was helpless too, that all she could ever do was dry the girl's tears and hold her and feed her creamy *gulab jamuns* steeped in rose essence. Sweetness and prayer. Everyone would think her foolish and a poor mother if they knew that that was all she had to give; that and her belief that everything would turn out right in the end. And maybe she did help after all because Neela grew up to be quiet and composed, and was completely untroubled by the doors that slammed shut, and by all the people who turned and walked the other way whenever they saw her approaching. Her footsteps never hesitated, never changed course, and she floated over the earth, waded through the air as if it were water. She had a faith of her very own, Parvati remembered thinking one day as she watched Neela glide through the gate, looking neither left nor right, and going off to the shop to get matches and soap and split pea flour. She was unafraid of anything and those children, those very children who had been so cruel to her started to walk the other way whenever they saw her anywhere, and Neela would barely glance at them, would barely notice them at all. She did not seem to need friends and was content to be around the house and attend the *mandir*, and to laugh at Billa's jokes and antics whenever he dropped by to visit, as she was doing then in the kitchen. She was laughing as Billa made jokes and told stories in the lamplight which played about on her face and reddened it. She was just a child, a girl who liked to laugh and play like any other, Parvati thought, as she watched her and listened to what Billa was saying.

'One day when I turn into an old man, you'll have to come and save me, eh?' Billa said, and he put up his fists in a mock fight.

Neela laughed and looked at her own small fists and said, 'I will have to find another way, Uncle.'

'Oh, you will, you will,' Billa replied. 'I'm counting on you now.'

'Or you could just hush up your mouth and stay out of trouble,' Parvati said. 'You're always running off your mouth with some hotmouth talk and one day, one day I just know that it'll get you into trouble so big that you'll…'

'Alright, Parvati,' Rampat said. 'He's just making jokes.'

Billa got up to leave then and he was still laughing when he told Neela that he was hearing how the Maraj family with the big jewellery store in Georgetown was asking around about her, how they had heard about her beauty and her sweet voice, and wanted to make a match with her for their son, and how when she got married she would turn into a fine city lady and forget all about them and the village.

Billa laughed again and Parvati smiled and watched Neela. She had heard the rumours too, had heard how the Marajes had driven up in their big shiny car to see Pandit Tiwari the week before. 'You should see them, the mother and father sitting up in the back seat like a maharajah and maharani with the chauffeur with his eyes front and centre like he's in the army,' Billa said, puffing out his chest and strutting around the kitchen. 'Yes. I believe Pandit Tiwari will be coming to see you soon. You'll be invited to go and see the Marajes in their big city house, and to see if you like the boy.'

Billa was strutting around the kitchen, was busy with his antics and his talk, and Rampat was hunched over his dinner plate, so it was only Parvati who saw how everything changed, how, in an instant, all her fears rose up and appeared before her, and she knew that once they had shaped themselves like that, had appeared to her like that, that her eyes could never lose them again. For all the rest of her life she would never be able to take back that moment when she had blinked and found, when she opened her eyes, that Neela was no longer a child, an innocent amused by Billa's antics, but a woman, a knowing woman with a bigwoman smile and eyes that glittered hard like little lights. They shone as if wet, and her smile turned into a big laugh that parted her lips to show her teeth. It stayed low in her throat and growled like something strange, like something animal.

Parvati watched the woman and knew that she was not her Neela but a spirit that had come and taken her over, and she looked around the kitchen, looked around confused, but Billa's mouth was hanging open on a sentence that was left unfinished, and Rampat was hunched down even lower over his plate, and was looking at no one, was looking at nothing. They were no help, no help at all, and Parvati was gathering up her confusion into a quarrel, was readying herself to speak, to shout, and she was drawing in her breath and was getting ready to call out to Neela to stop it, to stop smiling like that, to stop laughing like that when the woman rose from the table. She pushed her chair back hard and it scraped across the floor with a dragging sound then toppled over and crashed, and Parvati watched her and trembled and drew back her words into the silence that followed. She had pushed hard against the table as well and the oil lamp rocked and threw high flaming shadows onto the walls all around them. The kitchen was a ring of fire, and Neela herself was fire-lit all over. Her lips, her tongue, even her eyes – they all glowed red and she threw her head back and laughed again. Her hips swayed, her hands danced and her laugh turned into a little song that came deep from the back of her throat. Her voice, her sweet voice which always climbed clearly to reach the highest notes rumbled low with a strange, haunting music.

Parvati heard her singing to her love to come to her, to come into her arms and sleep the sleep of eternity, and she heard her laugh again and saw her move over to the stairway that led to the upstairs rooms, saw her move up the stairs, leaving the music and melody to trail away behind her. She disappeared into the darkness at the top of the stairs and it was then that Parvati drew herself up straight and thought about Taijnie, and knew that it was her, that it was her mother who had come back to haunt her and to take her over like that, that it was her mother who was making her behave like that, like a badwoman who was casting her net, spinning her web. She had given the girl little thought over the years because she never wanted to remember the birth, and the death, never wanted to remember that the baby was never hers at all. But there was no turning away from it any more, no turning away from the fact even as Parvati remembered how she had held the baby close from the moment she was born, and how she had named her, how it was she who had named her. She remembered it clearly and knew that she was not going to let her mother, her badwoman mother step in and upturn her house and all the plans that she had for the girl who was her very own daughter, her very own Neela.

The night was pressing in. The oil lamp glowed softly on the kitchen table, and the outer darkness hummed and croaked and barked, but the kitchen was quiet and Billa left without a word, hurried away into the night, speechless, without saying a word. At any other time, Parvati would have laughed and teased him about it, about his speechlessness, but that night she watched him go and said nothing. She watched him go and watched how Rampat still had his eyes on his plate, and she wished that she could return to the moment when she had blinked, wished that she had kept a steady eye on the world instead. Then, she thought, it could never have slipped past her to go its own way like that, could not have run away from her like that, run away like water itself.

Rampat had not finished his dinner and when Parvati sat down at the table across from him, he pushed the plate away and got up. He was careful to not look at her, to not meet her eyes, and the moment when something could have been said passed, passed by them in silence, and he went out into the bottom-house to lie down in a hammock. Parvati watched him leave, watched him get up and leave the kitchen, and it gave her quarrel room to grow. He would let Neela do just as she pleased, live with them all her life, all their life if she wanted, and turn herself into her mother even and bring home a belly big with a child. Parvati breathed hard and turned to the sink to wash the dishes and made the pots and plates clatter and clang to fill up the silence. Yes, he would do anything to please her, his princess, even if it meant spoiling her whole life for good. He believed that was love, Parvati thought, to ask nothing, to say nothing, and to accept everything without question. But love expected, insisted, demanded, and it would be up to her to see that Neela did not end up in any kind of trouble. She was going to be married, good and proper, with all the sacred rites and she would have a nice life like everybody else. She was going to see to it. All that hip-swaying, hair-combing, night-swimming, sweet-singing nonsense would have to stop. She would have plenty of children and keep a nice home. Yes, the Marajes would do just as well, and they were wealthy so she would be comfortable and want for nothing. Neela would see how nice a life could be, Parvati thought, and she was going to keep an eye on everything and make sure that that Taijnie would never step in again and make any trouble with her badwoman ways. She was going to see to that, Parvati decided, as she put the last of the dishes away and saw that Rampat had dozed off.

What do men know anyway, she asked herself, sighing and letting go of her quarrel. All those years living with his family and suffering their insults – sure he had held her close and dried her tears but what did he understand about her heart, and how it had squeezed itself shut, and had drawn itself away from the world? Men knew nothing, nothing at all. It was only because she respected the closeness of family that she had not demanded that they leave and make their own home elsewhere. She would have lived on the streets if he had asked. And it was then, as if sensing her willingness to leave, that he had brought her the sea voyage, had brought it to her like a gift, a gift full of every kind of brightness in the world. But she had backed away from it, had been scared of the very idea, of the vastness of the thing. How far would they travel, and would they ever return, ever see their families again? She had never been on a ship before, not even on a small fishing boat she had told Rampat. She had put up arguments, defences, every imaginable obstacle in his path. What if they drowned, got lost, got swept away by a storm? Even humiliation could be borne for knowing how far the savaging would go, but the vast unknown of a journey out to sea to a strange land – he was asking too much, too much of her, she had thought for she knew nothing of ships and seas and sugar cane and was afraid to step away from the only world she had kept faith with, so she had turned away from his words, the words he had picked up in the marketplace, and she had heard him sigh and fall sleep. He would not force the journey on her and would not go without her, and she too had slept, pushing away all thoughts of the voyage out and away from all that they knew. But she had dreamt then of the world spinning and spinning around the sun, spinning faster and faster until it was a blur, until it seemed it would drop off into endless darkness. Then it had stopped suddenly in a burst of light, in a shower of stars, and she had awakened breathless, and with her heart racing, and she had seen in that instant that they must go, that they must journey across the spinning world, across the *kala pani*, and that it was their only hope. She had shaken Rampat awake then and had hurried him away before the sun came up, before she could have time to hesitate and change her mind, and Parvati always trembled whenever she remembered how close she had come to dismissing the journey, from the journey which had given them the baby, the child, Neela, and had brought them to the new world and all its possibilities. Rampat would have accepted her decision if she had wanted to stay. He would never have pressed the journey on her if she had said that it was pure foolishness.

She was his lotus blossom he told her in their most intimate moments, but she knew it was not only her prettiness that lit up his eyes. She was bold and she was dependable. Maybe he had seen it all when he had first looked at her, had first seen her. She was there every day that he came by to buy her sweets, was there day after day, year after year. Then she had dared to wear the joy-red sari he had bought for her, had married him right then, that very day when he had asked, had married him without questions, without plans or expectations.. She had taken the sari from him and wrapped it, pleated it, tucked it and drawn the richly embroidered *pallu* over her head then stood beside him at the *mandir* where they had exchanged wedding garlands and vowed eternal love, loyalty and respect for each other. He would protect her as they journeyed through life together, he had promised. He would be true and loyal and remain her life-long companion. He had looked into her eyes and had made the vows to her, to her alone without the benefit of a pandit since none of them would have agreed to marry them, she being just a girl from the bazaar, and he, a landowner's son. But the promises they had made to each other in their *jaimaal* wedding were all the richer for that. They were bound by nothing more than their own faith and trust in each other, and by their belief in the deities who were their only witnesses. The *jaimaal* was not without its romance for defying the world and its conventions, and everyone around her had thought her brave to dare the world so.

They had held their breath for her sake and she had never allowed them to see how her heart had trembled. Parvati sighed and looked at Rampat. He had fallen asleep in the hammock. He had his own ideas, her Ram, her Rampat. He was willing to take risks, and took care to guard her from the worries of the world, but he was not a man who could go it alone. He needed help to part the waves, to perform the daily miracles they had needed to survive.

None of their neighbours, besides Billa, knew of Neela's birth at sea, knew who her mother was and how she had died. Their shipmates were scattered in distant villages and estates and they would have forgotten all that had happened on the voyage out of India. Good fortune always closed over a troubled past, and even the great storm that had tumbled them around like playthings would have become a tale of heroics told from the safety of land. And the baby born out of the storm? She would have been long forgotten, or had become a footnote to a memory. Only Billa knew, and he had told no one. Everyone knew Neela as their own, and knew of no past, no past that held a mystery born out of the belly of the sea. Parvati sighed. It was going to be a long night so she let Rampat sleep.

Neela left early, well before midnight, and did not return until the sun was near to clearing the horizon, and all night Parvati's heart was clenched tight, was fisted up, and she hardly breathed. It was as if she was conserving her strength for all that she might be asked to bear. Several yards in front of her Rampat was crouched low on the canal bank. In the dark, he could be mistaken for a rock or a mound of earth left there by some careless workman. He did not move or shift about but sat out each hour in a stillness like a penance, like a pact made with the gods that if he did not move a single muscle everything would turn out well. But his stillness did not fool her. She knew his fear, all the thumping, pulsing, beating fear he felt as he watched the water and willed it to part, to give way and give him back his Neela. And just when all seemed lost, when the sun trembled between the earth and the sky, when it threatened to rush in and light up a whole new day without her, when Rampat would have sighed and would be preparing to push himself up from the bank and return home, and when Parvati was getting ready to go with him not caring if she were found out – just then, the water parted and Neela waded up to the bank. No telltale ripples announced her return. She rose up from the water as if she had been there, just below the surface all along and she sat on the bank, singing softly to herself and combing and drying her hair in the warming morning air. She seemed the same as before. Even from where she stood, Parvati could tell that it was as if the night before had never been, that it had all been an imagining – the laughter, the music growling low in Neela's throat – that it had all turned around in her head, in her head alone.

Parvati willed her heart to calm itself, to stop its hard beating as she hurried home. She had come back and that was all that mattered but Parvati feared, feared most of all that if they did not take care she might slip away from them, forever. All day the worry followed her about, and she planned what she would say to Rampat when he returned home that evening from the rice fields, and how she would greet Neela that day, how she would smile and laugh and talk as if nothing had happened. She would be bright with chatter like Daro and Loving, the young women who helped her with the kitchen work, though that morning their bright talk fell around her unheard as she mixed a batter for the savoury *phulouri*, and went through the motions, adding cumin, pepper, and salt to the split pea flour with barely a thought as to what she was doing. The bustle and chatter of the kitchen were restful. They made everything look normal and helped her cover up the confusion in her head. They would go and see the Marajes soon, as soon as the offer was made, then they would come out and see Neela and everything would be settled, the wedding date and everything. But what if they did not send an invitation, what if they listened to the many whisperings around the village about the girl, listened to all the foolishness that people said about water mamas and fair maids, and turned away instead? But Parvati did not believe that they were people who lived by ordinary rules. They would laugh and dismiss all that as empty village talk, as jealousy of a pretty girl who was obviously born for finer things, things they alone could provide. They would come to rescue Neela from all the country people, to fetch her away to the richer life she deserved, Parvati thought, and she worried then that they knew nothing about the Marajes, and that they could turn out to be mean and cruel, because money could do that to people, could give them biggity ideas about themselves. They could never do that to Neela, could never let her go off and live with such people, and Parvati thought then that there was always Parvesh if things did not work out. He with his long face and puppy-dog doting – it would make Dolly so happy if they decided on him. Rampat was sure to fret, but married to Parvesh, Neela would be just two streets away and that alone would console him well enough.

The kitchen in daylight looked innocent, ordinary, hardly looked like a stage for all the drama of the night before. Perhaps it was the night itself that had cast its darkness over Neela and turned her into a stranger with a stranger's laugh. All the drama had lasted for a second, no more than a second, and Parvati knew that if she were to ask Billa and Rampat about it, about what they had seen and heard the night before that they would both laugh and tell her that she was imagining things. The bright sunlight would do that, would make them dismissive, even forgetful. It had a way of driving out your night-time fears but Parvati remembered them and she looked around the kitchen and expected flames to leap off the walls and beat against her, to blind her, and her heart raced, and she stirred the batter faster and faster and raced against the thoughts that crowded up in her head and clamoured for attention. They would have to tell Neela everything, Parvati thought. But she had grown up not knowing, and they should probably leave it be, for what would be the good of Neela knowing who her mother was. She was the only mother the girl knew and Rampat, the only father, Parvati thought, and she blamed all the confusions in her head on Taijnie. It was all Taijnie's fault. She would not rest herself in the sea, but had come to take her daughter back for herself, and away from them, and it was then that Parvati knew it and felt it for sure, that one day the girl was going to leave, was going to run back into her own, true nature. You could not hold those things back, Parvati thought. It would be like trying to hold onto water itself, and everyone knew that that was not possible because water had a way of finding the tiniest crack, had a way of flowing on, of continuing its journey no matter how tightly you held it. How she wished that Rampat would say something, speak, make a row even, and tell her all his fears so that she open up to him about hers. Perhaps it was all too late, she thought, and it was when she thought that, thought that it was too late, that Parvati stopped everything she was doing and looked about her at the kitchen walls, at the walls which were bright with sunlight.

'Auntie, Auntie, what are you doing?' Daro asked and she peered closely at Parvati's face.

'You put sugar in the *phulouri* mix, Auntie,' Loving said, and she laughed and took the spoon and bowl from Parvati.

'You're not feeling well, Auntie?' Daro asked.

'She looks like she's seen a jumbie, eh?'

'Stewps. Don't talk stupidness, girl. Jumbies only walk about in the night-time. Come, help me take her out to the bottom-house to sit down.'

'Auntie, you sit down and rest yourself. We'll get everything ready today.'

'Run upstairs and call Neela. Tell her that her Ma is not feeling too good today.'

'No, no. I'm alright,' Parvati said. 'Just let me get some fresh air.'

Parvati let the women take her into the bottom-house where she sat in the shade of the sharp morning sun and took deep breaths of the warm air. Nothing could hide in the sun's naked glare. Neela's bigwoman behaviour, her turning into a stranger like that, Taijnie and her river-foam story, her own fears, Rampat's – she threw them all at the sunlight hoping to make sense of them but they kept slipping away, slipping away like water, like light. They slipped through her fingers no matter how tightly she held on. They had their own way. Not everything was possible after all, not even with the strongest faith in the world, Parvati thought, and she remembered that it was always the brightest sun that cast the darkest shadows on the earth and that there was no doubt about how brightly Neela shone. All Parvati knew was that from the very first time that she held her, held the baby girl in her arms, she had known that the girl would always be the centre of her world. Children did that. They were supposed to, were supposed to be your heaven and your earth, and she had grabbed at the chance when it came without thinking, without question. She was too greedy, and this was her punishment – that Taijnie was going to come and take over the girl for herself. She had befriended Taijnie when all of their *jahajis* and *jahajins* had turned away from her, had seen her for what she was, for the badwoman that she was and had turned away from her. But she had taken her baby to her breast, and the girl was now grown into her own self, her true self, and Parvati had nothing to hold to but her faith, her full faith in the world and all its goodness. She sighed then, and heard Daro and Loving come up behind her with their bowls. They were stirring their bowls of batter and bringing their bright kitchen chatter with them.

'Auntie, come tell us a nice story.'

'Yes, tell us about the time Uncle Rampat fetched down a golden sunset from the sky to make a bright sari just for you.'

'Yes, Auntie, tell us that story.'

It was their favourite story of the old country, and hers too. It was her most beautiful memory and when she smiled the young women put away their bowls and spoons and hitched up their aprons and made themselves comfortable. They knew the story, knew all its words, all its twists and turns but they never tired of hearing it. For them it glittered like a fairy tale and all the more because they knew the real-life prince and princess, so Parvati breathed in deeply and started.

The story would take her to a time and place where everything came out right and because she could do with such a journey right then, she smiled and looked out into the sunshine as onto a lit stage and began. 'He used to come every day after school, to buy my *methai*. Whichever tray caught his eye, he would point to it and I would wrap up the sweets or pastries for him.

'He was a shy-faced boy and I used to be shy at first too but it was because of his quietness that I made myself bold. It was left to me to fill up the silence so I used to chatter away at him and laugh and try to get him to talk. The truth is, I just wanted to hear his voice, you know, but he used to look at me with his big eyes and with his face pulled long and serious like an old man and he would walk away with his bag of sweets, all important-like, like he was a big man with no time for idleness with little girls. The first times I thought he was vexed with me for teasing him and I used to worry myself sick that he would never come again. But he always came and he stayed silent, giving me no words at all, just watching me put the *gulab jamuns* or *rasgullahs* into a bag during all those years. We grew up like that – him silent and me teasing him until the day came when all his words tumbled out and ran over each other so fast that I couldn't make head or tail of them. I had got so used to his silence that when he decided to open his mouth to speak, I almost fainted.

'It was a like a dam had burst to let out everything he had kept corked up inside of him. His words came deep from his belly. They were like thunder rumbling through heavy clouds but soft, too, like rain on rose petals, you know, soft and strong at the same time, like silk or velvet, and my head got all confused just listening to him. It was as if all those years he was preparing what to say and he said everything at one time.

'Well, my whole family came out to look. They had heard the strange voice and came out to look over the newcomer to the stall only to find it was the boy-turned-man who they used to jeer and call dumbo and tell that their Parvati would never give her *dil*, her heart to a man with no voice, no tongue, that only a man with words that came deep from the belly of the earth would win their beautiful Parvati. They had long sensed why he came each day to the stall but they always believed that one day he would stop coming because his parents owned land and lived in a big house behind high walls so they teased and mocked and laughed at him to prepare me for the day when he would disappear from my eyes forever.'

Parvati paused and looked into the sunlight, her face soft with the remembering, and Daro and Loving looked at each other and waited. The story had secret spaces that would be carried to the grave and they only spoke of them when Parvati was not around.

'She was afraid.'

'That his family would find him a rich bride.'

'That he would disappear – poof! – one day just like her family said.'

'And she would go mad thinking he was a dream she had made up...'

'...to please her *dil*.'

'And her with no words to make him real.'

'No words to remember him by.'

'He would pass like a shadow over the earth, like a jumbie in the dark.'

Parvati had to let her heart rest and release its tightness before she could continue. She remembered how she used to drop off the edge of the earth with the sun if night came without him, remembered how she would fall and fall, and how her heart would sink with the fading light and threaten to lay itself down in the dark. She died like that many times only to be jolted into sitting upright, into making her back regal, and into letting her smile play about her eyes when she would see him sauntering up among the bazaar stalls, stopping before this or that one before standing before hers to peer at the *methai* on display as if he had chanced on them for the first time and was astonished by the sumptuous spread of *gulgullas* and *laddoos* and *barfi*. She always giggled, always forgot that she had died moments earlier, as she had wrapped up his selection of sweets for that day. He was late sometimes, but in the end he always came and he never knew how she had suffered thinking him dead, or worse – wed to another. Unlike her family, she did not believe he would disappear one day even though he gave her nothing to hold to beyond the next day's hope that he would walk again among the bazaar stalls, seeking out hers, seeking out her. Like the sun rose and the sun set, that pattern too was fixed, and she remembered how she prayed, prayed that she would just see him every day for all the rest of her life. Then, in an instant, in a moment like magic, like a conjuring trick, her prayer was answered and she was given everything, and there in the bottom-house, in the sharp sunlight, she knew that they could not have turned the world over on its head like they had, and could not have been given so much only for it to go wrong. They had been tested and had come through it all and, when she remembered that, she drew herself up straight and continued.

'When he came that day with a parcel in his hand and started to speak, his voice ran through the streets, flowed out like a river and everyone left their stalls to come and look. He trembled at first but then he pushed out his chest to give his words more room, and they came out strong, strong and deep, each one richer than the one before. I could not breathe. My heart stopped, my head was spinning round and I was listening to his voice but I was hearing nothing. I only knew what he was telling me from the things my family was saying. All of them had crowded up behind me and were talking like a mad chorus, talking low and high and all over the place.'

'He wants to marry our Parvati,' Daro sang.

'But she has no dowry,' Loving said. They imitated the family's voices from the story they knew by heart.

'He's in love. *Pyar, pyar.*'

'His parents will throw them out for sure.'

'No bazaar bride for their son.'

'No bazaar girl for a daughter-in-law.'

'Don't do it, *bayti*, you'll be sorry.'

'But look at our daughter's eyes, her smile, her face shining like a moon.'

'He holds her *dil*, her heart.'

'Do it, Parvati.'

'He'll give you a good life.'

Parvati laughed at Daro and Loving's jangling music then continued. 'They made such a commotion, and my Ram was standing in the middle of the street holding out a parcel to me and, when I opened it, all our breaths stopped. The whole world was one big hush, I tell you. Everyone saw the brown paper wrapping come apart in my hands and watched as a whole sunset spread with golden light fell at my feet.'

Daro and Loving clapped their hands.

'Was it beautiful?'

'How did it feel?'

'It was a red river running down the middle of the street – yards and yards of the finest, reddest silk with golden threads and beads that bloomed like a flower garden, and my Ram, he picked it up at one end and wrapped it around me, and threw the golden *pallu* over my shoulder. How everyone cheered and clapped!' Parvati paused and blushed. 'I married him that very day.'

The young women cheered and clapped as well, then returned to the fires and the sizzling pans of the kitchen. The story ended there for them. The prince had found his princess in a country of palaces and crowns, of silken rivers and sunsets that fell out of the sky, and like all fairy stories it did not look beyond the happy-ever-after ending.

The memory was layered now with time and distance. They were like packing placed around treasures to keep them safe, and the memory never dimmed for Parvati. In fact, the story with all its magical twists and turns, its unexpected outcome grew brighter with each telling and always restored her faith. Rampat had been given to her and all the years she had lived with his family, keeping her footsteps close to the walls of the house where she was protected by the shadows, were only a trial, a test. She had passed it, and she could be generous now, forgiving even, even about the taunts that had rolled off her sisters-in-laws' tongues. They were the cruelest. Their many children had made them so. They were the favoured ones, and Parvati had run between their apartments, ordering their rooms and carrying out their every behest all day and all night especially if any of the children were ill. She had no children of her own, they would remind her, so, dear Parvati, help us with ours – we have so many. They would say this and laugh and send her off to the kitchen to fetch warm, sweetened milk, or to make them *gulgullas* or *kulfi* or *barfi*, whatever sweet they craved that day.

When Rampat's parents played with their grandchildren, spoiling them, Parvati would watch from the shadows of the walls and pray. Perhaps she was to accept that Rampat was enough, that she had already been blessed beyond all expectations. She had thought that many times but had always rejected the notion immediately because in the ordered world children made a home complete. She knew that to be true; even her own chaotic family was part of that order and, being sure of that, she had kept her calm even when Rampat's mother would send her off to the kitchen to help the servants, saying, 'Go, Parvati, and help them with their work. Nal and Saraswattie and Pooja have so much to do already with their many children.'

But all that was another life, another karma. If she met them now, Parvati would hold out her arms and they would embrace her. She was whole now, not a shadow, and they would see that in an instant. Even so, she still trembled whenever she remembered how close she had come to rejecting Rampat's plan that they sail away on the *S.S. Ganges* to a new life. Such a break demanded more from her than she thought possible, then the dream had come and she had seen everything clearly. Rampat never asked her about her change of heart and she could never have explained it to him, how she knew for sure that they had to travel around the spinning world to meet their fate. It was the same way that she knew for sure that Neela's marriage would settle her, would plant her feet firmly on the earth and that, if they failed her, she would slip away from them forever. Parvati needed no night dreams to guide her but dreamt open-eyed about the wedding in the bright sunlight.

'Now it's time for another wedding, eh Auntie?' Daro called out to her. It was as if she read her thoughts and saw, as Parvati did, the *maro*, the wedding tent that glittered in the morning sun, saw the palm branches arched over the gate, and the lotus lilies that were strapped to every tent post with bright ribbons.

'Yes,' Loving joined in, 'now it's Neela's turn to be wrapped in a silken sunset', and when Loving said that, Parvati saw Neela draped in a sari, richly red and made heavy with golden threads and shimmering beads. How the girl blushed and fidgeted with the bangles on her wrists and the fresh flowers in her hair. She was a beautiful *dulahin*.

'She will be a beautiful *dulahin*, eh Auntie?' Daro said. 'I hear the Maraj people have been asking round about her.'

'Yes,' Loving added, 'they have a big jewellery shop in town.'

'Imagine the golden bracelets and the earrings she will wear, eh?'

'They want Neela for their son.'

'Their boy, Vijay.'

'You and Uncle hear about this, Auntie?'

It would appear that everyone already knew everything. In a village where little happened, a big car bearing rich people would invite speculation, and gossip would fly, and stories would be made up. Neela herself had become part of that pattern, that weave. She was the reason why the milk went sour, the calf died, or the baby was born dead. She was always the reason, the explanation, for the villagers might pull away from her, but they were equally drawn to her by a natural curiosity, by a fascination with the unreal. She was not only a fair maid and a water mama, but a sea spirit with unearthly powers, a *devi*. She could heal, do miracles, cast off devils. They made her over into everything that they were not.

The stories about her magic, about omens and signs had taken on a life of their own and had spread about the countryside, and even when Neela was still a child, people used to bring their sick and crippled and dying to take life from her hands. It was Parvati who always turned them away, who sent them to the pandit or *moulvi*, or to the dispensary or the hospital for prayers or medicines or both. She was the one who listened to them tell how nothing had helped so they had come to Neela, that she was their last hope. Many times she cried with them, like she did over the little boy who was badly deformed and unable to walk, and who had to be carried in his father's arms like a baby. Doctors had looked at him and shaken their heads, had dismissed him and turned to those they could inject with cures, so the parents had come, had travelled many miles, to place their son at Neela's feet. They had heard it said that she could become water itself then turn herself back into human form.

'If someone can just draw out the bad spirit from him, our Ramesh will become well. Oh, Auntie, let your daughter put him in the water so that his bones can melt away like hers. Then we can set them back properly. Then our Ramesh will be able to walk and run like other boys. Oh, Auntie, please let her make our boy well.' The parents were young and they had cried, and Parvati had cried with them for Ramesh's legs which were curled up and useless, and for his eyes, which were blank. She had talked to them in a low, steady voice and had told them that her Neela was just a child with a different spirit and that people took that to mean all sorts of things, but that she couldn't cure their Ramesh, that the Lord Bhagwan gave their boy life and He alone knew what was best for him, and for everyone.

'I, too, when I look at my Neela, I have to steady my heart this way,' Parvati told them. 'We don't always understand everything in this world and God saves his biggest challenges for the bravest. You must have faith.' She had said all that knowing that there was no faith in the world strong enough to steady your heart as you watched your child die.

She began to recognize those who came seeking cures even as they stood at the gate. Their eyes gave them away: they were always hollow and haunted. They would stand still and silent and wait to be invited in, and Neela would see them and disappear up the stairs, and after Parvati had soothed them and sent them on to find cures in other places, she would find her daughter sitting before her mirror, combing and combing her hair with her golden comb, and singing softly to herself. She was only a reflection in a pool; she disappeared when a pebble was thrown. The words she sang in front of her mirror were always like that, that she was only a dream, an imagining. When she was still small she had touched her face once and said, 'Ma, I can only ever see my face in the mirror. I'm only a reflection. I'm not real.' She had said that, and Parvati had laughed and pinched her cheeks and told her that she was as beautiful and real as the mirror showed, but as she grew older, Neela added more to her song, added that the whole world was only a reflection in the eyes, that it was a trick, a trick to tempt the greedy, the evil.

She sang like that and smiled and touched her face then said, 'And when they reach for it they find nothing, nothing but their own greed and their own evil, and it kills them.' Neela had laughed, and Parvati had trembled and hurried out of the room and, sitting in the shade of the bottom-house, she remembered the laugh, remembered how it had come low from the back of the girl's throat, how it had growled and rumbled. The signs were there all along but she had chosen not to see, not to hear, had chosen to rush away instead, and Parvati decided then that she would go and talk to the girl plainly and tell her everything, everything she knew, and let things fall where they might, and she was just about to get up and find Neela, when

Dolly came bustling through the gate. She was walking quickly, was bursting with some news.

'Parvati! He's coming this way. Oh, what news here today!' Dolly spoke all the way from the gate to the bottom-house.

'What news? Who's coming?' Parvati asked.

'Pandit Tiwari. He's coming with the news. Girl, everybody knows! The Maraj people came to see him and he's coming to talk to you and Ram to fix up a meeting then is big wedding, eh?'

Just then the pandit unlatched the gate and joined them in the bottom-house. Dolly was right. He was there to arrange a time, was suggesting a Sunday lunch for Parvati and Rampat to visit and meet with the Marajes at their home in the city. 'They're good people, nice people. They keep a big *yagna* every year to give praise and thanks for all their blessings. Neela will be in good hands,' he said

Daro and Loving had put away their bowls to listen. 'We've got to start making the *methai* for the wedding from now, eh Auntie?' Daro asked.

'A big seven-curry to cook!' added Loving.

'And plenty music and dancing, eh?' Dolly said.

'Yes, *tassa* and *dolak* and *dantal*. Everything!'

'Imagine the bangles she'll wear!'

'And the henna for her hands and feet.'

'And a sari that lights up like the sky itself, eh Auntie?'

Pandit Tiwari laughed and Parvati told Daro to fetch him a glass of fresh milk. He was happy to be the one to bear the news, and Parvati could tell that the match satisfied him. He was always protective of Neela and he probably felt that all his years of keeping her safe from all the talk that followed her about had paid off. The Marajes were good people, he said again, and laughed at the antics of Loving and Daro who were drumming on the kitchen table and dancing, were taking turns to swirl and twirl across the floor. They were already celebrating and knew of nothing that could cast dark shadows, even blot out the sun but Parvati watched them and she trembled. She had planned that moment for so long, for so many years, that moment when she would see her daughter well married into a nice family, but she had never thought beyond the wedding, never considered all that could be discovered. She had been caught up in her own fairy tale, her own fantasy and had never thought to look beyond the glitter of the occasion, but now that the moment had arrived, had become real, she trembled and worried and wondered at all that might happen, at all that might come loose. She sat in silence amidst all of Daro and Loving's drumming and dancing, and no one noticed or they thought, perhaps, that her silence was her way of accepting the good news, that she needed a moment to catch herself and to reflect on all that was about to change. And the pandit had not come expecting objections, anyway, for the Maraj son was nothing if not a match made in heaven. Even Dolly said so.

It was funny how she had put aside all her hopes for Parvesh so easily, Parvati thought. Even a distant claim on the Maraj wealth made everyone giddy, and they would all come to the wedding just to feel close to it, and to watch Neela as she stepped round and round the sacred fire. They would watch her closely to see if she hesitated or slipped, to see if her feet wandered, and Parvati trembled again. For all their big-heartedness in choosing a village bride for their son, the Marajes would expect nothing less than perfection in a daughter-in-law, especially one who would be expected to be properly grateful for the sumptuous life her marriage would bring her. They would not tolerate anything out of turn. They would not stand for any sea-slipping, throat-laughing, hair-combing nonsense, and Parvati decided that she could not bear all the worry alone and that she would have to talk to Rampat that night, would have to be plain and open and tell him everything that she feared, and that there was still Parvesh, and that Dolly would be like a mother to Neela and protect her, and that Parvesh with his quiet ways would not question anything. She would be safe with them, and close by. It would be like she had never left home, at all. She knew that Rampat did not take to the boy but there was so much more to consider.

'Neela!' The exclamation from the women in the kitchen broke into Parvati's thoughts. Neela had come downstairs to the kitchen.

'Look at our *dulahin,* our bride!' they said and they flocked around her, all of them, and they were all talking at once. Pandit Tiwari smiled then got up to leave, and he raised his hand in a blessing. 'Sunday then,' He said. 'I will let the Marajes know to expect you and I'll pick the most auspicious date for the wedding to give the couple a good start.' Parvati saw him to the gate then turned back to join the commotion in the kitchen. She thought it would help her to put away her trembling, her worry, for Neela was laughing at everything the women were saying to her, at all their teasing, which only encouraged Daro and Loving and Dolly to get even louder. They only saw how the girl laughed, how she giggled and laughed with them, and it was only Parvati who saw how her manner changed, only Parvati who heard how her laughter stayed low and rumbled in her throat. She had not imagined any of it the night before. The girl was her mother's child, was Taijnie's child, after all, and she could not help but wonder if they were going to lose her for good, and if the girl was going to slip away from them and disappear from the earth like Sampson's mammie and granmdmammie had. Such tales were told of men that died, or drowned, or sickened and pined away until they were dust but those were stories that were told to frighten children on moonless nights, were jumbie stories and fairy stories. They did not live, those tales. They did not laugh and sing under your very eyes and next to your heart but only lived in the dark night-time, in every sough of a branch, and under every big rock where children found them and ran screaming every time.

But Parvati saw how Neela laughed and clapped her hands when the women danced around the kitchen, danced around her, and she felt that she was just imagining things, that it was her own fears that were chasing her, fears she had had from the moment she had held the girl in her arms, and had known that she could be taken away from her one day. But the girl was happy, was laughing, was acting like every young girl with a suitor at her feet, was behaving like she herself had done that day when Rampat came and poured a red and silken river before her. The girl was no different and Parvati heard how she started to sing as Loving and Daro and Dolly took turns at drumming on the kitchen table. She sang about a handsome prince who rode over mountains of waves to meet his love, his love who bore a bouquet of flowers picked from the sea. Parvati listened keenly to the words and followed the story of the song and heard how the prince lay in a bed bluer than the sky with pearls for his eyes and plumes of water to crown his hair. 'She tended him for all eternity,' Neela sang, and when she finished, Daro and Loving and Dolly all cheered. It was only Parvati who heard what the song said, and heard how the notes stayed low in Neela's throat. It was only Parvati who trembled.

The whole day passed like that for her. Parvati trembled then laughed, felt fear then went giddy with happiness, and she longed for the day to end, for Rampat to come home so that she could talk to him, tell him everything, so that she could hear him say that she was worrying herself about nothing, was fretting up herself about nothing, about nothing at all. But when, at last, she sat across from him on the verandah, and watched him take long drags on a cigarette, she found that she was exhausted and had little to say. She had held everything she knew and everything she feared so close to herself and for so long that it had become a comfortable habit, and she found she could not, after all, say words that would cast suspicions on her Neela, that would make her out to be a lie or a stranger, and Parvati turned her face into the falling light and told Rampat only about the Marajes' invitation, told him all that Pandit Tiwari had said.

His face remained closed for the longest time and Parvati was becoming irritated, was about to cut the air and break into his silence with some sharp words when he asked, 'So, what do you say?'

'You're her father, Ram. Let me hear what you think, eh?' She spoke lightly, joking almost.

He fell back into silence then, and she could see from the quick puffs on his cigarette how much he too trembled, how much he too feared. The years of watching over her had come to that, that they would have to let her go, and Parvati saw the worry of it gather on his forehead and settle around his eyes, and she sighed and looked out at the darkening sky, watched it get darker and darker, locking it down for the night. She sighed then and said that there was always Parvesh, that he was a good boy and that Dolly would look after her like a mother but Rampat cut her off with a sharp no before she could even finish.

'No,' he said, this time quietly like a thing decided that need not be mentioned again. 'It'll be alright. We'll go and meet the family and see for ourselves what kind of people they are. If they're kind and good like the pandit says, it'll be alright.' He paused then added, 'It'll be good for her.' Then as if he had said too much, he laughed. 'I mean with a husband and family and all that to look after she will be busy, eh?'

Parvati sighed and smiled and sat back in her chair, settled back into it comfortably. It was decided then. It was easier than she had expected and she told Rampat then, told him all the plans that Dolly and Daro and Loving had for the wedding, all the dancing and singing that they planned to do, and when he laughed, when she saw how easily he laughed, she let all her worry slip away into the night. She had let a whole set of foolishness come over her for the truth was that she was probably looking for all kinds of signs everywhere because of what their *jahajis* and *jahajins* had said on the day the girl was born, all those mad whisperings they had made, and she had taken their madness for truth and had looked for signs where there were never any, where there was never anything at all.

But all week, Parvati could not help but trouble herself with the fresh fears. She worried that the Marajes would turn out to be biggity people because money had a way of doing that to people: it gave them biggity ideas about themselves, and she went to their house expecting that, expecting them to have airs, and to act all vain and pretentious. She had convinced herself so much about what to expect that when the boy's parents, Uma and Suresh, greeted them with smiles and with their arms extended to embrace them, Parvati had to stand back and catch herself, had to steady herself a little before she, too, reached out and put her arms around Uma and kissed her on the cheek. They turned out to be the nicest people, and the boy, Vijay, was no prince, no maharajah, after all, but he had a nice face and a nice manner and Parvati could not help but think that Neela was a lucky girl to have found such a good match among such nice people. Neela would live like a maharani with cushions at her back and spreads of carpet at her feet. Everything about the house and the Marajes were like that, cushioned and comfortable, and it was not until she had eased back onto the settee and was looking closely at Vijay and thinking that he would make a good husband for their daughter that she realized that she would be losing the girl forever, that after the wedding, Neela would belong to the Marajes, that she would come to live there among them in that large spread of a house with its many windows and high ceilings and she would be lost to them forever, would be lost as much as if she had disappeared, had run off like water itself. Vijay had two younger sisters, pretty girls, and Neela would find herself among them, would have new parents, and sisters and a husband then a family of her own, and she would drift away from them, from the village, the village with its small houses and narrow lanes, and become a fine city woman just like Billa said she would.

Parvati thought that and had to flutter her handkerchief about her face to stop herself from feeling faint, from feeling all her fears come over her again. But she also wanted to laugh at herself, to laugh out loud when she realized that all her worry had been nothing more than her fear of losing the girl to a marriage, of watching her disappear from them on her wedding day because the girl did not have real ties to them, after all, no ties of blood, and when they told her the story of how she was born aboard the *Ganges* far out at sea, how she was born to a mother who died, she would leave, would turn away from them and find that she had no reason to come around and see them any more. But Parvati knew that their Neela was not an ungrateful child, and that she would not behave that way, so she pushed away the worry of it, the worry of all that might happen, and she put away her handkerchief and turned back to the chatter and laughter of the conversation that was going on around her.

Suresh and Uma were talking of all their plans for Vijay, were saying that the boy was already managing the jewellery business and that he would take over from them, would inherit the city shop they had built. 'He will take over and modernize, expand,' Suresh said and he laughed and said that the boy was bright and had a good future, a bright future.

'And Neela?' Uma asked then, and turned to Parvati. She wanted to know everything about the girl. They heard that she was beautiful and could sing the most beautiful songs, and Parvati blushed then and said yes, the girl was beautiful and she was kind and good and that she liked to go to the *mandir* to sing at the *satsangs,* that she had the clearest, finest voice, and that everyone said that she sang like a real *devi,* a real goddess. She was a nice child, a good child, Parvati said, and Rampat laughed and said that their daughter, that their Neela was the best child in the world.

Everyone talked and laughed at once, and they moved to the dining table which was set prettily with china plates on a lace tablecloth. The curries and dhal and roti were all well made but when a dish of *gulab jamuns* was set before Parvati and she bit into one of the fried milk balls and found it tough, she smiled a little to herself and thought how she would surprise them, how she would surprise Uma and Suresh and Vijay with her *gulab jamuns* when they came to visit, when they came out to the village to see Neela. The ones set before her in the pretty china dish were made from milk powder but hers she made from scratch, from curds that were made from fresh whole milk and a squeeze of lemon juice which were poured into a fine muslin cloth and hung to drain for fifteen minutes. She then mixed the curds carefully with the best refined flour and divided the dough into balls, and in the centre of each milk ball she placed a green cardamom seed and two grains of brown sugar then rolled the balls carefully to remove any cracks in the dough before she fried them, fried them until they were golden brown. The last step was to have the syrup ready and warm, a syrup of sugar and water and crushed cardamoms in which the milk balls were steeped for at least one hour before serving. To make the sweet properly took care and patience but the ones set before her had been done hurriedly, had been fried for too long, and were tough. But Uma said they were the best in the city. 'I had them made specially,' she said, and Parvati smiled again at her little plan. They were to come out on the next Sunday for lunch and to meet Neela, and Parvati planned that she would get up early on Sunday morning to make the fresh curds, and the sweetest, creamiest *gulab jamuns*. It would be such a surprise.

All that week, Parvati planned the lunch. She got all the ingredients together, and listened to Daro and Loving as they laughed and chatted and decided on which of the seven curries they would cook first on Sunday morning. They were to come early and start the preparations for the *katahar, aloo, baigan, bhajee*, pumpkin, eddo, and the dhal that would be made thick then sizzled well with cumin and garlic that were burnt to a crisp. And all that week, she thought that she should sit down and talk with Neela, tell her about the Maraj family and about the nice life she would have with them, and that she was not to be afraid of anything at all. But the days were too busy and Neela seemed happy enough. She continued to laugh and talk and to let herself be teased by Daro and Loving and Dolly about the wedding and about becoming a *dulahin*. Every day was like a *sangeet* party, like a bridal shower in the kitchen with the women bursting into folk songs, and making fun of the *dulaha*, the bridegroom, and setting out to give Neela advice on all that she would have to do in the bedroom to have a good marriage, and Parvati shushed them when they got too bawdy, told them that that was enough now, and kept a close eye on Neela, watched to see whether her voice would rumble, whether it would lose its high-pitched laughter and stay low in the back of her throat. But all week Neela behaved like nothing more than a young girl who was being promised love and marriage and the whole fairy tale that went with it for Daro and Loving and Dolly spoke of the wedding that way, made it glitter and sparkle with crowns and gowns and sequined splendour.

All week they planned and prepared and reached for the best glass bowls from the backs of cabinets, and washed them and rubbed them until they shone. It was as if they were preparing for the wedding day itself, and Parvati wondered whether she and Rampat should not sit down with Neela and tell her something about how she was born, tell her about the ship out of India, and about her mother, her real mother, and Parvati cried whenever she thought like that. She could not help it and she would leave the kitchen and all its chatter, would leave it to go and sit in her room and cry quietly to herself, and to tell herself that she always knew the day would come when they would have to tell their daughter all about Taijnie, tell her that she was not theirs at all. But when she suggested it, said that it was time, Rampat said that they should let the Maraj family come first, and when the date was set and everything was ready then they would let her know how she came to them out of the storm at sea, how she came to them like a blessing, like a gift. Rampat was sure of it, was sure that that was best, so Parvati left it alone, left the girl's story unsaid and untold, and trusted that he was right. The week was filled with enough bustle and busyness anyway, and when Sunday came Parvati rose early, well before the sun, to make the *gulab jamuns*, to make the balls of milk that would burst sweet and creamy on the tongue.

She followed each step carefully and was placing each of the fried balls into the syrup, and laughing a little to herself at how surprised Uma would be when she tasted her *gulab jamuns*, was laughing at her little surprise when Daro and Loving arrived to start all the cooking and preparations for the lunch. They arrived with their bright chatter and scrubbed the table which sat just off the kitchen, scrubbed it clean and spread it with a newly bought square of plastic which was bright with big red flowers, and Dolly came with lace slipcovers for the backs of the chairs. They were hot pink. 'They brighten up the place real nice, eh?' she said, and she was making ready to leave when Parvati invited her to stay, insisted that she stayed. 'You're like family, like my own-own sister, Dolly. Come, sit down and rest yourself. The Marajes will be here soon, and you look so nice all dressed up in your new lace frock. Come, see that the girls set the table nice.'

Daro washed the best plates, all edged in gold and blooming with delicate pink roses, and placed them evenly around the table then put a vase filled with hibiscus, crotons, and streams of bougainvillea picked from the yard right in the middle, between the bowls of rice and dhal. Even Rampat commented on how festive everything looked, and when the Maraj car drove up just then and parked outside the gate, when it hummed and purred and spread itself across the dirt lane, all sleek and silver and hugging the ground, Parvati felt her heart flutter and tremble again. But she breathed in hard and closed her eyes and told herself that she had travelled far, had come all across the world, had survived a storm that had tumbled them about like playthings, and that she had been granted such blessings, such blessings from the gods that nothing could go wrong now. She had no doubt that the boy would find Neela beautiful, that he would have no objections, but when Parvati thought of Neela, she held her breath and prayed that the girl would not take a sudden turn, would not do anything rash, anything indiscreet, and that the hard glitter in her eye and the low growl in her voice would not return to intrude on the day.

Parvati breathed in deeply again, and when she opened her eyes and saw how Uma and Suresh and Vijay smiled, and how they held out their hands again in greeting, she let all her fears just drop away. She had faith, such faith, she thought, and she held out her hands to her guests and welcomed them to her home, and when everyone was settled in the sitting room, Neela stepped in quietly with a tray of sweet drinks for everyone, and Parvati saw how Uma held her breath and how Suresh clapped his hands in delight. He called out to Vijay, then, called out to their boy who had stepped out onto the verandah to look at the narrow lane and the small houses that were set among the spreading trees. 'Vijay, come and meet Neela,' he said. 'Come, my boy, and see how beautiful she is.'

And when the boy stepped inside and looked at Neela, Parvati saw, at once, that he was nervous, that he was suddenly unsure of himself. Neela was even more beautiful than he had expected. He could never have imagined such a face, such hair, such grace, and it took him a full minute to catch himself and to mumble a greeting, to nod in her direction and say *namaskar*. But his parents rushed in to fill his silence. They were delighted. They clapped their hands. They spoke. They laughed, and just then Dolly came up the stairs to announce that lunch was ready, and as they were moving down the stairs, as Parvati turned to lead her guests down the stairs, she saw Neela lift her head and smile at the boy, at Vijay. It was a brazen smile, her badwoman smile, and when Parvati saw how Vijay stepped back, stepped back startled, she felt the clamour run through her heart again.

She sat at the table and trembled but the bright chatter did not give her fear and worry room to grow and soon she, too, was caught up in the laughter and conversation when she saw how pleased Uma and Suresh were with everything. They complimented Daro and Loving on their cooking and made the women blush like little girls. And Parvati was glad she had invited Dolly to stay. She kept up a running conversation with Uma which gave Parvati the chance to sit back and turn over all the wedding scenes before her eyes. She had done that so many times before, but there at the table, with the prospects of the event becoming real, even elephants loomed large and peacocks wandered across lawns that were acres wide, weaving in and out of the bits of conversation that floated up around her. Everyone was talking at once and she heard Dolly telling Uma about her cake shop on the main road, Rampat talking about the rice depot and export prices, and Suresh answering questions about the jewellery business and bringing Vijay, bringing the boy into the conversation.

The boy, Parvati thought, and looked again at Vijay, looked at him more closely. He was no prince, after all, and Parvati gave up her open-eyed dreaming and let the elephants go and the peacocks scatter. He was broad-shouldered and squat and had a square head, and he was no more than an inch or two taller than Neela. His eyes were his best features. They lit up his face when he smiled and he smiled a lot as he talked with his father and Rampat. He had a nice face and a nice manner was what she thought again, and he looked sure and steady. The pandit was right: the Marajes were nice people. Parvati sighed again and packed away her worry for good. It was time. Neela's footsteps would surely keep to the earth now. With the whole world in all its goodness and richness at her feet, she could do little less. Everything that went before was nothing but childish play, even boredom perhaps with the same-old, same-old country life they lived. She would live in the city and become busy and bustling. Her footsteps would surely keep to the earth, would flit about above it as busily as butterflies and she would come to know the city streets as well as her father did, would become a businesswoman, too, along with her husband, with Vijay, since the business would eventually be theirs. Parvati remembered then her own youthful days in the bazaar and how she once sat among heaped basins and platters of sweets. She remembered the thrill of the sale, and how the heaps dwindled and the coins jingled merrily as she threw them, one after the other, into the small box that she kept at her side. Neela would know that thrill, too, the thrill of the sale, and she would take an interest in the world around her, all those big and important matters that the city men, those politicians came and talked about.

Parvati never felt that any of the talk about building wider streets and bigger schools had anything to do her, and in truth, she did not pay much attention to any of it. She liked her life just the way it was. She wanted nothing to upset it. She was wholly content with her house and her neighbours and with Neela, most of all with Neela, but she thought that once the girl started to live in Georgetown, she might take an interest in all the political talk, like the talk that was coming from Suresh and Vijay. They were going on about all that the politicians were saying, about all the promises they were making about home rule, about getting independence so that everyone would have a better, brighter future. They were repeating all the words she had heard many times before, the same ones that Rampat always brought back from the meetings he attended.

He would often return with Sampson and Billa in tow and they would sit in the bottom-house until late at night turning over all that they had heard. Billa was always the loudest, and she did not mind their talk too much, even when they started to argue, did not mind their talk just as long as that Reverend Davies was not with them. She did not like the man or his work. It was a shameful thing for a big man to do, to steal people away from their gods, their ancestors, and all that they ever knew about themselves. He was nothing but a thiefman, a common thief, and Parvati could never understand why Rampat was friends with him, why he cared to listen to anything that the man had to say. She remembered how she had found Rampat sitting in the bottom-house one evening late and when she had asked him what was the matter, he had started to tell her how the reverend had seen violence, big violence with flames and conflagration, had seen violence that afternoon after a young man who turned out to be Sampson's son shook his finger in Billa's face. But she had cut into the story and had told Rampat not to listen to a word that that man said, that he was not to trust anything he said because he knew nothing about their life and how nicely they lived with everybody.

But he was like that, her Rampat. He had a big heart which had room enough to hold everyone, even that white preacher man, and Sampson, who used to whip them for anything, for anything at all, and that Billa. She never knew what it was that ever drew Rampat to the little Tamil man. It was since they were aboard the *Ganges* that she had noticed it, had noticed their closeness, and when the man turned out to be bound for Coverton Estate like them, the friendship grew even closer. She supposed he was lively company, and he was a good and honest man, never mind all his bigmouth ways, so she had not minded Rampat's friendship with him too much. But the reverend was another matter. Parvati never spoke to him at all beyond a polite good day whenever he joined the men in the bottom-house to go over all the latest political talk. She would bid him good day and turn back to her kitchen. She always made sure that he was aware of what she thought of him.

Every day, she saw the product of his work among the villagers, saw how it turned people inside out and upside down until they did not know who they were. The Premnath family – she used to sit next to the mother and her daughters at the *mandir* – had all become Christians, Presbyterians. It gave them biggity ideas about themselves and that was what vexed Parvati most, that the reverend's people felt that their new religion made them better than everybody else. The Premnaths were an easy catch for him for they had new money from rice lands and a rice mill and they thought that they needed a new god to go with their new wealth and status and all their new ideas about themselves. All the parents ever talked about was how their children were going to get educated in the Christian schools and go away to study to become doctors and lawyers. They thanked Jesus for their new life and guarded themselves against everything from their old. It got so that they would not even wear a sari or *kurtha* any more. They were afraid that that alone could draw them back to their old ways, and Parvati thought that it was a risky business, indeed, if pieces of clothing could pose such great dangers to their new ways. Even the poor drunks that turned Christian found money to buy shirts and ties and hats to wear to Sunday service. They wore new airs with their new clothes and all Parvati could think was that it was an ungodly business, indeed, when a church and a religion gave people such grand ideas about themselves. She said as much to Rampat when he spoke about Reverend Davies' good work among the poor but that was just like him, it was just like him to be all understanding and forgiving, and she kept a close eye on the reverend whenever he came by because she was sure that he was after her Rampat's soul. She did not ever believe that he could be swayed by anything the reverend said, but Parvati knew that you could never be too careful or too watchful.

Her own deep contentment with the world came from drawing it in closely about her. It kept her safe, that world which she knew well, knew how it would act and feel and talk, and she never felt any need to look about her too much because it was out there, beyond what the eye could see, where trouble lay. The journey out of India was enough distance for one lifetime. She had had her full share of adventure and newness and strangeness and had drawn in enough of the new world about her to make it comfortable and familiar. It was why all the political talk of a new brightness and a new future never interested her for her life was already full and blessed, and she only had to look around the table to see all her good fortune, and see how well everything had turned out.

Dolly was still deep in conversation with Uma and Parvati thought, not for the first time, how Dolly was part of the goodness she had found in the new world. She was like the big sister Parvati had left behind in India. Dolly had the same kind face and the same little-girl laugh that she had been prepared to miss forever, and she had taken to her at once when they met at the *mandir*. And when Dolly found out that Parvati could make the sweetest sweets, it was she who got Parvati her first order to make the *prasad* and *methai* for a wedding in the village, then suggested that she make enough sweets and pastries, each day, for her shop by the main road. It was the best suggestion ever, and it gave Parvati a bustling business and enough money to pool with Rampat's to give them a nice life. It had all turned out well, and Dolly became her whole family in the new world besides Rampat and Neela. They shared secrets and kept each other company, and they always went together to the *mandir* or to *jhandis* or wedding houses about the neighbourhood. They laughed at the same things and found that they liked the same kinds of people, and Parvati was not surprised to find that Dolly did not like Reverend Davies either. 'The man makes being a Hindu a sin,' Dolly said and shook her head. 'But that there is the real sin: turning people away from themselves.'

It was Dolly who also suggested outings and excursions and Parvati liked that about her for, left to herself, Parvati would be quite content to stay in her home and her yard and not ever go anywhere else in the world. But Dolly liked to walk about. She liked to meet new people and visit new places, and the outings she planned for them were always nice for Neela, so Parvati always went along with them. They had even gone to the city a few times, had taken Neela with them when she was a little girl, all dressed up in a frilly pink frock. Parvati had taken her around the city to show her off. That was how she saw those trips, that it gave everybody a chance to see the beautiful child clutching her hands and to know that she was her mother. Those were the only times that she allowed herself to feel boastful. She would walk along the pavements talking with Dolly and holding tight to Neela's hand, and Parvati would talk and laugh and look at the shops but the truth was she did not like the city very much. There were too many streets and too much busyness. But it was there that Dolly was in her element. She dove into every shop and turned everything over before she settled on buying some trinket or trifle, a bunch of brass pins or a pot spoon. And Neela liked the place, too. She liked the shiny shops and the streets bustling with horse-drawn carts and honking motor cars and cyclists going off in every direction. The place must have looked like a big adventure to her little-girl eyes and Parvati went along with them and kept up with their prattling well enough, but the truth was that she was always glad to get back home to her yard and narrow lanes and the neighbourhood where she knew everyone. She had never even gone to Paradise. There was no need. She had no friends there and Sampson and some of the friends he brought with him from time to time were all the people she knew from the next village.

It was Rampat who liked to bother his head with those things, about knowing Georgetown and all its streets, and finding out about Sampson and how they lived and how they had come to the colony. But those were longtime stories. They had nothing to do with life now and Parvati had no time for them. 'This time is not longtime, Ram,' she would say to him as she bustled about her kitchen, only half-listening to him go on about the country and its history, and the politics of the place, of the coming changes, of home rule and independence, and of getting the vote. He liked to keep his head busy and bother it with all those matters, and Parvati thought that when he became a grandfather it would be just the thing to settle him down.

She laughed at her pretty picture. She could see their grandchildren running and jumping about in the yard and Rampat settling them into the hammock and telling them stories about India just like he used to do with Neela when she was a baby. All those years of watching the girl grow into a beautiful young woman, a young woman about to start out on her own life – Parvati laughed again as she looked at all the faces around the table, and laughed even more when Daro and Loving came around and set small glass dishes of *gulab jamuns* before everyone, and said how Auntie Parvati had made them especially for them, how she had been up since early that morning to make the sweet. Parvati saw Neela eat hers hurriedly then signal to Vijay that they leave the elders to themselves. Uma and Suresh exchanged pleased glances as the young people went back up the stairs with Neela leading the way. Everyone stopped to watch them go, to watch them run back up the stairs and disappear at the top, then all together, they laughed and talked and their comments rushed in, overlapped one another and became a hurrying, sparkling stream that slipped out through the windows and out into the sunshine. It was a festive noise, and Parvati was laughing and watching closely as Uma took a small piece of the *gulab jamuns* in her dish and brought it to her mouth, was spooning it along with the syrup, which was heavy and fragrant; Parvati was watching and waiting to see the delight on Uma's face when she tasted the sweet, was waiting for the surprise when a scream, a scream that was frightened and pained, a scream that was like no other she had ever heard cut into their chatter, cut into it and stopped it dead.

For all of the rest of her life, Parvati was to remember that moment – the talk and laughter, the sunshine, the smiling faces and the *gulab jamuns* – she was to remember that moment as the last time, the very last time that she ever felt at ease in the world. From that point on everything changed, and was lost forever. The scream was not a high-pitched, female scream. She registered that at once. The notes did not shiver and shriek; they had a deeper, bellowing sound, a masculine sound. It was the sound of fear, of deep-bellied fear, and Parvati was the first one to get up from the table. She pushed herself up and her chair toppled onto the floor, and she pelted herself up the stairs, her footsteps urgent, her feet bare, slapping and banging on the treads as her fancy, beaded slippers flew off her feet. Fear drove her, whipped her up the stairs. It ran with her. It was no longer an imagining, a worry in her head, a dread locked away behind her eyes. She was running up the stairs, pelting herself up to meet it, to face it. It was there in the scream. It sounded familiar as if it had come out of her own head and she knew that she had been expecting it, had been waiting on it all her life.

The ease she had felt only moments before around the table, at the pretty picture of laughing, contented people – she had only been fooling herself. This was what she always knew to be true, this sound of terror. Her heart shifted, actually moved in her chest and pressed up hard against her ribs. It was heavy with dread but it was a dread that brought with it a distinct relief, for, at last, she would face it, would have to. It would be over once and for all. Once and for all, she said to herself again. She had allowed herself to be fooled by the bright chatter and the laughter only because she wanted so much to believe that that was the reality, and that all that she had come to know and understand was only an imagining in her head, the way Neela always said, that the world was a reflection of the light, that the real was only imagined, a dreaming in our heads. No, no, no, Parvati screamed to herself as she raced up the stairs, the top seeming mountain high, unreachable, shifting farther and farther away as she ran to meet it.

'Oh, my Lord Bhagwan,' she prayed, 'I would give anything, anything! I have done wrong. I have been greedy. I wanted to be a mother. I wanted a child to love and nurture and watch grow. I was glad when Taijnie died. Yes, I was! I was glad when her little life bled away. I believed that I could be a better mother, that I could love her child more, that I alone deserved her. There, now you know how black my heart is. I took her, took her for my own and pretended to the whole world that she was mine, my own, my daughter, my flesh and blood that I birthed through long and hard labour. I lied. I stole. I was greedy. I am a sinner and I kept it from everyone, even her. Oh Lord Bhagwan, forgive me, forgive me. I would give anything, anything. Cast me down in my next life for the sinner that I am, only give me this one salvation now. I will make it right. Only save me, save her, save us.'

Parvati held her heart to still it when she reached the top of the stairs, when she saw, at once, how Vijay was pinned to the wall, how Neela was leaning in on him, crushing him, and how her tongue, her red tongue was playing all over his face. The girl was laughing. It was her badwoman laugh. It was Taijnie's laugh, the laugh that came from low in her throat. Vijay screamed again when he saw Parvati, screamed for help. He was frozen stiff and unable to move, unable to thrust Neela from him. One hard shove would have done it but she held him down with some fiendish strength until Parvati moved in and pried Neela away from him, loosened her grip and added her own screams and shouts to the mad laughter, the bellow, to the tumble of feet on the stairs as everyone followed her into the drawing room. She got the boy away from Neela just as his parents reached the top of the stairs. They arrived just in time to catch him as he collapsed into their arms, sobbing, sobbing unashamedly like a child, a frightened child.

'What happened, son?' Uma asked.

'What did she do to you?' Suresh asked.

'Did you trouble the girl, son?' Uma asked.

'Uma! What are you saying? You know our Vijay is not a boy like that,' Suresh said.

Parvati was still struggling to hold Neela against the wall and she called Rampat over to come and help her. 'Who are you? What did you do to the boy? Answer me!' Parvati said to Neela, but quietly so that no one would hear her.

And when Neela said nothing and tried to push her away, Parvati said, louder this time, 'Tell me. Tell me now!'

But Neela only laughed and when Rampat came over he only stroked Neela's hair, gently, softly, as if to hush a fretful child.

'What did you do to Vijay?' Parvati asked again.

'Enough, Parvati. Listen to what you're saying. She's our child,' Rampat said.

'This is no child. This is a woman, a knowing, grown woman,' Parvati replied.

Dolly, Loving, and Daro had all crowded into the sitting room and were standing about open-mouthed. Vijay was still sobbing, quietly now, and his parents continued to ask questions but without waiting for answers.

'What happened?'

'What did she do to you?'

'We heard such things…'

'Such things were said…'

'But we thought it was all nonsense!'

'Jealousies.'

'And fairy stories of water mamas and so on.'

'She was crushing me. She was going to break my bones,' Vijay said, in a rush, a rush of fright, and he told them then that Neela had opened her mouth and he had seen the whole world spinning around inside it. That was when he had screamed. The boy told the story and Parvati was surprised to find Rampat laughing, and was even more surprised when he started to tell Uma and Suresh the story of the young Lord Krishna who had stolen some butter once in a childish prank and how when his mother told him to open his mouth, she saw there, instead of the butter, the entire universe spinning around inside it. But he never got to finish his story for Uma cut him off and told him that his daughter was no divine being, no goddess, but only a jumbie woman, a water mama. They had heard such things, she said, had heard such things about the girl but had dismissed them as country people's superstitions, as imaginings in their head. And when Rampat continued to laugh and tried to make light of what Vijay thought he had seen, Uma gathered herself up to her full height and said, 'Our boy is no fool.' She turned away then and added, 'Come, Suresh, We're done here.'

They left. The Marajes turned away and left, and Parvati heard the low purr of the car as it moved away. She was still holding Neela against the wall but collapsed then into a chair and held her head in her hands and cried openly.

'It's over, it's all over now. She's her mother's child. This is Taijnie's work. Our *jahajis* were right after all.'

'Parvati! You're her mother,' Rampat said, sitting down across from her.

'No, I'm not! I never was. She never belonged to me. She has her own nature and it's not mine, it was never mine. My daughter would want to be married, would want to settle down but this girl, this woman here, she has her own way about her. She's a stranger to me.'

Parvati knew that Dolly was standing just behind her with Daro and Loving, knew that she was standing there and listening to everything that she was saying. She had never told Dolly about the girl, that they had brought her home from the sea when her mother died, had brought her home and made her their own. She had never told her the secret even when Dolly had shared all her confidences with her, had even told her about Rampat's, how he planned to buy a car and drive it home and surprise her and Neela. Dolly had heard it from Lakhram and told it all to Parvati, had told it to her and shushed her and told her to make sure and say nothing to Rampat about it, and Parvati had told the secret to Neela and they had stood many times in the kitchen and watched Rampat smiling to himself after a trip to the city, and Parvati would always chuckle and say to Neela, 'Look! The maharajah planning to bring home the biggest elephant from the hunt.' Dolly had shared that secret and many others, had always told Parvati everything she ever knew about the world, but Parvati had held her own secret close, had held it to herself alone. She had been too afraid, too afraid to let it out, to let it go. That would have been like giving up Neela, like letting go of the girl herself to say it out aloud, to admit that she was not her mother. She wanted to turn and say that to Dolly, to tell her how afraid she was, to explain everything but she feared that it was too late, and Parvati sighed and gave it all up then, and said, 'Blood tells in the end. She is her mother's child and she'll turn out just like her, just like her! She'll bring home a belly one day and…'

'Parvati!' Rampat slapped her hard across her face. 'Stop this. Stop it at once. Neela is our daughter, our child, and no one else's. How can you say such things?'

Her cheek stung and Parvati looked at Rampat in surprise and wonder. He had never raised a hand to her in all their years together and to do so then over Neela, over Taijnie's daughter! She put a hand to her cheek. The day was destroyed. It lay in tatters about her when it had held such promise, when she had woken up before the sun and made the curds and shaped the milk balls and watched them turn as golden as a promise in the hot oil. She would never be able to eat that sweet again. It would turn bitter on her tongue, as bitter as her memory of that day, and there was to be no salvation, no redemption, and nothing would ever be saved and made whole. Parvati collapsed then into sobs, and wailed and rocked herself back and forth.

'Loving, Daro. Please, you can go now. And Dolly, it was good of you to come, eh?' Parvati saw how Rampat managed to smile, and how he tried to make light of everything as he saw the women down the stairs.

Parvati did not look at Dolly and Dolly said nothing to her. She, too, would leave, would go out of the gate and leave, and Parvati rocked back and forth, and felt the silence of the house settle all around her. It was a tangible thing, like something she could touch, could cut with a knife. The only sound was that of her own wailing. Then Neela laughed. It was a girlish laugh, not the low growl that Parvati had come to fear, and Parvati looked at her and started on at her again, accused her of everything, and asked her over and over why she had chased away a nice boy like Vijay, and his nice family. She asked it over and over until the girl, eventually, said, 'You know, Ma. You always knew. I had to save him.'

She had turned into the sweet girl again, the Neela who was all innocent and pure, and before Parvati could ask her anything more, Rampat placed a hand on Neela's shoulder and said, 'What your Ma said just now about your being born and about Taijnie and...'

'It's alright, Pa. Don't worry so.' Neela hugged her father and kissed Parvati on her cheek right where it stung then went to her room and closed the door, and Parvati heard her singing, singing softly to herself, and even without being there, without being in the room, she knew exactly how the girl was sitting before the mirror and combing and combing her hair with the golden comb. She was going to leave, Parvati thought, and she placed her hand on the spot where Neela had kissed her. She had tried so hard to shut away all that she knew, had tried to turn away from it, hoping all the while that that alone would work to change everything, hoping that if she refused to see it, it would go away. How foolish she had been, she thought. She had wanted to believe that she could hold onto water itself and weave it and work it like magic and shape it into a pretty picture that would please her eyes.

'Ram, Ram,' Parvati said in a calm voice. 'What will happen to us, to her? The house is like a deadhouse, Ram. Only this morning it was like a wedding house and now this, as if somebody died here.'

'Shush, Parvati. It'll be okay.'

'No Ram. It's all done now.'

The sun had started to drop away below the horizon, was starting to draw down the day's light. Soon it would be dark, and Parvati shivered, then sobbed loudly, openly, and Rampat came and sat beside her and wiped away her tears.

'Hush, Parvati' he said. 'Remember what a sweet baby girl she was? Remember her first smile, the first time she called you Ma? You were so happy, we were so happy. That's not nothing, Parvati. Try to think about that, eh? Come, lie down, get some rest.' Rampat lifted Parvati's feet onto the sofa and placed cushions under her head. 'Rest, now. It'll be dark soon.'

Yes, Parvati thought, closing her eyes against the falling light, it would all be dark soon and the canal would lie still under the night sky until it was broken by soft ripples, by someone entering into it with hardly a stir, a young woman it would be, all silver with golden hair. Her thoughts trailed off into dreaming as, exhausted, she fell asleep.

She only awakened when she heard the hushed footsteps going down the stairs, but she lay on the sofa for a long time, several minutes, several hours – she could not tell how long – before she got up and followed. There was no hurry. She knew even as she stepped out into the night how it would end and how the next day would begin, and she felt that all the life she had lived, all the things she had done, and all the seas that she had travelled had happened only to bring her to that moment, to that moment when she would have to accept the inevitable.

She stood in the narrow lane and closed her eyes and saw Neela smiling, laughing, a tiny girl against a vast sky, a vast sea, a vast earth. But she looked at home in it, not solitary at all, not alone or afraid. She was laughing, and running, running, running. Running from or running toward? Parvati sighed. Would she ever stop wondering, questioning, hoping, she asked herself, taking her time to walk through the narrow lane that led to the canal, or was it a mother's fate, her entire fate to always worry so? She would always be Neela's mother, would always worry, she thought, for she had come through too many years of watching over the child to ever rearrange her feelings. And the girl had known, had known all along how much she knew, how much she had kept to herself, and it was a comfort to Parvati that Neela would always know all that she felt about her.

When she reached the bank of the canal, she saw that there was no moon or starlight and that the water was a blank, that there was not even a ripple to mar its surface. It was as if it was shut tight, had closed in over a secret. There would be no witnesses that night, she thought, and she sat and watched Rampat watching the canal. They sat like that, unmoving, all through the dark night, and Parvati could only guess at all that Rampat felt. His stillness was like a penance for a sin, like a prayer for salvation. He would be praying, crying even, she thought. But her own tears were spent, and her prayers were all used up. It was not the fault of prayer, or faith, or nature. She had just been too afraid to look closely, to see clearly and had been more than content to build her own dreams and imaginings around all that she had feared most: that their *jahajis* were right, had been right all along about the girl, about the baby born out of the troubled sea when they had muttered into the wind that her fate was bound up with dark days, with dark days ahead, and that it was not their part, not their part at all to question any of it. In the end, her dreams had not been enough to hold her, to keep her, and Parvati sat through the darkness, resigned, and knew that the sun was going to rise on a world without her.

And so it did. Dawn came and Parvati looked about her and marvelled that all those many years had passed and she had never seen the canal at that particular time of day when it danced with a hundred bits of light that were shed by the sun's first rays. They were like fallen stars. She lay among fallen stars, and they, too, would drown, would disappear forever as the sky lightened. It was a different world although behind her, across the dam, she heard all the usual morning sounds of the village, the sounds of doors and windows being flung open, of brooms swish-swishing in yards, and of pots sizzling on open fires. It was as if nothing had changed, and Parvati got up then and went over to Rampat and placed a hand on his shoulder, and he rose after a long, last look at the canal then headed home with her, and she saw how he did not even look back when a bird flew down and dipped and splashed into the water.

PART THREE
BILLA

Is all that we see or seem
But a dream within a dream?

EDGAR ALLAN POE, *A DREAM WITHIN A DREAM*

Neela is Gone • Pondicherry • Fighting Sampson • Savo
Neela is Found • Buying the Truck • Cheddi Jagan
Mahendra is Married • Forbes Burnham • The Shining Days
The Split • The Devi is Lost • Billa Falls

THE GIRL WAS GONE, had vanished as if she had never been except that Billa knew the truth of it, knew that she had left to follow the path of her true purpose, the one to which she was born for he had watched her grow, had always protected her, but when he had seen the avatar appear that night in Parvati's kitchen, had seen the hard glitter of her eyes and heard the laughter trembling low in her throat, he had known that the *devi* was expanding, was moving beyond the limitations of their world. Their Neela was an innocent, a village girl who sang sweetly sentimental ballads but the one that appeared that night, had appeared for no more than a moment, was a prowling, knowing city woman, so, when he heard that the girl had left, had disappeared, Billa was not too surprised even though he, too, had wanted to believe, like Parvati, that Neela would get married and settle down, and that her feet would stay firmly planted on the earth. He had wanted to believe that, but when he went to their house that day and found it silent and shuttered, and found Rampat and Parvati weeping over Neela's disappearance, he wanted to say to them that they should not grieve for their Neela had come into the world for good reason even though that reason was not yet clear to them. He had known that about her even before he saw her, even before she was born for it was there on the *S.S. Ganges* when he had seen the lightning flash and had heard the crack of thunder break behind dark clouds that the knowledge had come to him. He had read the signs, and when the sea had risen, and risen higher still, he had known that the baby would be born and that it would be a girl, a *devi*. The world itself birthed her and for its own purpose, and Billa wanted to say all that to Rampat and Parvati to comfort them but it would have been a hard thing for them to accept just then, a hard thing for them to know that the child was never theirs at all, and he thought it best to let them give themselves over to their grief if only because he was sure that the girl would return to them one day. She was never ungrateful or cruel as a child and Billa was sure that she would find her way back to them, back to the village once she came to the end of the journey to which her fate was bound. Nothing was without reason, not birth or death or the steps of any journey, and because he knew that to be true, Billa had faith, faith like he had had from the moment he first knew of the *devi's* coming. It was because of that faith that he had believed that everyone knew, that all their *jahajis* on board the ship were aware of the true nature of the child that was born to them for he did not believe that they could have heard the heavens roll and seen the flash of silver break the sky and not know, so when Parvati had brought the newborn child on deck to show her off, to show off her pretty baby girl, he had stepped up immediately to look into her eyes, and to see how, beneath the flutter of her long black lashes, they were large and dark and watchful.

It was true that he still did not know why she had crossed the *kala pani*, why she had come with them to the new world but he had long accepted that it was her karma, that she was sent to help them survive all that lay ahead. They had need of her for they were to arrive as strangers in the new land and he could see how she would be a continuity, a link between their two worlds and a reminder of their past, of the far stretch of history that had brought them to that moment and to that journey that was taking them to the other end of the earth. It was not a journey they could have undertaken alone or without the accompaniment of prayers and devotions to the deities, and Billa had stood before the *devi* so that her eyes could look upon him and he had even felt the need to prostrate himself there on the deck of the *Ganges* and to let her *darshan,* to let all of the *devi's* blessings fall upon him.

But the mad mutterings of the *jahajis* who had listened to the sailors' readings of the swollen seas had done their worst and all about him his shipmates had shied away from Parvati and the baby in her arms, had pulled away and turned their backs on them and had chanted mantras to keep away the evil eye. But even if they felt she was a bad omen, an evil that had come into the world he knew that they were not ever going to offer up a sacrifice to appease what they believed to be the anger of the gods. And he could not have ever suggested it, could not have suggested that they should sacrifice even a small bird to still that anger, and to calm the worst of their fears. If he had, he knew how they would have looked on him with horror.

It was the way of the Hindus from the north to believe that their *poojas*, that their prayers performed with flowers and fruits, with water spilled from a cracked coconut, and with crowds of red-throated hibiscus placed before the feet of the gods were true measures of their belief and the depth of their faith. And if he had told them all that he knew and how he understood the world, they would have turned their backs on him for he was only a Tamil, a South Indian, and they would have turned away from him as if he, too, were nothing but a stain on the world for being a devotee of a different deity.

He worshipped Mariemmen, the dark-skinned goddess of his community, and no one could have ever turned him away from her for she kept him safe, had saved him from certain death on more than one occasion, and he always made sure that he did his duties and performed the ritual sacrifices that she required. He sprinkled her with blood, still fresh and warm, for her intercession in his pitiable life for he was only a man, a common man, and when the skies thundered and the seas rose up to meet them, he was reminded, lest he forget, of his true place in the enormity of things. He was puny, and were it not for the grace of the gods, a non-being. It could all be taken away in an instant and he had already known such moments when death threatened and darkness fell, but he had survived, had survived, perhaps, so that he could bear witness to the coming of the goddess. That was how he had felt on board the *Ganges* when the girl was born. He had felt blessed.

There were only two others like him, men from the south, on board the ship, men who had strayed far from home, had gone north leaving behind Tuticorin, or Chittoor, or, like him, a sprawling street slum outside Pondicherry. He had not approached them, and they, too, had left him alone, but he had seen secrets in their hooded eyes and had wondered if they had read as much in his. They, too, had stayed far from the baby but Billa knew it was more to keep attention away from themselves than from any fear they had of looking on the face of the child. They were probably men like him, men with a past, men who had survived some horror, and after he had looked at her, at the baby who was formed out of the formless sea, he had stood at the ship's rail and looked out at the waters, at the eternal circling waters and felt oddly comforted. She would be beautiful. She was a promise of good to the world.

He had already told Rampat as much, that he should not worry his head about what their *jahajis* were saying. He had even recounted the story of the birth of Ganga Mai to still his fears, the poor man being so worried, and his words must have found their way to Rampat's heart and eased its burden because after that day the man was always at his side, was always seeking him out. Whenever he went up to the rail to stand and watch the sea slipping away under them, drawing them closer and closer to the other side of the world, Rampat would appear and stand beside him. It was as if the man drew strength from him, and Billa had not minded that, for he had strength enough for two. He could not remember what they ever talked about but it was mostly to do with the rich and abundant life that awaited them in the golden sugar lands of the Demerara. They had exchanged dreams standing at the *Ganges*' rails. They had talked of themselves as men of adventure, as braves rushing forward to face the unknown, and said that only the daring, safe in the knowledge of their own strength, could take such risks. That was how they had spoken of themselves but, in truth, the dreams they had summoned up there at the ship's rails were little more than rakish escapades that placed them in foreign fields then saw them riding back to their families in India on white steeds with pockets full of gold. It was showing off. It was boyish swagger. How much better the reality had turned out, Billa thought as he had set out for Rampat and Parvati's house that day for they were all doing well and the Marajes had come the day before, on Sunday, and he was sure that they had looked at Neela's beauty and had decided immediately that it was their very good fortune to have found such a bride for their son. He was expecting to hear that the date had been set and he was planning to offer the use of his truck to fetch the tall bamboo poles that would be needed to pitch the *maro*, the wedding tent, and to fetch the loads of freshly cut *purine* leaves that would have to be brought to the wedding house first thing in the morning.

He would get his sons and their friends to help him cut and load the broad leaves that spread themselves out below the tall stalks of the lotus blossoms that grew in the trenches everywhere. The boys would have fun doing that, in wading out knee-deep into the trenches and cutting the leaves that curved upwards from their stems to form natural bowls. The food eaten from a *purine* leaf at a wedding house or a *yagna*, a big prayer service, was the sweetest by far – the rice and dhal and richly cooked vegetables that were served with all kinds of chutneys – and Parvati would be in her element with all the sweets to prepare, all the *gulab jamuns* she would make to burst sweet and creamy on the tongue. And amidst it all would be Neela seated beneath the *maro* in a glittering red sari. She would be a beautiful *dulahin*.

He set out that afternoon for Rampat and Parvati's house to hear all the grand news, and Savo had told him that she was going to wait up for him no matter how late he returned, to hear all the news he would bring back about the boy and the family, and everything that Parvati was planning to cook for the wedding. She was like that, his Savo. She liked to know everyone's business and liked to put her mouth into everybody's story, and she even went so far as to agree with Parvati that he was too loud, too aggressive, too everything, but if there was ever a fight to be fought or a quarrel to be settled, it was him, Billa, that they all turned to. He always told them that it was Savo's own talk-name, her own gossipy ways that were bound to bring trouble one day, but Savo never let up. She and her friends liked to dissect every quarrel that flew through the open doors and windows of the village: who was right and who was wrong and who should get thrown out or sent back to their mother. They played judge and jury on everybody.

But even with all that, Savo always knew better than to indulge in any of the talk that followed Neela about. She knew enough to keep away from that topic, at least when he was around, and he had laughed as he left the house, left her washing up the lunchtime wares, and had said yes, yes, that he would bring her all the news, all the news of the wedding, and he had left for Rampat and Parvati's house, had walked briskly along the lane, and had swung through their gate and said Sita Ram, Sita Ram by way of greeting and had moved towards the bottom-house where Rampat and Parvati were sitting side by side on a bench, and he had continued to laugh and talk even though they did not turn to look at him, did not turn to him with any reply.

And it was not until he was nearly in the shade of the bottom-house that it came to him that the place was still and quiet. It was like a deadhouse. There was no sound of Daro and Loving, or of Dolly. There was no sizzle of hot oil and no clang of pots, none of the busy sounds that went on all day like a celebration in Parvati's kitchen. There was no sound of any life at all, and it was then that he saw how Rampat and Parvati were sitting up straight and staring at the empty space before them. They were not moving or even blinking and they did not look up or say anything and it was then that Billa drew up a chair and sat down across from them. He took off his felt hat and placed it carefully on his knee. He did everything slowly, drew out each movement and gave them every chance to react, to move, to say something. But there was nothing. They never looked at him or broke their silence and when Billa leaned forward and peered closely into their eyes, he saw that they were dead. The world was gone from them, had left. Something dreadful had happened but no word of it had reached Billa. He had left for the city before dayclean, before sun-up and had been busy making deliveries all morning and no news had reached him, no news that any ill had befallen his *jahajis*. And Savo knew nothing either or she would have said, so, whatever it was that had happened, the news had not yet travelled. The Marajes must have refused the girl. Billa could think of no other reason that could make Rampat and Parvati look so mournful and he leaned forward and was making ready to laugh and say that there would be better suitors, more handsome ones, that the girl was good and beautiful, and that if the Marajes wanted to turn up their noses at the best match they could ever make for their boy then let them.

He leaned forward and was making ready to speak, was gathering up the right words to say when Rampat started to cry. He cried like a child, openly. He made no attempt to hide his tears or to wipe them away, and it was Parvati who spoke first. She spoke without expression and told the story, all of it, in a low voice that stayed well within the confines of the bottom-house. It was not meant to escape beyond, into the sunlight, into the next yard and the next, and Billa understood that he alone would be told the story, that he alone would know what, until then, they had kept to themselves. He heard everything then, of the days and nights of endless worry, of seeing and not seeing signs everywhere, of hoping, of praying, and of the waiting and waiting by the canal on countless nights.

'Last night she left, went into the water and left,' Parvati said and she, too, then covered her face with her hands and rocked back and forth and wept.

'Billa,' Rampat said. 'You're my own, own *jahaji bhai*, but this thing we kept to ourselves. We watched and hoped and prayed that her feet would keep to the earth but, in the end, she left, she ran off like water itself. If I didn't know better, I would say that we made her up purely to please our eyes and our hearts. But you were there when she was born. You know, you saw.'

'Yes, yes,' Billa said. 'I know everything.'

'She was always her mother's child, Taijnie's child,' Parvati said. 'She never belonged to us.' She drew comfort from that, from placing the blame of it elsewhere and Billa saw how old she had grown in a single night, how her skin which even the day before had stretched out smoothly over her cheeks, had collapsed, had given way to fold around her mouth, her nose, even her eyes. She was an old woman and childless and she covered her face again with her hands and she wept.

Rampat, too, looked aged, bent; and his eyes had become empty. They no longer held Neela in their sight so they roamed and shifted back and forth, up and down as if searching the farthest corners of his sight for any sign of her, as if he expected to find her skulking there just out of the range of his eyes, expected to find her and draw her back to make her the focus again of all that he ever saw but, after a few moments, he grew tired and gave it up and settled for staring out again into the space in front of him. Then he wept again, openly, like a child.

It was late when Billa left them that evening, left them sitting in the dark bottom-house. Night had crept in, had taken over, and when he left to make his way home he did not think to pat their hands and leave them with empty words of comfort and hope. It would have been unthinkable, even cruel to belittle their loss that way. Their grief was beyond the reach of words and it was enough that he had stayed with them and shared in it, and if he had said to them that Lord Bhagwan knew best, it would have been true, but it would have brought them little comfort even though Rampat and Parvati were not unlike him. They had the kind of courage that braced itself against disappointment and loss and, since Neela had brought them great joy, they were to accept the sorrow that came with it. It was the way of the world that it weighed and measured the two sides of everything like the gods themselves who created and destroyed, were both darkness and light, sadness and joy, each avatar a semblance to its own time and purpose. Rampat and Parvati knew the truth of that but they had never read the signs at Neela's birth like he had, and had never known over whom they had kept watch. They had believed that their Neela was a wayward child, a girl who liked the water, perhaps, because she was born from it, but they had never looked much beyond that and, for them, it was enough that she always returned with the sun whenever she went out to the canal on those many moon-filled nights and moonless nights. He knew because he had seen them, had seen the separate, still figures in the early morning light when he had gone fishing in the canal, had seen them sitting patiently as if they were afraid to disturb the very air around them with their breathing. No one knew their secret, but him, and he had never told anyone.

He came on it quite by chance when he went down to the canal in the early morning hours to cast a net to keep his hand in, to catch again the feel of his days in the Pondicherry fishing boats when he had helped to throw the large nets into the bay then drag them in jumping with fresh *sankara* and *sura* and *pama* and *koduvai*. It was a little adventure, and he always took his youngest son, his lucky son, Krish, with him on his fishing escapades even though Savo fretted herself whenever she heard him tiptoeing around the house and creaking up the floorboards to get Krish, all yawning and sleepy-eyed, out of his bed. The boy would fetch the bucket and he, the cast net, and they would catch the canal water where it was sweetest, where it was well away from the sea and its salty brine, and he showed the boy, small as he was, how to hold the net then throw it, how to fling it wide into the canal then draw it in carefully and feel the weight of the net in his hands as he drew it in and know it was filled with fish. They caught *houri* and sunfish, and Krish would pull the jumping fish from the net and fill the bucket. The boy was lucky that way. Whenever he brought him, the fish just jumped straight into the net, ready to get caught. That was what he told Savo when they returned with the bucket full of fish that she would clean and fry in deep, hot oil until they were crisp and golden. He would tell her that the boy was lucky, and that without him there the fish just watched him full in his face and turned away from his net. The story always gave Savo fresh excuse to fret-up herself and she always told Krish not to listen to his father's stupidness. 'Everybody makes his own luck,' she said each time. 'Your father has his luck and you have your own just like your big brothers.' But the boy was always ready to get up and follow him with the bucket the next time Billa woke him up. He would walk beside Billa, stay close by his side. He was happy to be chosen, was happy for the adventure and even if he looked about him as they made their way up the sideline dam, looked about him for a good spot to cast their net he never saw the two figures seated by the canal.

His young eyes, his six-year-old eyes knew nothing about searching the morning air for intrigue and mystery so he did not believe that the boy even saw Rampat and Parvati, saw how they were crouched close by the water, and how they watched it. Krish passed right by them but his eyes saw nothing, and Billa was careful to slip by quietly in the dark and to stay far enough away so as not to disturb them. But seeing them keeping watch over the dark waters of the canal always reminded him of the journey out of India across the *kala pani*, and he would tell Krish, would tell the boy how he saw a *devi* being born out of the sea, how the clouds had thundered and the lightning had cracked the sky and how the sea had risen up from the very bottom of the world to bring her into the universe. He never gave her a name but told the boy that she walked among them, had come to guard and protect them and keep their world safe. He liked to tell the story, liked the way it stormed and thundered then calmed itself when the *devi* was born and when the boy tired of that tale, Billa would tell him then about the large nets he had cast out into the Bay of Bengal when he had gone out on the biggest boats to catch the biggest *sura*, the shark, which had large pointy teeth and looked fierce even in the tangles of the net. 'We would bring the fish back to the Pondicherry market and sell them for a nice price,' he told the boy. The boy listened but never asked where was Pondicherry or the Bay of Bengal or the *kala pani,* and where had the *devi* gone and the ship, the *S.S. Ganges,* that had tumbled them about at sea. He was a child and everything was possible, was within reach. He did not yet know the true measure of the world so nothing was strange or distant to him, and Billa was glad of it for if the boy were ever to poke about the stories, if he were ever to ask questions, things might slip out, might get said out of carelessness and once they were out there would have been no way to take them back. So, while he spoke freely and told the boy all kinds of stories, there was one story that he told only to himself.

No one knew it or had ever heard it and he recounted it only to himself if only to touch its darkness again and know how far he had come. The boy, Krish, who would be sitting some feet away with his bucket, waiting to fill it with jumping fish, never heard it and never knew the true distance that his father had travelled. Pondicherry, Billa would say to himself. He would breathe the name softly into the cool morning air. It was the naming of another world. He went fishing there, it was true but that was an occasional job, one that he took when there were no fights around, when he had bested every challenger, or opponents had backed away and were unwilling to face him. He fought dirty, they said, and the word got around that everyone should stay clear of him because he bit and kicked and used every possible trick to win. But he had to, Billa thought. It was a matter of surviving. Krish would never know what that was like: to grow up on the streets, to leave home because one mouth less to feed was the best gift he could give his mother, his father having died and left her penniless with five children. He was the youngest son, like Krish, and he must have been only a little older than six or seven when he had walked away one day from the flapping scrap of a tent that they called home, had walked away to make his way in the world. He could never remember what had happened on that particular day to make him leave. His big brother might have quarreled again about the difficulties of earning enough to feed them all including their two sisters, two girls with no prospects of marriage. His big brother always talked that way but on that day, Billa must have tired of hearing it and he had left, had walked from the edges of Pondicherry, from the slum tenements of the city to its centre and the bazaar. He had arrived and looked about him and immediately a stallholder had called out to him, 'Here, boy, help this lady with her packages' and several bundles had been placed all over his shoulders and arms and he had followed the woman to a walled house. She was a servant and had given him some small coins and a glass of milk for his trouble and he had rushed back to the bazaar with the coins in his pocket. All day he had fetched packages and helped stallholders to shift boxes and lift bundles, and by the end of the day, he had a merry jingle in his pocket. That was the good of it. The bad was that he was prey to the bigger boys who beat him up and took his money. It was after a couple of beatings that he had put up his fists and learned to fight.

The fetching and lifting and carrying at the bazaar gave him muscles. He got a broad chest, bulging arms and a flat stomach. He did go out on fishing boats whenever there was work but he became known for his muscles and his strength, and that was what had attracted the first challengers. The first fights were nothing but a few minutes scrapping in the heat and dust of the Pondicherry streets but when he won fight after fight, one of his challengers, a man he had beaten several times, took over as his manager. That was when the betting started. It brought in nice sums of money and, if he fought dirty, it was only because every other fighter did the same. He watched them and learned their tricks, learned them fast enough to beat them in every fight. He became light on his feet and quick with his fists and his reputation grew. He became a champion and his odds got better and his purse grew and he saved enough to get himself a nice place to live and that was when he started to think of visiting his home, of making his way back to the edges of the city, to the slums, and to look for his family, maybe even set them up in a good place to live. The plan played in his head, and he turned it over and saw that it was good. His mother might still be alive, and his sisters might not be too old as yet for marriage. He could provide them with dowries. It was a good plan and he made ready to leave in a week's time. He bought saris for his mother and sisters and *kurthas* for his brothers. He would buy fresh sweets, fresh *methai* from the bazaar to bring to them. He would not arrive empty-handed and they would be glad to see him – he was sure of it. They might not even recognize him for he had left a boy and had grown into a man. That tickled him, that they might peer at him, a stranger bearing gifts, and that he would have to introduce himself to them, would have to laugh and fling out his arms and say, 'Billa!' and that he would watch their faces as they too laughed then reached out to embrace him.

Everything was set and on the night before his departure he went for a stroll about the city. He walked through the streets that had become so familiar to him, had been his home for years. It was late and the streets were nearly empty. A few people who knew him called out to him. He had friends. But he also had enemies. In the fighting business, you collected enemies, men who rankled at losing, whose egos were bruised, and men who swore revenge. He was always watchful because of it but on that last night before leaving the city for weeks, maybe months, he was smiling to himself and was thinking only of how the years had been good to him. The gods had been kind. He felt blessed. He walked slowly, casually, carelessly even. He stopped and started between his remembrances and was paying no attention to the streets' shadows, to the areas between buildings, under sheds and awnings where the night fell the darkest. And that was how he came to stop at the head of a dark alley and he was kicking the dust about and chuckling to himself at a particular memory, was laughing a little to himself when a shadow leapt at him out of nowhere and slashed him in the stomach, cut a gash clean across his belly. He felt the blood run and felt the pain of it and heard the shadow laugh, and Billa did not ever know how he had held together his open, bleeding stomach while his hands, those same hands, found a piece of wood and lashed the shadow hard across its head. He heard a crack and saw the shadow fall and become a darkness on the earth. It bled. It did not move. It stayed on the ground and a pool of blood widened around it. And Billa ran.

He did not think. He did not believe any good would come of that. He ran blindly with no plan, no direction, and did not stop until he reached Calcutta. He ran, holding the gash in his stomach together with his hands then with bandages ripped from his *kurtha*. He ran from town to village to city. He passed through Madras then made his way up to Vishakhapatnam. He left Tamil Nadu behind and ran north through Andhra Pradesh and Orissa until he reached West Bengal. He ran all along the coast of the Bay of Bengal. He did odd jobs for food. Or he stole when no jobs offered. He learned dialects and he learned Hindi and Bengali. He found that he had a quick ear for new sounds and phrases. The instinct to survive, to live, gave him that. The cut on his abdomen healed over and left a long, rough scar. An inch or two showed above his dhoti and marked him as a man who had faced danger and survived; and it was Mariemmen who saved him. He prayed to her and sacrificed a small bird, sprinkled a clean rock with its blood in a back street of some town, some small fishing town along the coast where he stopped long enough to place the rock on a tree stump. It was the best he could do by way of a *murti* and an altar and he prayed to Mariemmen to save his life, nothing more. He did not care about wealth or health or happiness. He prayed only for his life. If she spared it, he would use all of his life, everything until his death to atone for the ill that he had done. That was his promise. He did not, even in the dark of the night, and with no one around to hear him but the goddess, speak of the deed aloud. He never spoke of it until he cast it out into the early morning darkness, threw it out and saw it circle, fan out around him and become part of the new world. He felt safe enough to speak of it then, to name the deed and say the words aloud, but softly still and only to himself before he gathered it in, pulled it in and put it away carefully again into a corner of his mind where he kept it well battened down.

His life was spared. Mariemmen was merciful with her forgiveness and when he reached Calcutta he found that he had run as far north as the coast would carry him. But a Tamil man in those northern states could be picked out easily so he kept a close eye on policemen and anyone in uniform. He kept to narrow side streets and kept his head down and it was stumbling about like that, blindly, that led him to the edge of a small crowd where he heard an *arkati* talking about a ship that was going to sail soon to the new world of the west where they needed strong men to work in the sugarfields and to help turn around the sugar in the big, boiling vats. They would cut cane and *chaley cheeny* and make plenty of money and return as rich men after five years of work, the recruiter said. The words promised escape. The ship, the *S.S. Ganges*, was to leave in a few weeks' time and Billa signed up immediately without asking any questions. If there was cane to be cut he could do that. If there was boiling sugar to turn around he could do that. He was a survivor and he could do anything. He was fearless. Still, it was only when he was in the depot compound, was well behind the walls and fences and away from the city's eyes, that he started to feel safe again. The Englishmen at the depot looked him over and placed his name in the emigrants' register. He told them he was from Kanchipuram. He was careful not to mention Pondicherry. They did not ask how he had found himself so far north, so far from home. They did not care. They needed strong men and he looked the part, and it was in the depot compound, waiting for the ship, waiting by the Hooghly River to begin the journey, that Billa found his voice again.

He relived his fights to entertain his *jahajis*. He was a stranger in their midst and he set out to win them over by telling them stories about the mighty men he had fought and beaten back with the heavy hammering of his fists. Each time he spun a tale it took him farther and farther away from the one story that he would never tell. Each time his *jahajis* laughed and cheered it put distance between him and that Pondicherry night that had cracked and bled in the dark. He placed layers and layers of fabled time between himself and that darkness. His stories grew and he embellished them until he made himself fly like the gods, kill six-headed cobras with his bare hands, and down whole armies with a single blow even though the truth of it was that Billa never fought again. He found that he only had to put up his fists during an argument and everyone would back off. No one dared to take up his challenge, dared to test his bulging muscles and to discover for themselves how much of his stories were true. For his part, Billa never fought again because he did not trust his strength any more. He was afraid that it might unleash a further darkness which would overtake him and bring him down. He never fought again, that is, until Sampson stood over him in the cane fields that day and roared at the sky.

The fight stayed clearly in his mind because it was his very last and he always liked to remember it from its first moment, from the moment when the giant who watched over them circled him and looked at him from a distance. He would have heard of Billa's stories and would have taken note of his big muscles, and Billa, in turn, was careful to keep out of the man's way. He knew that Sampson was biding his time, was watching and waiting, waiting on the right moment to pounce. It was the way of a fighting man. There was only ever room for one champion in any world and Sampson had reigned over his for years. He was not about to have his position usurped and taken away without a fight, and Billa knew it, knew that he would have to face the giant one day. As much as Sampson was sizing him up, was taking note of his weaknesses and was deciding where he would land his hardest punch and how he would bring him down, Billa was doing the same. He measured the giant with his eyes and saw how big he was, how heavy and how tall. But Billa knew that his bulk would also made him slow, even cumbersome, and he decided that his best defence, when the day came, would be to dodge and weave and dance, that he would dance around the giant and make him turn and turn again. He would get him to throw his punches into empty air, would get him to become flustered and lose his head, and he would use the giant's own bulk to bring him down. That was his plan. It was a good one and he had even shared it with Rampat, had told him that fighting was not about muscles at all, that those were only grown to scare your opponent, and that it was all about strategy, that it was a head game, a game of wits. But his *jahaji bhai* was not a fighting man. Any show of muscles scared him. He backed away from confrontations but Billa, when he heard the roar break over him that day in the fields, that day when he had put his head down to take a little rest, had taken a sip of rum and was looking for a little quiet, when he heard the roar crash over him, he jumped to his feet and put up his fists at once.

He put his fists up and, as he had long planned, had dodged and weaved and ducked, and waited for his moment even as all around him, he heard how his *jahajis* held their breaths. They were preparing to weep for him. They had heard all his stories, had heard how many men he had taken down, but they knew that none had been like Sampson, a giant so high, so wide, so heavy. They felt that Billa was no match for him and that he would surely die in the fields that day. Billa heard it in their breaths, their breaths that were drawn in and held tight. He heard how afraid they were for him and he did not hold it against them for they did not know how much he had survived, and how hard he could fight, could lash out and protect his life from anyone who tried to take it from him. It could be a giant, a phantom, even a shadow – but they did not know that story so he heard how tightly they held their breaths as they watched him dance and dance around the giant. He was dancing to the drums in his head, to the *tapoo* and the *tassa*. He picked up a rhythm and made the giant turn and turn again, made him a partner in his dance, a clumsy partner who pivoted on his large feet, and when he judged that the moment was right, when he heard Sampson roar again, saw the sweat pour down his face, and saw him lean all the way forward and throw his whole weight into a punch that extended his arm to its furthest reach, when he saw the fist come to within an inch of his head, to within an inch of his life, it was only then that Billa leapt.

He leapt sideways and out of the way of the fist just in time to see Sampson's body follow his fully extended arm and fall, lose its balance and fall onto the dry earth with a thump. The giant was down, but Billa always knew that had his *jahajis* not picked him up and carried him off shoulder high around the fields, that Sampson would surely have risen from the earth and flattened him with one mighty blow. Billa always knew it, felt it, always knew that Sampson was right when he told his side of the tale, told how Billa's *jahajis* had saved his life that day.

His life had been spared once, twice, and it humbled him, even made him philosophical, and he wondered then, in the stillness of the night, as he walked away from Rampat and Parvati's house, walked away from the news that the girl had gone, had left, whether he was not destined for some particular task, for something other than looking after his family and building up his nice, little trucking business. He had come far, had crossed oceans, had survived much and, perhaps, he had been spared so that he could find Neela, find the girl and bring her home for he had watched over her since her birth and he felt that if there was anyone who could find her and get her to return, it would be him. He knew her better than anyone, knew her true nature when even Rampat and Parvati turned away from asking too much, from knowing too much, and he thought then, in the darkness of his bottom-house, as he eased himself into his hammock quietly so as not to wake anyone that, one day, he would bring them such news, such good news that he had found the girl, had found their Neela. He had no plan about how he was going to proceed but he had been through enough in his life to trust that he would find a way, and Billa closed his eyes then against the darkness and stillness of the night. Crickets and tree frogs chirped busily all around him but the house itself was quiet.

Savo had not waited up for him, after all, and he would tell her in the morning that there was to be no wedding, and she would be full of questions about why and why not and he would be careful not to say too much, not to tell about Rampat and Parvati watching over the canal or about Rampat saying how the girl had run off, had run off like water itself. She was a good woman, his Savo, but she liked a good story, always liked it so much that she could never keep it to herself. It was the worst thing that he could probably say about her – that she liked to run her mouth with a story and stretch it to its limits but he knew that she meant well and that she meant no one any harm and, for all that, for all her gossipy ways, she was the best thing that had happened to him in any world, new or old. That he had won her for his own made him the luckiest man alive for when he first set eyes on the pretty woman with the flashing eyes he had known that his Tamil ways and beliefs, his animal sacrifices, and even his dark skin would not recommend him to her family. They came out of Bihar and would not be looking for a fighting man who liked his drinks for their daughter. But Billa had a way of getting lucky, and he had found out, by pure chance, that Savo's *nanee*, that her mother's mother had been a South Indian who had come straight out of Tamil Nadu and had attended the Tamil temple regularly.

As soon as he had heard that, Billa had oiled his curls and brushed his moustache, the moustache he had grown since coming to the colony, and he had stepped up then to Savo, had stepped up to her as bold as you please one day when she was walking along the lane that led to her house. He had struck up a conversation and had recounted one of his more fabulous stories to her and she had giggled, and when he had seen her walking along the lane just a few days later, he had fallen in beside her and told her then the tale of a warrior prince who had fallen in love with the maharajah's only daughter and how the prince had slain dragons, great beasts that shot fire from their mouths, and had won her heart. He had put everything into the story, had filled it with every twist and turn he knew and had drawn it to its happy ending when the warrior prince knelt at the girl's feet and placed his hand over his heart and declared his love. He had even acted it out there in the dusty lane under a bright, noonday sun, and when he had fallen on one knee and spoken of the prince's love, how it was good and deeper and wider than the ocean, and greater than all eternity, when he had spoken like that to her he had seen how Savo's eyes had shone, and he had known, on that very day, that he had won her heart forever. It was his greatest victory – his Savo, his sweet *dulahin*. Not all his fights, all his championships taken together could equal that, and on the very next day her family had come over to his house to see him and to make the arrangements for the wedding. His *jahaji bhai*, Rampat, and the Tamil priest had sat with him to receive them and he remembered well how he had told her father and mother that he would take good care of their Savo, and that she would never want for anything. He had more than fulfilled his promise for they lived well, had a good business and three sons, three healthy boys who were their life itself.

It was more than he had ever imagined possible when he had stood at the rail of the *Ganges* and made up such foolish stories with Rampat of finding treasures in the new world, treasures that were nothing more than gold or silver or glittering jewels. They had managed, instead, to make a future out of nothing, out of nothing but crumbs and broken promises, and small coins saved up one bit at a time. It gave Billa a swagger and he knew how others saw him, how they talked about him and his bigmouth ways. How Parvati fretted with him about that! It was bound to get him into big-big trouble one day, she always promised. But she meant well. She was always trying to settle everybody into their life, trying to make it better for them. It was what she had tried to do with Neela. She had decided on everything, the wedding, the bridegroom, and how many grandchildren she would have. She had laid out her daughter's whole life like new clothes spread glittering on a bed, and all the girl needed to do was to slip into them, wear them.

Poor Parvati, Billa thought. He felt sorry for her and for Rampat and he only had to think about his boys, his sons, and the way his heart would squeeze itself shut if they were ever to disappear from his eyes for him to understand their grief. It was unthinkable, and when the yearly *yagna* came around at his temple, Billa went to the temple grounds and prayed for guidance, and it was then, after his sacrifice and prayers, that the knowledge about the girl came to him, and he followed it up, followed the story that found its way to him and he found the girl in the city, and every day after that he wished that he could tell Rampat and Parvati all that he knew, but it would only have grieved them more to hear that the girl was a singer in a city nightclub, that she sang with notes that came low from the back of her throat and looked out at the world with a hard glitter in her eyes. It would have been too much for them to take. They would never have accepted that such a woman could be their Neela and they might even have turned on him, might even have pulled away from him for ever thinking that their child could turn into a badwoman like that.

He had seen how Rampat had kept his head down and refused to look at the girl, and how frightened Parvati was that night when the avatar first appeared, when she had appeared to them for just one moment all red in the lamplight and with the strange laughter rumbling in her throat like something earthy, something animal. He himself had hurried away into the night to stop himself from speaking, to stop himself from telling Rampat and Parvati that they could calm their fears of all that they could not understand if only they would perform a sacrifice to the gods. He had hurried away because he had known how they would look at him if he were to ever speak of such things. Close as he was to them, they would have turned on him with anger, even horror. It could have threatened their very friendship, and he could never have told them that he would never have found the girl had he not prayed, had he not at the yearly *yagna* at the Tamil temple taken the warm blood of the sacrificed goat and sprinkled it on Mariemmen and asked that he be granted a boon, be granted knowledge of the girl and her whereabouts. The *tapoo* drums had entered his head and he had danced in the temple yard with the other Madrasi men and women, had tied the red and gold plaid of the Madras kerchief around his waist, over his clean white dhoti and danced to the *tapoo*, had lifted up his hands and prayed that the girl be found and be returned to the village and to Rampat and Parvati who grieved so much for her. It had brought so much honour to his life to save her from the low talk that had followed her about the village, from the gossip and the foolish talk about water mamas and jumbies, so Billa had prayed that he would find her even if it was only to keep watch over her again as he had always done.

He had sprinkled the blood of the goat on Mariemmen and danced to the drums, and no one could ever have convinced him that it was not his devotion to his duties that did it, that led him to the nightclub in the narrow street that turned off from one of the wide avenues in the city. The place was called The Cove and a rough billboard said that its main attraction was a songbird from across the seas. She was nameless and appeared as nothing more than a sketchy outline of a woman in red with red lips, and hair that flowed off the edges of the narrow board, and Billa went to the nightclub late one night fully prepared to be disappointed because he knew how rum talked and he was almost certain that the story he had picked up in a city rumshop of a water mama who came up from the river at night to sing at the club then returned to the water, to the Demerara, was nothing but pure stupidness. It was rum talking. It was idleness and drunkenness, and he knew better than anyone how rum could stretch out a story and make it drown itself in rivers then bring it back whole and fully formed again. But he also knew that such tales were always spun outward from some grain of truth for that was how his own stories were formed, and because the one he heard in the rumshop came to him just days after the *yagna*, just after his sacrifice and prayers, he did not push it away even though it sounded like nothing more than a drunken fantasy. So he found The Cove one night late and pushed through its door and ordered a drink and waited to see the singer who, the story said, rose out of the river each night to make her appearance to the world.

He pushed through the door and wondered if the singer was who he thought she was and whether she would recognize him. He was pulled both ways. He wanted to find the girl yet wanted the story he had heard to be untrue, for he wanted Neela to remain the sweet girl they had always known even though he knew that it was the way of the gods that they moved in and out of your very lives to create, to destroy, to change and transform the world in order to fulfill the fate that was already written. He could not deny the girl her true nature and in the half-light of the club, with its tinny dance music coming from a phonograph, and with the men pooled around small tables, their eyes fixed on the small stage and the spotlight, fixed on the small circle of light where she would appear, Billa felt the need to offer up a prayer, a silent prayer to calm his fears of all that he was about to see. And when she did appear and he heard the first notes of her music, heard the voice and the low notes tremble at the back of her throat then climb and take the air in flight, when he heard the voice he knew at once, without even looking, that it was her. He was glad then of his prayer for when he did look up he saw that she was as red and glittering as he remembered. She roamed about the stage, threw out high notes to the men like a whip then laughed and drew them in again, drew them back low into her throat. The spotlight followed her every move as if she were its very incarnation, an incarnation that would disappear into darkness if it were ever to stray or become extinguished. The men never looked away from her and Billa saw then how well she had fitted herself to the city, to its cunning and its danger, and he understood then that if the purpose to which she was born required the likeness of such a woman, of such a wily, cunning woman, a woman who could turn men's heads and wring their hearts with a look and a promise of desire, that if it required a woman such as that then it was something quite dangerous, quite unimaginable. And that fate was bound to the city. He was sure of it, for the girl would not have come there otherwise, and no one needed to tell him that some horror was destined, was already written, and he prayed there at the club, muttered a silent prayer for his safekeeping, for all their safekeeping.

He made a vow, there and then, to keep a steady eye on their world and to listen closely to everything that was said especially in the city, the city that he always saw as sinister and deceptive, as a place of pure trickery. He never shared Rampat's love of the place. His *jahaji bhai* saw romance in every tree-lined street and every bright shop window, and saw it even in the sea wall that stood guard at its northern edge, stood guard over the Atlantic. It was an engineering feat, Rampat would tell him, for men to build a wall of brick and stone, to build a wall so stout, so strong that it could keep out the very sea itself. It was the Dutch who had built it, had built it so well that it had stood for centuries. But Billa believed none of it. He had stood on top of the wall many times and laughed at the very idea. It was foolishness to think that something manmade could ever keep out the sea and no one who knew the true depth of the ocean, who knew its breadth, its volume, its weight could ever feel safe behind such a wall, such a puny, manmade wall, its width no more than the length of a man, and its height no taller than Billa's shoulders. The sea would one day simply climb over it, ease itself over it and take back its rightful place. Billa was sure of it, was sure that the city would drown, and that the jungle would also creep in from the southern boundary to reclaim its space, for Georgetown was cut from it, hewn from it – from that jungle.

Billa had heard many stories about the jungle that were told by the men from Paradise, the dominoes players who came with Sampson, the burly men who went up river to mine for gold and diamonds, who went looking for treasure and lived to tell such tales.

'There are *camoudi* snakes so fat, so long they could swallow a man whole,' they said.

'And small-small fish with teeth like razors that could eat a man to the bone in minutes, in minutes,' they said.

'And jaguars.'

'And wild hogs.'

'And spiders as big as your hand.'

'It's a wild-wild place.'

'With rivers that froth up white and could swallow a man whole just like a *camoudi* snake.'

'And it stretches all the way south, all across the border with Brazil, all the way across the equator.'

'It's the Amazon, man.'

'A place where a man has no shadow.'

'Where a man walks alone.'

'Aye. And men fought for that jungle and the shadowless earth.'

'Killed for it.'

The men spoke like that of danger and death. They spoke casually with a cigarette perched on their lip and between the hard slapping of the dominoes, and it was their very casualness that made their stories terrifying. There was no attempt to convince anyone of anything. They just told the tales all stark and brutal and would leave off to laugh and slap the dominoes hard on the small table and say, 'Beat that!' then continue telling how they had seen a man disappear, had seen a man being eaten alive as if it was nothing, nothing at all. But Billa knew well enough how a story could swell and grow bigger with each telling so he took the tales with a pinch of salt and would laugh with the men when they stretched their hands out to their furthest reach to show how big the iguanas in the jungle were, how long; or when they rose up to grapple with the air and show how they had taken a jaguar down with their bare hands.

'The jungle is right there,' they said. 'And it's still a wild-wild place.'

It was easy enough to look about at the coastland with its green paddy fields and golden sugar cane, with its flat earth and the ocean lapping gently at its edge and feel safe, feel distant from all that wildness and from the continent's bloody history, but the place had bled and taken slaves and taken lives. It was raw and untested, and Billa was always afraid that in such a place, where nothing much existed beyond the present and a brief and brutal past, that the ground could shift from under them at any moment. It always made him feel vulnerable, exposed, and he always felt the unease most in the city where the jungle pressed in and the sea threatened. And he felt it that night at The Cove, felt all the dangers and heard all the threats in the low, trembling music of the singer in red, and he hurried away and knew that he could never bring the news to Rampat and Parvati, the news that their Neela had become part of the city's darkness.

In the broad light of day, it was difficult to believe that it was not all an imagining in his head, all the danger he had sensed when the singer had slipped and slithered across the stage like something dark, like something animal, so he told no one, not even Savo, about all that he feared. He held it close and to himself alone and took comfort from his faith that whatever it was that threatened, whatever it was that might crash about their ears, that they would surely survive it, as sure as they had survived everything before. Rampat and Parvati had done well to draw the world in close about them since Neela left, and they hardly ventured out any more. Their home and the village became all of their world, and Rampat never went into the city any more to look about to buy himself a motor car. Billa had learnt about the secret from Lakhram, but it was a secret that was forgotten, pushed aside, and Billa could see how Rampat would no longer feel the need to get about the place, to drive about the countryside or the city – not without Neela by their side. It would have been pointless, and Billa felt sad whenever he saw how all the pleasure was gone from their lives. Even when they laughed, and that was rare, their eyes stayed as dead, as dead as they were that day when he had gone around expecting to share in the news of Neela's wedding. But there was never any wedding, never any of the merriment of drumming and dancing, and a sleek new car dressed with flowers, and Billa always wondered whether it was that that made all the bright, new political talk attractive to Rampat, whether it was all the promise of a shiny future, a future that shone like a wedding house itself, because Rampat liked to pick up the political talk that was flying about the place and say that everything was going to turn out bright and beautiful. It was as if he was hoping that Neela would be part of all the brightness and all the promise.

It was he and Sampson, Rampat and Sampson who liked to talk to Billa like that. They would go on and on about home rule and all the ways thing would get better with their own people running the country, and the talk had a way of springing up everywhere and anywhere, on the street corners in the village, or at everybody's bottom-house.

'The country will be our own, man,' Sampson liked to say. 'We worked for it, slaved for it, eh?'

'And they're saying that everybody will get to vote, eh?' Rampat would say. 'Not just the big property owners but everybody.'

'Think about that, eh? We'll be living and working in our own-own country.'

'We'll be our own bossman.'

'That's right. Nobody to tell us what to do, eh? Nobody to push us around.'

That was how the two of them would carry on about the big future that the politicians were promising and Billa would allow them to go on and on before he would suck his teeth and tell them that they sounded like children who believed in nancy stories, who believed that all the fairy tales they heard were true-true stories. Those city politicians wore shiny shoes that never yet walked down a sideline dam to cut cane or plant paddy or catch fish – that was what he always told them. He said that those men did not know how they lived or what they dreamt about, and that all they wanted was to make themselves big. 'Once we give them our votes, they would forget all about us, all about their promises,' he would say, and Sampson would always reply, 'Like you want the white man to rule over us forever, man?'

'No, no, brother, don't get me wrong. I just don't trust those city men and their city talk,' Billa would tell them.

'But they're men of business, businessmen just like you, Billa,' Sampson would say and laugh. 'Like you don't trust your own self, eh? I catch you out good and proper, eh? They're men just like you, Billa.' Sampson always laughed when he spoke like that about Billa, talked about how he had become a big and busy man with his trucking business and everything, and how it was he, Sampson, that was going to the dominoes matches and telling the story of their big fight. 'It's only my side of the story everybody hearing so I'm winning the fight every time!' Sampson would laugh and Billa always laughed with him but the truth was that he had left the fight behind and had no need of it any more.

His side of the story could get lost forever and Sampson could have the whole of it for the truth was that when Billa looked back on his younger self he seemed to be nothing more than a fabled figure, an imagining in his own head. The boasting, the loudness – he did not need them any more. And he had also eased up on his drinking. That pleased both Savo and Parvati. He had grown into a man, Parvati said. He had become responsible, Savo said. He even felt that he had needed the drinking to fill himself up where there had been nothing but emptiness, so he was more than ready to let Sampson have it all, the fight and the victory. It added even more to the man's high spirits. That was something that Billa always liked about Sampson, the way he was always ready to laugh, to live it up. He lived in the present, Sampson liked to say, because that was all that mattered, and Billa could well understand his friend wanting to put all of his history, all the cruelties and horror of it behind him. But to live in the here and now and to let the future just take care of itself, looked risky, even reckless. That took a kind of bravado that Billa did not have. He needed to have control, to feel that he was shaping the future, every single day of it, and making it into the thing that he most wanted. But that took responsibility and it could become worrisome, even burdensome, and there were many times when he envied Sampson's flash and flair, and his easy-going ways. He was a real sweetman. He worked for good money as the estate driver but he also spent freely on women and drinks at the dance halls on the weekends. He liked his popularity, liked to be known as a man, as a big man with money to flash around, and he liked the freedom to sport and play around at the end of every week, and Billa knew that it was all of that that had made him laugh so much when Billa talked about buying the rusty, old truck that had lain for years at the back of the rice mill, had talked about buying the old truck and fixing it up and starting up a trucking business.

Sampson had laughed hard that day when Billa first spoke of it, and he had told Billa that he was just throwing away his money on pure stupidness, and that he was going to buy himself into his own slavery. 'You'll be hauling and fetching for everybody from morning 'til night, and for what, man? Stewps! I couldn't take myself back there, man. That is backwardness, man. Stewps! I count the money in my hand at the end of the week and I know it's coming to me clean and straight the next week and the next, eh? Working all day and every day and even in the night-time to make a lil living? No, sir! Not me! Life's too short, man.'

And Sampson was there again with the same kind of talk the day that he and Lakhram and Parvesh dragged the truck, all old and rusty and falling apart, into his yard. 'That truck's not worth nothing, man,' Sampson said. 'Rice miller Ally catch you good and proper to get you to take that piece of rusty old iron off his hands.'

'You're right, Sampson,' Billa said. 'It's nothing but a piece of junk. It'll take a lot of work to shine it up and make it work again.'

'But the engine can get fixed up, man,' Lakhram said. 'The chassis and the gears and the brakes – everything.'

'And we'll paint it bright red, eh?' Parvesh said. 'Bright red with white stripes right here on the bonnet, eh?'

It was what Billa had seen whenever he had passed the old truck again and again: he had shone it up with his eyes, had painted it a bright red, had oiled its engine, and replaced all its lights and, whenever he was done, the truck was always a thing of real beauty, and that was when he had started to ask around to find out about the possibilities of the venture. It would be a risk, and he could lose all his savings, so he had asked around the whole neighbourhood about possible jobs if he were to start up a trucking service, and Rampat had stepped up immediately and said that Billa could take his paddy bags to the mill and his rice to the depot in Georgetown. Two villages over, Boysie Karran had told him that he needed his fruits and vegetables to get from his farm to Stabroek Market in the city every week, and his neighbours on all sides had asked when he would get the truck because they were buying new furniture or moving to a new house or needed bamboos fetched to hoist their *jhandi* flags, their prayer flags. The word had flown around and Billa had felt that he was losing business even before he got started. And how Savo's eyes had lit up! It was she who had urged him to quit his job at the factory and take up the business full-time once the truck got fixed up. There would be too much business, too much, she had said, for him to only do it part-time and on weekends. She had passed the news of the business venture on to everyone she knew and was giving cut rates to her family and friends even before Billa closed the deal with the rice miller and hauled the truck into his yard where he and Lakram and Parvesh tinkered with it every spare moment they got until they brought it back to full life.

But Billa had to give it to Sampson – the business was a lot of hard work, endless work. Yet he did not mind it. He liked being behind the wheel of the truck, the red, shiny truck, and going up and down roads, and streets and sideline dams. It made him an adventurer. He met new people and went to new places, and he liked the constant movement, the driving about from place to place. It was almost like a bonus that the business turned out to be a success, a real success, and everyone who had promised him work made good on their word so he fetched Rampat's paddy to the mill and his rice to the depot in the city, and he did a weekly run for Boysie, fetching fruits and vegetables from his farm to his stall at the big city market. That was a nice arrangement for Boysie always had a little bonus for him, a pumpkin or squash, or a nice set of mangoes for the boys. Boysie was a good man that way and he became a good friend, and Billa always looked forward to meeting up with him for the man was always good for a laugh and was always up with the latest about what was going on in the city, so Billa would always settle back behind the wheel of the truck as he set out for the city and the market square and know that Boysie would have a good set of jokes and news to tell him.

It was what he was doing that morning as he started out on the drive which was always pleasant, especially in the early morning hours before the road got busy with cars and trucks and bicycles and donkey carts. The main road cut through villages that were much like Coverton and Paradise with houses set back in yards that bloomed with hibiscus and croton bushes. It was a pretty picture and, when he had weekend jobs, the boys liked to come with him. They liked the truck, liked the driving about as much as he did, and they would sit up in the cab with him or stand in the bed of the truck and look out at the passing scenery. The big boy, Mahendra, had started to drive the truck about the village since he was fourteen. He liked the feel of the machine under his hands, and Billa knew how it was because it was what he liked too, liked shifting the gears and turning the wheel and feeling how the whole machine swung to his command. All the boys – Mahendra and Vickram and Krish, small as he was – already talked among themselves about what they would do and where they would go once they got their own truck. Mahendra was going to move into the city. There was plenty of work to be picked up there, he said; and Billa expected that Vickram, because he was closest to his mother, would remain in the village. And there was Krish. Billa always chuckled whenever he thought of his youngest son, his lucky son. That boy would just shine and shine. He was the star. Billa did not need to worry his head about Krish because whatever he chose to do in life, he was bound to succeed. He could be anything he wanted, anything at all. The boy was born to them after the other two were already grown and had started out to school. He was a pleasant surprise, like an unexpected gift and Billa had decided that if the baby was a boy he would name him for Lord Krishna even if it was only because Savo glowed all through her pregnancy, glowed like Devaki when she was carrying the baby Krishna.

And when the boy was born and Billa saw his cherub of a face and how his eyes tapered at the corners, how they were shaped like a lotus petal, he was sure of the name, was sure that the boy should be named for the god. Everyone spoiled him, indulged him and doted on him, and Billa thought of him as his lucky son just for coming to them like a blessing when everything was going so well. He was like icing on a cake, like the sugar on the *methai*, but in truth, they were all good boys and they were his life. He was proud of all of them and he saw how the boys moved about and patterned themselves on him, how they watched him closely, watched how he walked and talked, how he prayed and performed all the ritual sacrifices at the temple, and they watched who he drew in around him as his friends. They were good and strong and honest and Billa was sure that they would grow and settle themselves into bright futures. He was doing his part by showing them how to live, how to live well and to have faith in the world, and he was working hard so that he could give them all a good start in life, give them each a truck of their own one day so that they could build something good for themselves for they were the very blood of his veins and Billa wanted them to have successful lives, and he knew that if any of them were to ever sicken or die, it would be a grief beyond all grief. It was no stretch for Billa to understand how Rampat and Parvati felt about Neela's disappearance because if any of his sons were to disappear from his eyes' sight, the light would go out of his very life.

All the years that had passed had not changed Neela for Rampat and Parvati. She was still the young and beautiful girl who sang sweet notes into the air. She never faded for them and Billa knew that they woke up each day to greet the sun only because each day brought fresh hope that on that day she would return. Without that, they would have long since given up. Even though Billa visited them often, he never knew what to say to them, what comfort he could bring so he took the tack of bringing them all the news from the city, news that he picked up at Stabroek Market, or along the roadside. They would smile and nod their heads, might even laugh out loud but their eyes always kept settled in their sadness and he still had no news to give them that could change that. He could not tell them how many times he went to the nightclub in the city just to sit in the half-light and wait until late in the evening when the singer in red would appear. He had come to know some of the regulars, had become a regular himself, and he would chat and pass the time and pick up rumours and gossip of what was happening in the city. It was almost always the same crowd, a crowd of men – English civil servants, Portuguese and Indian businessmen, and African and Creole professionals, doctors and lawyers mostly – and the talk was almost always about politics. The men at the club spoke like Rampat and Sampson, spoke about all the good prospects, and were always as upbeat as Rampat and Sampson were.

'It's the first step, man, to have our own people running the country.'

'Then it's independence, freedom!'

'Let's drink to that, eh?'

'Hear, hear.'

If the English minded the talk they never showed it. They looked indulgent, arrogant even, and it made Billa feel that he was on the wrong side of the whole idea of home rule and independence but he still could not bring himself to trust the politicians who were part of that scene, and part of the city. Some of the men spoke of them with an easy familiarity, spoke of them as friends, as family, and when he listened to that kind of talk, he knew that he was right to feel the way he did, for it was those people, the businessmen and the smooth-looking professionals, that the politicians were representing. They would be looked after, and people like he and Rampat and Sampson, the people in the villages would still be lost, would still be left behind, even with all the promises of development and progress and better rights for workers. Billa simply did not trust them with his future, did not trust them to honour him and his work and any of his beliefs.

And it was on that day, on that very day when he sat back in the seat of his truck and headed for the city market and Boysie's stall and was thinking of all the news that he would pick up that he came to thank god that he had trusted his instincts and had not given away his loyalty to any of those city politicians, for he no sooner arrived at the busy market square, a place that boomed and screeched and rang with bells, that he heard the good news, the news that was to change their lives forever. It was no surprise that it was there that Billa first heard of it for the whole country brought its goods and produce to sell there at the big city market and it was always right there, too, that Billa would pick up all the latest reports and gossip, whether it was from Boysie or one of the vendors. It was there under the big clock that they had landed on the beachheads in Europe and had followed Gandhi to victory in India and, on that day, Billa picked up a buzz as soon as he arrived, as soon as he stepped out of the cab and the men gathered to unload the bags and baskets of pumpkins, eddoes, spinach, mangoes and watermelons from Boysie's farm. A big talk was going on between them. They were excited, and Billa always liked to recount to everyone, for years and years after, how it was right there on that day at Stabroek Market that he first heard the name Cheddi Jagan.

He remembered the day and the time and remembered everybody who was around that morning, could call them each by name and recall exactly what each one said about the young man who had gone away to study in America and who had come back and was forming a political party to fight for them, for all of them. Billa was always fair to the story and would start by telling how he had sucked his teeth, how he had sucked his teeth and turned away and said that he had had enough of politicians, that they were all city men, were all tricksters, and that this Cheddi Jagan would be no different.

'But the boy is just like us, man,' Boysie said.

'Yes. He grew up poor on a sugar plantation on the Corentyne coast,' Janak said.

'His father is an estate driver,' Harold said.

'His mother is a good Hindu and did a big *pooja* for the boy when he came back from America,' Kishun said.

'The boy is smart,' Rogers said.

'Got a scholarship.'

'The boy is bright.'

'He will fight for the working people, the poor people.'

'He will get us the vote.'

'For our own-own government.'

'And he has everybody with him.'

'Africans and Indians.'

'No, no, Billa. This is no city man.'

'This here is a man like you and me.'

It was then that someone pushed a newspaper under his nose, and Billa's eyes widened and his heart lifted when he looked at the newspaper and saw a starboy there, saw a handsome, smiling young man with hair slicked back from a broad forehead. The boy was like a film star. He was leaning forward, leaning out from the newspaper with his handsome, smiling face and it took just one look at the photograph for Billa to know that Jagan was a man that he would follow anywhere, and follow forever. He had not yet heard the young man speak but he knew that whatever he said would be a truth that he would understand. Jagan had grown up in Port Mourant, a big sugar estate, had grown up a Hindu, had walked bare-footed along rutted dams and cast out nets to catch trench fish, had grown up in a bottom-house just like theirs that swung with hammocks and listened to all the stories of the village, listened to all its news and plans and possibilities. The boy had gone abroad to study, and had come back a dentist but he knew too much, had seen too much. He knew all about the exploitation of the working people and how the white masters worked the masses for profit, for their profit.

'That is how the boy talks,' Kishun said.

'About struggle and freedom,' Boysie said.

'It was the Enmore killings that did it, that turned the boy into a politician,' Rogers said.

'The white people killing those five estate workers like that,' Janak said.

'Shooting them in the back like that,' Harold said.
'Pooran.'
'Surujballi.'
'Rambarran.'
'Hari.'
'And Lallabaghee.'
'The colonial police shot them.'
'In their backs as they were running away.'
'The police had their orders. The men had got past the fence.'
'But you get nothing if you don't get past the fence.'
'Jagan said that.'
'A bright boy.'
'A good boy.'
'A boy with our future in his hands.'

Any time that they remembered the killings, the cold-blooded murders, it always made them fall silent, and Billa was glad to hear that the martyrdom of the five sugar workers had moved the boy, had moved Jagan to turn it around and make something good out of it. They would not have died in vain, after all. The shootings happened just after the big war, just after India got independence, and they had all felt the bullet in their backs. It could have been any one of them or their brother or their father, and villagers from Coverton and Paradise had climbed into the bed of Billa's truck and he had driven all along the eastern coastline until the sea wall ended and the seaside stood bare and unprotected except for mangroves and crab grass and beaches full of broken shells, had driven until they got to Enmore Estate where they had joined the procession for the burial of the dead. They had wept for the five men and their families, for the poorness of the huts they had lived in, and for the cruelties of the world. The men had been fighting for the right to join a union. They had joined a strike for workers' rights, for the same rights that workers in England, the 'mother country', had enjoyed for over one hundred years. But those were white rights was what Billa heard, was what they all heard. They were not for coolie workers on colonial estates, and the white masters had said that the strikers must not get past the fence, must not put foot on estate property but the strikers did, they had, and the order was given – shoot! – and the men had dropped dead.

It was just another waste of good lives, like all the lives lost before in rebellions and uprisings and strikes. The proper rituals were done, the proper prayers said and the earth was laid over the slain men, and no one paid any mind to the government when it set up a commission to investigate the shooting, and no one ever spoke about the commission's findings that the police were right to shoot, that they had to shoot to protect estate property from the strikers, from the poor, unarmed workers. It was as if the men were being shot to death all over again, so they had ignored the report and its findings. It was their only defence against the injustice of the thing, their only defence against their helplessness – until that day when the news broke that Cheddi Jagan was going to stand up for them, was going to speak for them, was going to lead them to freedom, to victory. It was the biggest news that Billa had ever picked up at the market square, the biggest news he had ever had to take home to Coverton and, as soon as the truck was unloaded, Billa put his foot down on the gas pedal and raced back all the way home, back home to Savo and the boys, and to Rampat and Parvati and Sampson.

But when he arrived, he found that the news had already travelled, had already reached the villages. Savo was full of it and so were his boys. Mahendra was going to join Jagan's party and fight, fight for freedom, he said. He was going to move to the city; that was where everything happened, he said. He was going to move to the city and join the fight, and it was that day, too, that Billa saw how the boy made broad gestures, how he shaped his plans with his hands, and he saw that his big son was grown into a man. He could see that the boy was ready for the world, and he knew that it was time to get the boy his own truck and settle him into his life. Marriage offers had come from several families in the village but Savo had looked them over and found them wanting. None of the girls were nice enough for

Mahendra, she said, and Billa had left it to her, was depending on her good judgment in those matters. The boy was eager to work, to get all grown up and he had left school at fifteen and was doing short drives about the village, had left school because schoolwork never interested him. It was Vickram and Krish who liked school better. They liked books and reading and it was they who had read the story from the newspapers about Jagan and his political party to Savo and Mahendra that day, and the story had got around, had spread itself out all around the village and had brought all the drums out, and when Billa set off to Rampat and Parvati's house with the news, the beat of the *dolak* and *tassa* and *tapoo* accompanied him.

He walked along the narrow lanes to the rhythm of the drumming, and everyone hailed him with the news that Cheddi Jagan, a boy like their own, like their own-own son was going to fight for them, was going to fight the English and bring them to freedom. It was like the words of a song itself and the music turned down every one of the narrow lanes with him until he reached Rampat and Parvati's house and it was there, in their bottom-house, that he heard that Jagan was coming that very weekend to hold a massive rally in the marketplace in Coverton. The boy was going to come and talk to them, to tell them his plans and everybody was going to be there, Rampat said. He and Parvati laughed and Billa saw how the laughter almost reached their eyes. It crinkled and creased all around the edges of the sadness that had settled there but, in the end, the sadness stayed. Only Neela could remove that. It would stay until she returned and their eyes could hold her in their sight again. Not even Jagan and all that he promised could do that, but they were going to the rally, they said, were going to hear what the boy had to say and they even left their bottom-house to help get the marketplace cleaned up and to see a stage built. Banners and flags were hung everywhere so that the boy would get a proper welcome for Cheddi was their own son, was a boy just like theirs, everybody said, and on the Saturday, long before he arrived, the market square was filled with every villager for miles around.

All the drummers were there and the Indian drums thumped and the African ones rolled from every corner of the crowd and they only stopped when Jagan stepped onto the stage, when he appeared high above them amidst the banners and the flags, appeared before them like a hero. They all cheered and whistled and shouted and they only stopped when the boy stepped up to the microphone and stretched out his arm, stretched out his arm like a blessing, and asked them to be silent. Then he spoke and Billa heard how his voice was strong and clear, saw how he stood tall, and how he was more handsome than his photographs. He appeared like a triumph before them and made all the ancient stories of the gods live. The earth could be flooded, the villages destroyed, and there would come out of the sky a deity in a golden chariot to hold the land high above the waters and to save the people of the world from certain destruction. Those were the stories that were written, the stories he knew to be true, and when Jagan spoke, when he stood before them and spoke, Billa heard clearly all the things that Jagan said: he was going to be a champion for justice, was going to lead them to freedom, was going to be a fighter for everyone, for all races and all religions, for everyone who had ever worked the fields, and he was going to lead them to a future that would be good and bright and prosperous. His words flowed like music itself. They had rhythm and repetition like all the best songs and Jagan said to them that they, the workers of the world, were going to be freed forever from exploitation by the white masters who owned the tools of their labour; that they, the workers of the world, would be united in their stand for freedom and justice, and that they would all work together to bring independence to their country and would throw off the shackles of colonialism and capitalism and stand together as a free and united people. He spoke like that to them, and when he was done, when he smiled and thanked them for listening and stepped back from the microphone, when he raised his hand and waved to them, they all cheered and clapped and chanted, Jagan Jagan, and rushed to place garlands on his neck and to lift him high on their shoulders and parade him about the square.

There was too much happiness. It could not be contained. It flowed and overflowed and Billa's heart swelled big in his chest and he was glad, very glad when he and Savo agreed to a match for Mahendra just then for the wedding preparations were the best excuse for merriment. And when Mahendra told them that Jagan himself would come to the wedding, Billa's heart swelled even bigger. He was so proud, so proud of his boy. Mahendra had gone and joined up with Jagan's party, had joined up with the party just like he said he would, and Billa had bought the boy a solid secondhand truck right off to get him started on his life. The boy was already driving about and doing well for himself in the city, was getting good work on building sites, and was using the truck to do party work as well, was fetching stages and banners and microphones for all of Jagan's rallies all over the country. It was all of that, all of Mahendra's success that had brought them a nice offer from a family two villages over who had their last daughter to marry. He and Savo went to meet the family and when the girl's father said what good work Mahendra was doing, what good work the boy was doing with Jagan's party, and how proud they must be of their son, Billa knew right off that it was the right match, the right family for Mahendra. Savo agreed. The girl, Radika, was nice-looking, she said, and she would make a good wife for their boy. The girl's family were small rice farmers and the wedding was fixed for a Sunday after the second crop of the year, for a day in August, and Billa and Savo invited the whole village, sent out the invitational grains of rice, the *nowta,* to all their neighbours.

Savo included everyone in the wedding plans. Parvati was going to make the *methai* and the *keer,* the sweet rice pudding, and Dolly was going to manage all the cooking on the wedding day. So much rice had to be cooked, so much flour bought to make the *roti,* and Savo pressed Billa into asking Boysie to get them his best pumpkins and *bhajee* and eddoes for the seven-curry, and to send the many pints of split peas that would be needed for the dhal. Singers from the *mandir* were going to come along with the *dolak* drummers, and everybody was going to dance when the boy brought his bride back to the house. 'Even Jagan,' Savo said. 'He would have to dance at the boy's wedding, eh?' It was too much for Savo that Jagan himself would be coming to their big boy's wedding. It made her laugh and prattle all day, and she shone up everything she got her hands on, the brass pots and glasswares and every piece of furniture, then she turned to shining them up too, Billa and the boys. They were to get their hair cut and they were all to go shopping in Georgetown for the best *kurthas*, and she was going to get herself a bright sari with bangles to match. Everything had to be just so, Savo said, and she brought her forefinger and thumb together like a dancer.

And when the wedding day came and the sun shone and Mahendra brought Radika home after the marriage ceremony at her parents' house, when they came through the gate all glittering in their rich wedding clothes, a shout went up, and the drummers and dancers and singers all came to the gate which was dressed with streamers and tinsel and lotus flowers and arched over with coconut branches, they came to the gate to greet the *dulaha* and *dulahin*, and Savo was there to circle their faces with the sacred flame and welcome them home. And when Jagan came later, came fresh from a rally he had held across the river, across the Demerara, when he came and stepped through the gate, another shout went up, and the singers and drummers and dancers rushed again to the gate to welcome him as if he were the bridegroom himself. Savo garlanded him with a *mala* of marigolds picked fresh from the yard, and everyone pressed in to touch him, everyone wanted to shake his hand. Even old people bowed and touched his feet in reverence and Billa saw how easily Jagan moved among the crowd, how he gave everyone his whole attention and when Sampson pressed up to shake his hand, Billa saw how Jagan smiled and spoke to him. He came up to Billa, too, and shook his hand and said he was glad to meet him, to meet Mahendra's father, and he said that the boy was a good boy and that he would go far in the party, that there was a lot of work to do. He said all that to Billa and Billa told Jagan then, told him that he could depend on him, could depend on all of them for their full support. Even when he left, when he stood beneath the arch of coconut branches and waved and left, he left behind the high excitement that followed him about everywhere, and the drumming and dancing went on until the early hours of the morning, until everybody was tired and could not dance any more. Even Sampson stayed until after midnight and when he got up to leave, Billa walked with him through the dark lanes of the village.

Sampson had grown old and did not get about much any more but he could not have missed the boy's wedding, he said, and Billa walked with him that night, walked with him as far as the bridge that led over to Paradise and listened to his friend talk. His conversation had changed. He hardly ever mentioned the dominoes matches or their big fight or how he was winning it all the time. He, too, had let it go, because he was not as well as he once was and the recounting of the tale needed a voice with vigour, needed action and drama to make it live and Sampson had developed a steady cough. His lungs, he said, and tapped his chest. The doctors said it was because of too many cigarettes, he said, then he laughed and said that they could say what they liked but he had enjoyed his sweetman days at the dance halls, and he had a whole lot of good memories to keep him company. He laughed again and the laughter broke away into a bout of coughing, and they stopped on the bridge to let him rest a little. It was then that Sampson told him that he did not think that he would live to see Jagan become prime minister, to see one of their own boys become the leader of the country, and Billa waved his hand and told him that that was nonsense and that he still had many good fighting days left.

'I talked to the boy, talked to Jagan,' Sampson said.
'Yes, I saw,' Billa said.
'He said he was going to fight for all of us, all of us, eh?'
'Yes.'
'We talked together like men, like big men, like fighting men.'
'Yes.'

'I told him he had my vote for sure,' Sampson said and started to walk again, to walk over the bridge to his home. 'I told him I was going to give him my vote and that he was to do good things with it, eh? I told him that we're all behind him one hundred percent, eh?'

'Yes, yes,' Billa said and he watched Sampson shuffle off into the night and disappear. He worried about his friend sometimes, worried about him living alone, and being sick and having no one around to help out. He did not know any of Sampson's family, any of his children other than the one boy, Martin, who he had seen that one time when he had come to the dominoes match and had shaken his finger in Billa's face. Sampson had laughed it off and said that the boy's head was full of stupidness he picked up in the city and that Billa was not to pay him any mind. Sampson never spoke of Martin again and Billa did not think it his place to ask whether there was anyone who could come around to help, so he brought Sampson food sometimes, and would send men over to fix a broken door or window. But he was careful with his charity, was always careful to make it appear that it was nothing, nothing at all. He would say that Savo had cooked too much food, or that he had a set of carpenters fixing up his house so it was nothing at all to get them to spend a little time repairing the steps or floorboards of Sampson's house. He was always careful like that because Sampson had a big pride. He still had his status – was still the estate driver, the sweetman, and still the champion fighter. He thought of himself that way, and still straightened himself up to stand up tall like he had done that day when he had shaken Jagan's hand. Sampson had stood shoulder to shoulder, and eye to eye with the boy, and had taken his hand in a firm grip. He might be a little slower, a little frailer but he was still someone to be reckoned with and he liked to laugh whenever Billa appeared with a bowl of soup or a slice of cake, liked to laugh and say that Billa was only coming around to show off himself now that he had turned himself into a big-shot businessman with a big delivery business and all that, and Billa always waved a hand and told Sampson to stop his foolishness, that he was the same Billa that

Sampson ever knew, the same Billa that he had tried to beat up in that big fight. They always laughed at that and Sampson would say that old as he was that he could still take Billa down any day, any day he chose.

It was watching Sampson become a lonely, old man that made Billa mindful about his own old age, about how he and Savo would manage. They had talked it over many times, talked over plans for the time when he would become too old to drive the truck about and make a living. Mahendra and Radika had already moved to the city and once Vickram got married, he would get set up in his own place, too, but Krish would stay. They would leave the house for him and when he married, he and his bride would live there with them. That was the plan, and they had talked to the boy about it and Krish had laughed and said that Billa would never get old, that his daddy would never get so old that he would never be able to drive his truck about the place any more. And it was true what the boy said for Billa felt strong, as strong as he was when he worked in the canefields, as strong as he was when he fought in the dust of the Pondicherry streets, and he could never see himself as an old man shuffling off into the night. He would go down fighting, he always thought, go down as he lived, a fighting man, and all that talk that Savo talked about them relaxing in their hammocks and playing all day with their many grandchildren – she already counted them, named them – was nothing but pure stupidness for he did not know what he would do with himself if he just had to sit at home, sit around at home all day and not bustle about in the world, not poke about at its edges to see what would turn up. But it was a nice picture: he and Savo playing with their grandchildren. It was part of the prettiness of the world, the happiness of the world, and whatever the threat was that he had felt at the nightclub and in the heart of the city, the threat that had rumbled and slithered across the stage of the nightclub, he had long since pushed it away as stupidness, as a story that had played around in his head, and he forgot that happiness had a way of doing that to a man, that it was a kind of drunkenness where everything appeared so bright, so shiny, that he could do nothing but believe that it was going to go on forever and ever like that, just like in a fairy story.

And, when not too long after Mahendra's wedding, Billa heard the African drums rolling out from Paradise, he went over the bridge to meet Sampson, to meet him and the dominoes players and all the men and women of the village. He went over with Vickram and Krish and some of the men from Coverton to see what the celebration was about, and they got the news then that Jagan had found a partner in his fight, a partner in a young lawyer, a bright boy just returned from England, a boy named Linden Forbes Sampson Burnham.

'The boy has my name, a good name!' Sampson said.

'Look at them, look at them,' Jacob, the school teacher said, and he showed around the day's newspaper which had a big photograph of Jagan and Burnham holding each other's hand high above their heads and smiling big smiles.

'Boys like our own-own sons, eh?' said Ruby, the fruit vendor.

'We will vote for them, vote for both of them,' said Nat, the carpenter.

'And they are bound to win.'

'This will be our own country then, eh?'

'They will make everything better for us.'

'Jagan and Burnham!'

'Our boys!'

'Our sons!'

'Massa day done!'

'Massa day done!'

They danced to their drums then, and pulled Billa and his sons and everyone along and they danced all along the main road that cut through Paradise, and they sent up a cheer of Jagan and Burnham, Burnham and Jagan, and Billa and Sampson slapped each other on the back and talked as if the battle was already won, as if the fight was already over for no one doubted the outcome, so they slapped each other on the back and talked as if the future was already there, bright and shining before them, and as if all their work, all that they had ever endured was already avenged with a sweet, sweet victory. And when they all went out to hear their boys, to hear their sons speak at the rally that Jagan and Burnham held together at the market square in Paradise, they all cheered and cheered for both young men. The boys had different styles, had different ways of talking and presenting themselves and Billa saw, at once, how together they made a first-class team. Jagan had a way of picking plain, simple words to make his points. He kept to a down-to-earth, country-boy manner, and he jabbed and punched the air just like a fighting man, and made broad gestures that gave shape to his words, gave them force and conviction, so when he said to them, 'The ruling classes will be swept aside by our revolution and we will emerge triumphant' Billa had no doubt that the promise would be fulfilled. And, when, after he spoke, Burnham took the stage and took the microphone and looked out at them, Billa heard how softly his words fell on the ear. They passed by as barely a whisper but then the boy gathered up his words in perfectly rounded tones, and swept them higher and higher still until they were spread out all around like something grand, like something marvellous. The boy had style. He was flamboyant, even stately. 'Freedom will ring,' Burnham said. 'Freedom will ring throughout the land and we will all, my friends, awake one day soon to the sound of her sweet music.'

'The boy! The boy talking poetry, man' Sampson said.

'The boy talking the white man's language sweeter than the white man himself,' Nat said.

'The boy born with honey on his tongue, pure honey,' Ruby said.

'My boy! My boy Burnham!' Sampson said.

'Starboys!' Jacob said.

'A team to beat,' Billa said. 'A team to beat.'

'The boys will work for all of us, eh?'

'You heard them, man. Better pay, better housing, better schools and hospitals and everything.'

'We'll live like kings!'

And Billa heard Savo join in and say, 'Starboys! The boys like starboys!' and he saw her join the rush to garland them, to garland them with *malas* made from fresh-picked marigolds and he watched as Jagan and Burnham were lifted high above them and were paraded around the market square. His boys were there – Mahendra, Vickram and Krish – and he saw them move with the crowd, watched them laugh and cheer, and he felt a swelling pride that he was able to give his boys such a future, such a grand future. They would be the inheritors of the new earth and would give shape to it and continue to build it long after he and Savo and Rampat and Parvati and Sampson and all of them, all the older generation, were gone. The journey out of India had been a blessing, a real blessing, never mind the brutal work of the cane fields, and Billa knew enough about life to own that nothing good came out of it until it was tested, was tested even beyond all endurance. He felt that he had come through well and that his boys were going to reap the benefits.

Mahendra was already on his way to his future, was already making a life for himself, and Vickram had also turned into a man, a good, steady young man. He had chosen his own bride, a nice girl from their own village, and he and Savo had met the family, and wedding plans were being made, and Billa had already picked out a good secondhand truck for the boy, had bought him a truck to set him up in life like he had done for Mahendra.

All of it was good and it was all that goodness of the new world that made Billa go back to The Cove one evening late to sit before the small stage where the singer in red appeared, and to watch her, to watch her closely and see for himself how foolish he had been to believe the rum-filled story that she was something unearthly, something special. He sat there and looked at her that night and sucked his teeth in disgust for he saw, at once, that she was nothing but a city woman, after all, an old, washed-up city woman with a voice that croaked from downing too much cheap rum and rough whisky, and he laughed at himself for ever thinking that she could be their Neela, the sweet-faced girl that Rampat and Parvati had picked up out of the sea, the girl who sang like a *devi* and had left, had disappeared from them for no reason, no reason at all. He was glad that he had not ever told them about the singer and the nightclub, that he had not ever hurt their heart that way with the stupidness he had picked up and believed to be true, and he was sure, as sure as he ever was, that the girl would turn up one day, would return home to Rampat and Parvati, would arrive back as much as she had left, and for no reason they would ever understand.

Billa was surprised that he could laugh it off so easily but he felt that holding on to all that feeling of threatening danger would be nothing more than being ungrateful for all the good fortune that had been granted him since he arrived in the colony. He even felt that holding on to the feeling alone might make the threat good. Then, anything that happened would be his fault and he did not want that particular responsibility. And he only had to look around him at the club and listen to the busy chatter and hear how everyone was laughing and talking at once, talking about independence and freedom, and about the prosperous future before them to see that the singer had become irrelevant, and that she was nothing, nothing at all. No one looked at her or listened to her any more. She had become background noise to all the new talk, all the busy talk about Jagan and Burnham. They were all that mattered and Billa heard someone say in the back of the room, 'Let's drink to them both' and immediately everyone raised their glasses and shouted and cheered.

'To Jagan, the revolutionary!'

'To Burnham, the sweet-talking diplomat!'

'Hear, hear!'

'Winners both!'

The few Englishmen who were still about had retreated to the edges of the room but they did not appear too put out, too worried by anything they saw or heard for they were still in charge, were still the masters, and Jagan and Burnham would have to deal with them, would have to talk with them to win the country, and Billa saw how they spoke to each other in voices that reached high above the noise of the drinkers and the music, the low, warbling music that was coming from the singer. She still slipped and slithered across the stage, still looked out at them and laughed but with the whole world turning itself around in such wondrous ways, in ways that no one ever thought possible, she no longer appeared magical, could no longer hold their interest, and it was then that Billa got up and pushed his way out. He left the club and the singer behind and he did not even turn around to look at her when he heard her laugh, heard her make that trembling sound that came deep from the back of her throat.

But there came a day when Billa regretted it, regretted all of it. There came a day when he wished that he could go back and undo all of his foolishness, undo all of his unbelief for he was sure that it was that that had angered the gods: that he had given himself over to the happiness, to the moment's happiness and had become unmindful of all the signs, all the warnings that had been revealed to him, for he had no sooner walked away from the club and its music and its laughter, had no sooner turned his back on the singer in red that the news came of the troubles that were to unravel all around them. It was Boysie who told him about it when Billa trucked in his weekly load of produce. It was Boysie who gave him the news first, but he had laughed and made light of it and said that the boys were too sensible, too smart to let a little fight blow up big and come between them, for the boys were fighting, he said, about who should be the party leader, who should be the candidate for prime minister in the elections campaign.

'Jagan says it's his party,' Boysie said, 'and that he's the leader.'

'But Burnham wants it, too,' Janak said. 'He wants to be prime minister.'

'The boy is ambitious,' Harold said. 'He won't play second fiddle to anyone.'

'Aye,' Boysie said. 'But they'll work it out, man. Don't worry.'

'Yes, the boys have too much sense to let a lil quarrel mess up all the big plans, eh?'

'They won't let us down, man.'

'There's too much at stake.'

Billa laughed with the men, laughed and made light of the boys' fighting but he did not tell them what he knew for sure as a fighting man himself, what he always knew: there was only ever room for one champion in any world. But he wanted to believe that politics was different and that Boysie and the men were right and that the boys would find a way to settle their differences. There was too much at stake, too much, he thought, for the boys to go and throw it away on a little squabble for they were bright, were educated men and Billa was sure that that alone would give them the good sense not to let their quarrel boil over and get heated and out of hand. He thought of them as if they were his own sons, as if they were his own boys who were caught up in some childish quarrel, like fighting over marbles or a game of cricket in the backyard. It was Mahendra who was always quick to put up his fists, and it was Vickram who always backed away for he was the quiet one, and there were so many times when he and Savo had to part them, had to pull Mahendra from scrambling on to Vickram's shirt. But, for all that, the boys were inseparable and would give their lives for each other, and that was how Billa saw it, how he thought of it when he heard that Jagan and Burnham were quarrelling. He believed that the very next day would bring them news that the boys were working together again for, in the end, they were men who read books and knew things about the world, and they would know enough to not let their little differences undo the whole of the future.

He took the news that way and when he went home and saw Krish sitting around with his nose in a book, he chuckled a little to himself and wondered whether he should make a joke and ask the boy whether the book had a good solution for settling a quarrel. Krish would probably have an answer, if he were to ask, for the boy liked to read and was always walking around or sitting around with a book opened in front of him. The boy would go far and he would be there to see him make something of himself, maybe even turn the little business into the biggest trucking service in the country. He was the tallest, the brightest and the most handsome of his boys and Billa had no doubt that he would achieve much.

The boy looked up at him. He had heard him chuckle and looked up at him, and Billa saw that his schoolboy's face was all serious as if it was bearing the weight of the whole world, but he continued with his joking manner and was starting to ask the boy about finding the answer, an answer for Jagan and Burnham's fighting, when Krish said, 'I'm reading the story of how we came to be here, Pa.' And Billa laughed out loud then and said that no book could tell the real story and he started to tell the boy about the *kala pani*, and the adventure of the journey over seas and oceans, and of storms that threw the waves up high as mountains and tumbled them about like playthings, and how when they came to the golden fields of sugar cane they had wielded their cutlasses like swords and cut down the tall stalks of cane, downed them as if they were armies of mighty men. He started to tell the boy all that but he got no further than the adventure of the sea voyage before Krish cut into his story and said, 'People got sick and died on those ships and got thrown overboard, got thrown out into the sea. They're lying there at the bottom of the world, Pa.' The boy said that, told him that and Billa saw again how Taijnie, how the poor, little girl whose life had bled away, had just bled away from birthing her child had been wrapped in a sheet, had been wound tight in a sheet and thrown over the rails and he remembered how long it had taken for the waters to take her down, down, down.

His story of the crossing never told of any deaths, of any deaths at sea from sickness or childbirth, and he sat down then and let the boy continue with the story as it was written in the book, the story that started out with a planter back in the nineteenth century, a planter named John Gladstone who had sugar fields in the colony of British Guiana. The Englishman needed labourers to work in his plantations, to cut the cane and grind the stalks and turn around the big boiling vats of sugar after the slaves were freed, Krish told him, but he was looking for cheap labour and he got the idea in eighteen hundred and thirty-six – and here Krish pointed to the page and the date – he got the idea of recruiting Indians. 'Because we were so poor, Pa, and we were willing to go anywhere for the chance of a job. That, and because some were tricked and never knew where they were going or how far away it was,' Krish said. 'If they had, they would never have set foot on those ships.' Krish went on to tell him then that he did not know what to make of the man's letter, of Gladstone's letter which he had written to a firm of agents in Calcutta, the firm of Gillanders, Arbuthnot & Company.

'Hear what his letter said, Pa. It said: "Our Plantation Labour in the Field is very light; much of it, particularly in Demerara is done by Task Work, which for the Day is usually completed by Two o'clock in the Afternoon, giving to the People all the rest of the Day to themselves."'

Billa saw then how the boy looked up at him, but he found that he could not meet the boy's eyes, could not let him see his anger at the lie, at the boldfaced lie, and see his confusion at finding that it was all written down like that, so clearly, for everyone to see, but he was glad that Krish had to look at him to confirm or deny the story. Neither he nor his brothers had ever set foot in the canefields, had ever had to wield a cutlass and do the backbreaking work, and Billa counted it as the greatest success of his life that he had managed a good enough living so that his boys would never know the savagery of the thing. And he, himself, had put it away, had put it behind him for good, and had turned it into a tale of strength and daring, had turned the trickery and deceit of the planters and the *arkatis,* and the managers who ran the estates for their masters, the men who made the profits for their absent owners, had turned it all into a tale of good fortune. It was better that way, he always thought, that the boys should not feel weighted down by that past, but Krish had uncovered it, was laying it bare and he could not meet the boy's eyes as he continued with the story he was reading and told him then about the Vreed en Hoop plantation, the plantation across the Demerara River, the one that Gladstone had described in his letter, and how the truth of it did come out. And when the boy reached the horror of the story, read out loud about the first *jahajis* who came on the *Whitby* and the *Hesperus* in eighteen hundred and thirty eight, Billa found that he had to close his eyes against the words, against the horror of what they told.

'A freed slave, Elizabeth Caesar, gave evidence of it,' Krish said, and he read, '"The Coolies were locked up in the sick house, and next morning they were flogged with a cat-o'-nine-tails; the manager was in the house, and they flogged the people under his house; they were tied to the post of the gallery of the manager's house; I cannot tell how many licks; he gave them enough. I saw blood. When they were flogged at the manager's house, they rubbed salt pickle on their backs."'

When Krish read that, read it out in a clear, high voice, Billa trembled. He knew such stories, had heard of the horrors of how the earliest *jahajis* had been whipped and fined and restrained for the slightest of faults, for even being sick and unable to work. Even they, the last shipload of labourers, had the whip at their back and he saw again how Sampson had stood tall over them and how he had nudged and pushed and flicked the whip, the long, polished whip over their heads and laughed. He remembered it all and found that he still could not meet his boy's eyes for he felt ashamed then of his golden tales of adventure, ashamed that he had made them up, had spun them out of such horrors, and that the boy had found him out.

'And did you know, Pa, that that man Gladstone was knighted – became Sir John Gladstone – and that his son, William, became a prime minister of Britain? It says here that William got financial independence to go on with his career when his father eventually sold up his estates in British Guiana, including the one at Vreed en Hoop, sold them up when the squalid truths became known and became too embarrassing, too shameful to be borne.' The boy closed the book and said, 'It was a shameful thing that men did, Pa.'

Billa said, 'Yes, yes, son.' He found that his voice was small, was barely a whisper and that it only gathered strength when he told Krish about what it said in the 'Bhagavad Gita', that there were men who were born with demonic natures and that they were known by their greed and their cruelties and that they always suffered the fate of being constantly reborn. 'They never reach God for they live trapped forever in the cycle of birth and death,' he told the boy. 'It is good to remember the words of the Gita, son. It kept us strong, men like me and Rampat and Lakhram and all of us, and all those *jahajis* who came before us and suffered the worst. But we survived because we had faith and hope and belief, belief in the gods and their goodness and we have built nice little lives for ourselves, and you and your brothers, you will grow it all and make it bigger still. That is what Jagan and Burnham are fighting for – to free us from that past, from all that history and bring us to a shining world.'

The boy sat and listened to all that he had to say, and Billa wished that he had more book-learning and could say more, could put it over in wondrous ways to make the boy see how he should learn from the past, should remember it and honour it, but that it was the future, it was always the future that he must keep his eyes on. 'If you don't lift your head up, you can't see where you're going, eh?' he said to the boy, and the boy smiled at him and nodded.

He wanted to see the boy thrive, wanted to see him find his way in the world like his brothers had done, Mahendra with the work he was doing with Jagan's party and already a father, a father of a baby girl, and Vickram who had settled down to a quiet life with his wife, Padmini, in a little house at the back of the village. Both of them were working hard and had plans, big plans for their families and the nice life they were going to live. In a couple of years, it would be Krish's turn, and he expected the boy to start out his life as a man in an independent country. He told that to the boy that afternoon, told him that he would live a free man in a free country, and that Jagan and Burnham were going to make it happen. He did not tell the boy all that he had heard about the trouble in the party and that Jagan and Burnham were quarrelling over who should lead because he was sure that it would blow over, would blow over in a day or two, but when it became clear that the boys could not mend their quarrel, could not settle their differences and the news spread that they had split, that Jagan and Burnham had gone their separate ways, it was Rampat who told him first that there was going to be trouble, big trouble because of it.

But Billa hushed him and said that if the boys were going to fight each other at the elections then Jagan was sure to win for he had all of their votes, all the Indian people in the population, and that that was a clear majority. The boy would win for sure, he said, and he saw no trouble in victory, in winning, and it was only then that Rampat told him all that the Reverend Davies had said to him that day when Sampson's son, when his son, Martin, had shaken his finger in Billa's face.

'The Africans say they slaved for the land, that they came first, and that nobody is going to take it away from them, no matter how much majority we have,' Rampat said. 'They say we're buying up all the land, like my rice lands and Boysie's farms and that we're now buying up property in Georgetown and owning business. They say that we can buy as much land as we want but that they're the only owners, the rightful owners.'

'The reverend said all that to you?' Billa said.

'Yes. He saw big trouble coming unless we had good leaders, men who could weigh and balance both sides and make everybody feel good.'

'Jagan can do that, man. Remember how all the people from Paradise came out to hear him talk and how they cheered for him?'

'Yes, but they have their own leader now; they follow Burnham, now.'

'Jagan will do good for everybody, man. He's for the working people, all the people, and he will win, will win for sure.'

'And that means they'll lose, Billa. They'll lose and they will feel that they have lost everything.'

Billa sucked his teeth then and started to curse out Reverend Davies for knowing nothing, for just being a busybody who had only come among them to turn all the good Hindu people against all their gods and everything they knew about themselves. He never liked the man and could never understand why Rampat indulged him with his friendship, why he would sit and talk with him and listen to everything he had to say. A man who did work like that, who made people turn against themselves could not be trusted to know anything, anything at all, he said to Rampat, but his friend only shook his head and talked again about the trouble that was coming, that Burnham and his people were not going to sit down and take a loss easily, but Billa insisted and dismissed all that Rampat had to say, pushed it all away as stupidness.

'You want Burnham to win then, eh? Eh?' he asked, and when Rampat said nothing, when he made no answer, Billa sucked his teeth and talked over and over again right there in Rampat and Parvati's bottom-house about how Jagan would win for sure, and how big the boy would win, how he would win the elections fair and square and make everything right for everybody.

And so it was, so it came to pass just as Billa said it would that Jagan won the elections, and Indians everywhere, in all the villages all along the country's coastline drummed and danced and paraded their victory, and Billa even went to Rampat's bottom-house to laugh and talk about the future, about the bright future, and to tell him again how much good Jagan was going to do for everybody. And Rampat listened to him, to all that he had to say, and said nothing but only pointed out to Billa how quiet it was in Paradise. 'There's no dancing and drumming there, brother,' he said. Billa only sucked his teeth and said again that Jagan would work for everybody and, it always seemed to Billa that he had no sooner said those words, had no sooner pushed away all talk of trouble, of danger, that every day opened on a brand new threat. The city streets began to march and chant and sing all day and every day as Burnham led his people – all the civil servants and dock workers, all the teachers and nurses and clerks – led them on protest after protest against Jagan, against his budget, against his plans, against his Communism. That was the biggest mark: Jagan's Communism. He was a Red threat, a Communist threat and he was going to take away everybody's churches and schools, was going to take away their very gods because he believed in none himself. 'Jagan must go', the chanting went, and Billa heard then that Burnham was busily cutting deals with the British and the Americans so that they would make him the prime minister, would give him the position he wanted and throw Jagan out.

He was hearing rumours everywhere of guns and bombs, of CIA plots and counterplots, and it was Boysie who first told him about Burnham making deals with the Americans because they wanted Jagan, the Communist, out of power.

'Kennedy is going to give Burnham money to make trouble against Jagan and his supporters – that's us, Billa,' Boysie said.

'Yes, Kennedy feels too ashamed that Castro beat him up in Cuba and now he's taking it out on our boy, Jagan,' Janak said

'No Communists in his backyard he says,' Kishun said

'They have a thing called a Cold War with Russia, and we're right in the middle of it.'

'And the English just going along with everything America wants.'

'It's Kennedy calling the shots.'

'To get Jagan out and put Burnham in his place.'

'Burnham is their man.'

'He's going to do whatever they want.'

'They hope.'

'They think.'

'It doesn't matter.'

'The only thing that matters is that Jagan is going to get thrown out.'

'Big trouble coming.'

'Big trouble.'

And it was when he heard all that, heard all the rumours of guns and bombs and of the violence to come that Billa felt his regret, felt that he had brought the trouble on their heads, and that he who had known, who had understood everything and had always had faith, had turned away from it, had dismissed it all, and had truly angered the gods. Had he not seen the *devi* being born out of the formless sea? And was it not he, he alone who had stepped up to receive her blessings, had watched her grow, then seen her expand into the universe, seen her change shape and nature and substance to fulfill the karma to which she was born? But he had turned away from her, had even laughed at her, and Billa regretted it, regretted then that he had let himself be fooled by a fleeting moment of happiness, a moment that was not even an atom's weight in the eternity of things. He had shown weakness and had put away his faith and his prayers and all his understanding of the world, had put them away even as he always told his sons to hold fast to such faith, to such belief. But he was sure that he could make it all safe again, could make them all safe from the chanting and marching and all the troubles that threatened if he gave himself over to his prayers, and made a sacrifice and begged forgiveness of Mariemmen and all the deities. But he needed, first, to go back to the club and look at the singer and listen to her music, needed to go to her and prostrate himself before her right there at the club like he had wanted to do on the *Ganges* when she was born. He would prostrate himself amidst the low lights and the small stage and the tables full of drinkers and she would know how regretful he was, how remorseful and how troubled and she would forgive him his doubts, his loss of faith, and she would have mercy on his soul and his human frailty.

He planned it all, thought it through well, but when Billa drove all along the coast through the dark one night, when he plunged himself into the half-darkness of the club expecting to hear her voice, to hear her laughter and her music, he found only quiet, and the stillness of a place long deserted and long abandoned. No one dared to walk about the city at night any more. The dangers of the day, the chants and marches and protests, had spilled over into the night-time and made every corner, every street and alley, perilous and menacing, so when Billa pushed into the club, into its half-darkness, he heard the quiet, and saw at once that the stage was empty and that the spotlight from which the singer would spring whole and glittering and red was gone. He went from table to table and asked the few drinkers about the singer, about the singer with the low, trembling voice but they only looked at him, and looked away and shrugged, and said nothing. They were dumb, vacant. It was as if she had never been, and Billa ran out then, ran out of the club and drove all along the coast, all along the sea wall and looked out at the darkness and the heavy swell of the water that stretched itself out to the horizon and disappeared into the night, and he prayed as he drove through the night that his sacrifice and all the prayers he would say on the very next day would not be too late to pull everything back and make the world safe again.

But it was, it was all too late, and Billa knew it when he returned from a delivery just days later and found himself trembling at the edge of a crowd, at the edge of an argument that had broken out between the dominoes players from Coverton and Paradise. He who had downed large men with his fists, who had always felt so mighty, so invincible – he trembled at the sound of raised voices, of angry voices, and trembled even more when he heard Mahendra's voice among them. He heard it clearly among all the others. The boy was in the middle of a quarrel, a fight. He had come that afternoon to visit them, like he did sometimes. He had brought his baby girl and his wife for a visit, and had gone with his brothers to watch the men play dominoes and to cheer on the Coverton team. But Billa returned home to find the boy's voice raised high and to hear him say, 'Jagan's working for the poor people, for all poor people, man. Call that Communism if you want but it's about rights for the working people, people like you and me, man.'

'He's a Communist. Like Castro in Cuba,' someone said. The voice was heavier. It sounded like Benjie's. He was one of the best dominoes players on the Paradise team and was close friends with Sampson.

'It's independence Jagan working for, man, independence for all of us,' Bisram, one of the Coverton players, said.

'Stewps! He's only working for you, for his own people. Not us!' Billa could not make out the voice but knew it belonged to a Paradise man.

'Yes! Who will see to our rights, eh? Jagan is only there for you Indian people, his people,' Benjie said.

'That's not true, man.' It was Mahendra's voice again. 'And your man, Burnham, only sitting down and making deals with the white man, with the same people who brought all of us to work in the fields.'

'Yes, yes,' Bisram said. 'And what's so right about that, eh? Tell us! Tell us, man! He's a sell-out. He's making deals and taking money, taking pay from the CIA, man.'

'And why not take the white man's money, eh? They owe us, man. Burnham's smart,' Benjie said. 'You wait and see how he's going to outsmart them. Jagan should have made him the leader, man, and let him do the dealing.'

'Yes. Benjie's right. If it were Burnham in there as prime minister, we would have independence already. They're not going to give it to no Communist, man.'

'Jagan's for the working people,' Mahendra said again.

'No! He's for Indian people; not Africans,' Benjie said.

'That's what this comes down to, eh? Eh? Is coolie man and black, eh?' Bisram said. 'We'll turn on one another instead of fighting the white massa, eh?'

'Well, you all got your man Jagan in government and running the whole show and what we got, eh? What we got? We left holding water, left holding corn husks and that's not right, man,' Benjie said, and it was then that the first blow fell and Billa found himself rushing forward with the crowd, rushing forward into the very centre of the tussle and getting hold of Mahendra and dragging him away. Vickram and Krish were there with him to pull Mahendra away, to pull him away from the fighting and the confusion, and it was then that Billa looked up and saw Sampson watching him, saw Sampson looking at him straight in the eye then turning and walking away with the Paradise team. All the dominoes were left scattered in the grass and no one, not anyone bothered to reach down and pick them up.

Mahendra's knuckles were bruised and he had a cut over his eye and, all the way home, he said that he was not going to let anyone curse out Jagan, or him, or any of his people without putting up a fight. That was what he said and Billa wanted to show the boy some moves, some good moves that he could use to protect himself, show him how to stand guard, and how to punch with the right and protect with the left. He wanted that afternoon in the bottom-house to stand up shoulder to shoulder with Mahendra and teach the boy some tricks about fighting but when he saw the fear and trembling on Radika's face, and saw how she held their baby close, he told the boy, instead, that he should be mindful, that he had a wife and child and responsibilities and that he should take care with what he was saying because they were living in dangerous times.

'Remember that the Africans have a history, too,' Billa said. 'And they have feelings, too.'

'They're just sore losers. Jagan won the elections fair and square, won by every rule in the book,' Mahendra said. 'But they plan to beat us up and take it away, eh? That's fair? That's right?'

Savo was putting a plaster on the cut over the boy's eye and she kept saying hush, son, hush, and it was then that Billa felt a despair, a deep despair and it was that feeling of pure hopelessness that took him over to Rampat and Parvati's house after Mahendra and his family left to return to the city. He would be able to sit with them quietly and share in their feeling of loss, would be able to feel it as his own. But when he got there he nearly turned back for Reverend

Davies was there. He heard the man's voice, heard him talking to Rampat and Parvati, and Billa was going to turn back just so as to avoid the man except that Rampat had already seen him and he called out and invited him in, so he unlatched the gate and walked up to the bottom-house and sat down and, immediately, Rampat asked the reverend to repeat all that he was telling them for the reverend had attended one of Burnham's meetings in the city and had heard all that the boy was telling his people.

'Yes,' the reverend said. 'They all came out to hear him. He has America and Britain on his side so he's free to do and say anything he wants and he stood before his people and told them how it was they who came to the colony first, who came as slaves and cut the bush and cleared the land and dug the drains and were the rightful, the natural inheritors of the land. He told them that no one else had any claim to it. He spoke to them like that then stretched out his hand over them like a blessing.' The pastor stood up and showed them how Burnham had appeared before his people and how he had stretched out his hand. 'The man speaks beautifully. He's charming and when he stands up before the crowd he looks like an African king, a *kabaka*. That's what they call him, their king. It stands to reason that a king needs a kingdom, and he's charismatic. He'll be able to get them to do whatever he wants.'

'With guns?' Billa asked, and the reverend nodded.

'With bombs?' Parvati asked, and the reverend nodded.

'Even murder?' Rampat asked, and the reverend nodded.

'The stakes are high and Burnham is ambitious and he will do whatever it takes to win,' he said. 'And his people are hungry for victory, for victory at any cost. They feel they're owed it, that they slaved and that their birthright has been stolen from them.'

'But Jagan will know what to do, eh?' Billa said. 'He'll have a solution, eh?'

Billa watched the reverend shrug. 'America will crush Jagan easily if that's what they decide. It's Kennedy's decision and he feels he needs to make a statement, to show Russia how easily he can crush a

Communist. He needs a victory badly after the Bay of Pigs debacle and this will be an easy one. You all need to be careful, even here in the villages.'

The reverend had lived among them, among the Indian villagers, and the Hindus especially, for so many years, and Billa could see that he was trying to be sympathetic, but, for all that, Billa still could not change his mind about the man and all that he stood for. Whatever happened, however they got through the troubles, the reverend would come out on the other side of it still seeking their souls to turn to his god. And just as Billa was thinking that, the reverend said, 'We must pray, must ask for God's help and guidance. I'm holding a special prayer service on Sunday. If you feel like it,' he said and he then placed his hat on his head and left, walked off into the evening light, and Billa told Rampat and Parvati then about the fight that afternoon and how Mahendra got a cut over his eye, and they said they had heard, had heard about the dominoes players fighting over Jagan and Burnham.

'It has come to this, eh?' Billa said. 'Even Sampson walked away from me like I'm nobody to him.'

'Sampson!' Parvati said. 'I always said that man was no good.'

'But he and Billa have been good, good friends and that stands for something, Parvati,' Rampat said. 'Don't worry, Billa, Sampson is still your friend. Give it time and all this will blow over. The reverend is right: we must pray, brother. It is faith alone that has kept me and Parvati going all these many years. We must pray for God's help with everything.'

Rampat and Parvati had learned patience and acceptance, and Billa saw the good of it, saw how it made them at peace with the world but, even as he sat there, he felt again all his despair, and he knew that he could not ever sit back like that, sit still and wait on the world to show itself to him. Even as he sat there and listened to them, listened to them speak softly about hope and patience and God's will, he wanted to go back again to the temple and pray, wanted to drive again into the city to see the marches and hear the chants, wanted to go back to the nightclub and see whether the singer had returned for he was restless, restless like the wind, and he wanted to move, to act, to make something happen, and he wanted that evening to say to Rampat and Parvati that they should pray, that they should make a sacrifice, a blood sacrifice, should do something more than spilling the water from a cracked coconut before the deities, but, as before, he stopped himself short because he feared that they would turn away from him, and he knew that he could not risk losing them and all the closeness they shared. So, he told them, instead, how he had talked to Mahendra that afternoon, how he had told the boy to move back home to Coverton until things calmed down in the city, and how Savo had told the boy to let Radika and the baby come and stay in the village with them even if he wanted to stay in Georgetown and play hero with Jagan, and that the boy had told them that he had to keep close to the party's headquarters in case he was needed, but that he would send his family home to Coverton if things got worse.

'I made him promise that he would leave the city at the first sign of danger and he said yes, yes, Pa, and was telling me then that I should stop coming into Georgetown because things could escalate and get out of hand at any moment,' Billa said.

'The boy is right,' Rampat said.

'Yes, everybody's got to be careful these days,' Parvati said. 'It's not like long-time, like the days when we came here first and everybody was living nice together, and even Sampson started acting nice to us in the cane fields and all that. Everything's different now. Everybody's fighting for betterment – Jagan and Burnham – they're fighting for betterment but it's still fighting, and one is bound to win and one is bound to lose, eh?'

'Only prayer can help,' Rampat said.

'Only the gods can help,' Billa said.

It was how he felt, truly, and it made him pray constantly, pray for mercy and pray that he would find the *devi* again. He had turned away from her and lost her and he prayed and promised that he would give anything, would make any sacrifice if she would only return to their world and make everything right again. He prayed at the temple, and prayed with Savo and Krish when they did their morning *pooja*, when they circled the deities with the sacred flame, the eternal flame, and that was how it happened that on a Friday morning he stood at the sea wall and saw the day open with the sky on fire, and saw the *devi*, the *devi* herself riding in from the sea on waves that rose high above the earth and were rolling in to crash over the wall.

He was turning his truck into the city and heading for the market square with a load of fruits and vegetables for Boysie's stall, was doing his weekly run for Boysie, when he saw the line of fire to the south of the city. The horizon was on fire and he heard screaming and shouting and running everywhere and Billa knew that it was happening, that all the rumours, all his fears of threats and danger, and all the whisperings he had heard of troubles and plots and bombs had finally come to pass, but he felt prepared, felt he could handle it and he turned his truck off the main road and headed straight for Mahendra's house to get the boy and Radika and their baby girl, to get them to leave the city which was disappearing under smoke and ash, disappearing into a fiery darkness, and was booming and exploding everywhere as one building after the other went up in flames. He saw a big drum fly up in the air and burst open and scatter fire everywhere. It was a drum of red paint, and the paint spilt out like blood and caught fire; and all around him he heard those sounds, those pops and explosions as paints and thinners and all kinds of chemicals caught fire and threw off sparks that pitched about high in the air like fireworks. It was the old wooden buildings that were more at risk. The fire was eating into them quickly. The newer places, the concrete shops stood a better chance even though he saw how the fire was razing their roofs and making all their large windows, their modern plate glass windows just shatter into little pieces, into pieces that shot through the air like bullets. There was fire and ash and sirens and shouts and the sound of running feet everywhere, then, out of a small alley, Billa saw a group of African men come at him with sticks.

They were running after him, running beside the truck and shouting, 'Look! A coolie! Catch him!' and he saw how they held their sticks shoulder-high like rifles, and he knew that if they caught him he would surely die, so Billa pushed down hard on the accelerator and moved the truck through the smoke, moved it forward blindly and prayed that the road ahead was clear. His heart was racing and the truck was racing and he was pushing it on harder and faster and away from the running men, and he found himself praying, praying yet again for his life, for his life to be saved. He drove like that feeling the rush of the tyres beneath him, feeling the speed of the racing truck until he turned a corner with a screech, and he heard the shouts of the men fall away, heard them grow faint then fall away and disappear in the smoke. He had lost them and when he reached Mahendra's house he found that the boy was already bundling his family into his truck and was making ready to leave and Billa told him to go home to Coverton and to stay away from the city, told him about the African mobs that were about, and told the boy to hurry up and leave and that he was not to return to the party headquarters, that he was not to return to play hero and worry his mother's heart, but that he was to go, to leave the city, and that he would be right behind him.

He was planning to do that, was planning to follow the boy out of the burning city, and he was turning his truck around and heading back to Coverton when he caught the barest edge of a sound that was coming in on a quickening wind, a wind that was coming in from the sea. The sound was familiar. It was the sound of laughter, a laughter that was low and throaty and trembling and without even thinking, without any consideration of danger, Billa turned the truck with one swing of the wheel, turned the truck straight into the sound and drove steadily towards it. And that was when he found himself at the sea wall with the sky on fire to the south and the waters of the sea to the north of him, the waters that had risen high as mountains and were curled over at the top, were curled over and frothing at the top. And it was then that he saw her, the *devi,* saw her at the very top of the curling wave, and he fell to the earth immediately and prostrated himself before her as he had wanted to do on the deck of the *Ganges*. He fell full-length onto the sodden earth behind the wall and gave himself over to her will.

There at the sea wall, he offered up prayers, and asked for her blessings as the city burned and the sea moved in to drown the world. He had angered the gods with his unbelief, with his carelessness with his faith, and he asked for forgiveness for his human frailty and he asked that their world be saved, saved from all harm, and he promised again that he would give anything, anything at all to help save their world harm. He prayed to the *devi*, and to all the deities as the wind whistled and threw up higher and higher waves, and when he got up and faced the sea again, he saw that the goddess was once again the girl they had always known, the sweet-faced girl, Neela, and that her hair flowed and curled and swirled away into the waters of the sea, and that her voice was gentle and soft, was the sweet rushing sound of a sea breeze that ran high above the roar of the storm, and as he watched, he saw the wave grow even bigger, even taller as it readied itself to storm over the wall.

Billa stood there and watched the wave advance and felt that he was like a figure in the Ramayana, a mythical figure in one of the bold stories of feats and wonders, and that he was to be the bearer of good news to all the people of Coverton and Paradise, the bearer of good news to all his friends and family. He would tell them that the girl had returned, that the *devi* had returned to fulfill her karma and to save their world. He would, at last, be able to tell Rampat and Parvati all that he had known even from the day the child was born, tell them how he had watched the avatar at the nightclub and how he had doubted and lost faith and had lost her, but that she had come again and that he was going to make sure that she would never leave, that the goddess would always be with them whenever they had need of her.

But when he arrived home with news of the girl's return, he found the village in an uproar. Krish ran out to meet him and he was telling the boy about the *devi* and what he had seen, and how she had come in with the wind and was riding on a wave, a mountain-high wave just like a story out of the Ramayana, was telling the boy how the *devi* had returned to them, when he found everyone pressing in around him and speaking all at once, speaking to him about killing, about murder. Savo was clutching at him and crying and holding her grandchild, was holding Mahendra's baby girl and crying for her safety, for all their safety. 'They're going to kill us,' she was saying, was saying over and over. It was what everyone was saying, that the villagers in Paradise had picked up cutlasses and sticks and were going to attack them, were going to beat them up and burn their homes and worse. But he and Sampson were good friends, they said. He must go and talk some sense to Sampson, they said, and Billa stood before them and told them to hush, to calm down.

'Yes,' he said. 'I will go and speak to Sampson and the men of Paradise. We have been good friends and neighbours all these years and there is nothing in the world that should come between us. None of you will be killed here today. I give you my word.'

Billa said that to the villagers and to Savo and Radika and Padmini and he started off immediately towards the canal and the bridge, started off with a chuckle and a quick gait towards Paradise. His sons and some of the men fell in with him, and when they passed Rampat and Parvati's house, Billa waved and told them that he had such good news for them, and that he would tell them everything, everything he knew as soon as he got back from his talk with Sampson and the men in Paradise. He laughed a little to himself and saw already how their faces would lift and how the sadness that had settled around their eyes would leave for good when he told them that their daughter was going to return home that very day, that he was sure of it, for he had seen her, and he knew that she was going to return to them once her work in the city was done. He was still laughing to himself about all the good news that he had to give to Rampat and Parvati and all the people in the villages about the *devi* when he crossed the bridge and raised his hand to greet Sampson.

Sampson was standing in the middle of the street, and the village men stood with him, carrying sticks and cutlasses on their shoulders like rifles. Sampson had a stick, a long stick on his and when Billa raised his hand and smiled and made ready to speak, to say what good friends they had been, what good neighbours they had been all these years, and that they should not ever let anything come between them, make enemies of them, when Billa made ready to laugh and remind them of the many good years they had lived together, he saw Sampson raise his stick high, saw him hold it with both of his hands and raise it high, then felt it break hard, heard it crack hard against his head, and Billa felt the pain of it, felt the blood run down his face and was surprised at how hard the earth was when he dropped, when he fell against it.

PART FOUR
KRISH

each day demands we create our whole world over,
disguising the constant horror in a coat
of many-colored fictions
TALE OF A TUB, SYLVIA PLATH

The First Terror • Vickram Leaves • Ma Dies * Mahendra Leaves
The Devi Appears • Aunt Parvati Dies • Friends with the Reverend
Jagan in Office • Krish Regains his Faith • The Devi Will Return

WHEN HIS FATHER FELL at his feet that day and died, Krish did not know how he would ever breathe again. It seemed impossible that life could continue, could go on as if the void that was left where his father once stood could ever be closed over, and so easily. The world itself had dropped at his feet and died and all of its shining promise went with it, all of the faith and hope that his father held, all of his belief in the deities, including the *devi* who he said had come into the world to protect them and save them from harm; and Krish thought that it was too much of anyone to ask of him that he should continue to have faith, that he should continue to believe when none of it had helped his father. So, even when the villagers said how Billa had stood up to the rage and taken the blow to the head, had taken the fatal blow for all of them and saved them, even when they spoke of his death that way, spoke of his father that way, and said that he was brave and heroic, Krish could only think that he had lived an unfinished life, that he had been brutally cut down, and that it was not what he had ever wanted for his father. He had expected him to always be there to watch him grow, get married, have children, and live like he had, live large, and embrace all the world as his own. He never wanted him to give his life like that, to become a sacrifice like that, and when he went with him that day to Paradise to meet Sampson and the village men, Krish never expected it to be the end of the world as he knew it. He had rushed out to meet him, to meet his father when he returned from the city that day, and he was full of the story of the men in Paradise who had picked up sticks and cutlasses, had swung sticks and cutlasses onto their shoulders like rifles, like long guns, and were planning to attack them, to come and burn the houses in Coverton and to beat them, and do worse. He had rushed up with his story only to hear his father telling him how he had seen her, how he had seen the *devi* rising out of the storming sea, had seen her rise and curl at the very top of a mighty wave and that she was going to drown the city, was going to drown the wrongs of the world then return to them in Coverton. It was the same *devi* that he had always told Krish about on those moonlit mornings by the canal when they had waited for the fish to jump into their net, the *devi* that his father had seen being born on board the *Ganges*, the one who had left, had disappeared, and who his father always said was going to return one day. 'She's returned to us, son,' he had said to Krish just before all the villagers had crowded in to tell him that the men in Paradise were going to attack, were going to attack Coverton that very day.

Krish always trembled when he remembered how brightly the noonday sun had shone, how the day itself had shown no sign, no mark of terror, and how his father had moved forward, had proceeded over to Paradise without any moment of doubt or hesitation. He had laughed and talked and swung his hands and called out to Uncle Rampat and Aunt Parvati along the way about all the news he had for them, about all the good news he was going to bring to them later. He had walked like that, had moved ahead as if he were going to meet up with one of his stories, one of his own stories of battles and heroes, and Krish had moved along with him, had picked up his pace and swinging gait and had swung his arms as well and laughed when his father had laughed for he had told Krish such stories of his younger days, stories of going out on big boats, boats with sails as big as clouds that had swept him far out to sea where he had fought the biggest *sura* with the sharpest teeth, and it was always he, his father, who won the battle and landed the shark on the boat's deck. So, Krish had walked beside him and had expected nothing less than that his father would win, would triumph at whatever it was that waited on them in Paradise for he had also heard that particular story many times, had heard how his father had fought Sampson among the cane stumps and won. He always believed that side of the story even though Sampson liked to tell a different tale with a different ending.

Sampson always laughed when he came to their house and told Krish and his brothers all the stories that he knew, told them how he had challenged their father in the cane field one day and had won, had won the fight for sure, and Krish and Mahendran and Vickram would laugh and say no, no, that it was their father who had won, and Sampson would laugh his big laugh and slap his knee and say, 'No, no. It only appeared that way because his *jahajis* picked him up quickly and carried him off on their shoulders.' Krish had heard the man tell the story many times, those many times when he came to their home to pass the time of day with them in their bottom-house. It was his favourite story, the story of the big fight but he also liked to tell them other stories, stories of jumbies and water mamas, and about the water mama who used to live among them, who used to walk about the earth among them, and that he knew she was a real water spirit because his mammie and grandmammie were like that too, and they, too, had gone away in the water, had left to go and live among their own people. 'But they're going to come back for me one day. My mammie told me she'll come back for me and I'll know her for sure when she does no matter what she looks like or what form she takes.' Sampson always said that, and he would laugh and slap his knee – the Sampson that Krish knew as a child – and their mother would always come up to them and fret with Sampson about the stories he was telling the children. She would call them away and tell them, he and his brothers, that all those stories about water mamas were stupidness, that Sampson's stories about his mammie and grandmammie, and the one about Uncle Rampat and Auntie Parvati's daughter, about the girl who used to walk about the earth among them then disappeared, were nothing but foolishness, and it was she who told them that the girl had run away from home because she did not want to get married and settle down to any family life.

She said that Uncle Rampat and Auntie Parvati had picked the girl up out of the sea, had picked her up straight out of the sea water on the crossing from India and that the girl had run off like water itself, and that everybody knew that she had gone to the city to sing in a nightclub because she was nothing but a city woman, a badwoman just like her real mother was, the girl who had birthed her then died on the ship, the very ship that had brought their father from India over to the new world. She would tell them that story then tell them not to say anything about it to their father because Uncle Rampat and Aunt Parvati were his *jahajis*, his shipmates, and that he believed all the things they said about the girl because he did not want to hurt their feelings. 'Your father is a man like that. He has too much of a good heart to tell your Uncle Rampat and Auntie Parvati that the girl was no *devi* born out of the sea,' their mother said to them, and Krish knew that it was a true thing that their mother said when she told them that their father had a good heart, a big heart and that he would never have wanted to hurt the feelings of his good friends.

He never wanted to hurt anybody at all. His bigmouth ways were nothing but swagger to throw people off balance and he used it on drunks who brawled in the streets or threatened violence on their families. Their father only had to raise his voice and raise his fists and the men would back away from him, and Krish liked that about him – that he was a man who stood up to a fight. He had courage and Krish was proud of that but if he and his brothers ever asked him about the big fight between him and Sampson, their father always laughed and said that there were better ways to settle a fight than by fighting. It was a lesson he had learned the hard way, he said, that it did no good to strike a man, to pick up a stick or a piece of wood and lash a man over his head because it settled nothing and only brought too many worries on your own. He never went further, never told them how he had learned that lesson but Krish always felt that it had something to do with the story that his father told to himself in the early morning darkness, the story that he cast out over the canal in whispering sounds when they went out to catch fish on those escapades that used to fret his mother.

He was little at the time but old enough to know that whisperings held secrets and that secrets held good stories and, sitting by the bucket and waiting to fill it with jumping fish, he had strained to catch his father's words even though he had heard nothing that made sense, had only heard words like Pondicherry and Tamil Nadu and Orissa and Bengal and Calcutta. They were all foreign to him and even now, grown as he was, he still did not know the thread of the story that strung those place names together and gave them sense. Perhaps, had his father lived, he might have told them the whole of it, might have filled in the gaps and told them how he came to know that lashing a man over his head with a stick settled nothing.

Krish always believed that it was that very reason, that very lesson that had made his father go over to Paradise that day with his arms raised, with his arms raised in greeting. He had lifted his arms up and smiled, had even laughed, and was making ready to speak, to speak to his good friend Sampson when Sampson had brought the stick that he held, had brought it down hard on his father's head. Krish had seen the stick move, had heard the crack of it, and had heard his father cry out, then seen him bleed and fall to the earth, and he remembered screaming and he remembered holding his father's bloodied head in his hands, and he remembered that he screamed for his father and for a world gone mad for it was the first time that he came to know that about the world, that you could watch it, see it, feel it, hear it and that it could, none of it, make sense. He had seen his father fall, had seen him bleed, had heard him cry out, and he had felt that it was all too brief, too short a time for a life that had been lived so large, a life that had crossed oceans and battled every monster on earth, to be cut down and be gone forever. It was impossible that it could be taken like that without notice, without permission, without any preparation or sign since the world gave notice for much less. The wind would rise to announce a storm, and dogs would bark to warn of danger but in an atom's weight of time his father was lost, had bled away without any sign or warning.

He was a brave man, and proud, a man who was unafraid of battle. There was no other like him, and he had given Krish an idea of the world as a shining place, a place that was filled with every bright possibility, had handed it to him like a gift, and Krish knew that he was his lucky son, the shining star of his life who was expected to live and see the fulfillment of all that promise. But he did not know how he could hold fast to such ideas when the world had become so treacherous, and it was on that very day, as his father's life bled away into his hands, that he started to doubt all that his father ever told him about how he understood the world for he only saw that the world was a cruel and uncertain place, a place where there was no hope, no promise, no salvation, and he had screamed and felt the pull of hands take him back over the bridge, over the canal and back to their home where his father was laid out on a rough table in the bottom-house, and where the whole village gathered to weep and mourn and pray for his soul's journey. He had wept at other funerals since but that was his first and it was the hardest still because the death was so brutal, so unjust. None of the brutalities that followed, none of the injustices that came after ever cut as deep, and they always served to reopen the wounds, to lay them bare and cause him to remember again his father's last cry, the shock and pain of it, and the way he fell to the earth and died. He was no lucky son, after all.

He had not seen the danger coming, and had not even lifted his hands to fend off the fatal blow. He had only wept, had wept like a child for the suddenness of the thing, the savagery of the thing, and they had all, all of them relived the death with each new brutality that followed that first onslaught that began in the city that day then spread all through the countryside. Krish always believed that had his father lived to see how the world fell apart and disintegrated around them, how its brightness faded and how it became tarnished with horror upon further horror that he would surely have forgiven him his doubts, and understood his loss of faith. It was not a dishonour to his father that he lost all belief, all hope, for he loved him and wanted to keep faith with the world as he understood it, with the world that he knew to be true, but Krish found that it was not possible to do that in the darkness that moved in and stayed with them for years, for decades after. And when his brothers made the decision to leave, to take their families to safe ground, Krish could find no arguments to make them stay, not even the argument that their father always believed in the bright possibilities of their world and that it was wrong of them to give up that hope. Krish could not say any of it because he himself no longer believed it, and when his brothers joined the thousands who fled because they saw no hope of change, saw no hope that the violence against them would ever stop, he wondered at times whether he, too, might not join them one day; whether he, too, might not abandon every last hope and leave.

It was Vickram who went first, who left with plans that once he was settled in New York they would all follow, that he would get up all the necessary immigration papers to sponsor them. And it was Mahendra who tried to talk him out of it, who tried to tell him that Jagan was going to get things under control, was going to get the country safe and secure again. 'He knows the problems, man,' Mahendra said. 'He knows all that went on in the city and at Wismar just the other day, and he's going to set things right, man.'

But Vickram only sucked his teeth and said, 'He knows what? Look at what all the reports about Wismar say, man. Black policemen stood by and watched the beatings and burnings, even the rapes, and the killing of two Indian men and they did nothing. Their leader is Burnham and the enemy is us – Indians. The police don't take orders from Jagan, man. So who will protect me and my Padmini and my Shanti, my little baby girl, eh?'

'Have some faith, man,' Mahendra said. 'Jagan's working to reform the police force, to get Indians into the force. He knows what he has to do to make the country safe for everybody, man. Look, brother, Pa came here and worked hard to make a life for us here. He put his blood and sweat in this earth and you can't just pack that up in a suitcase and leave just like that.'

'Pa would not want me and my family to get killed,' Vickram said. 'He would want us to live, man. And one death in the family from all this madness is enough, more than enough. You've seen the people who have come here from Wismar? The Indians that the African people chased out? You've seen their eyes? They're dead, man. Jagan can promise me that that won't happen to me, to all of us?'

When Vickram spoke like that about the Wismar refugees, of the hundreds of Indians who had been burned and beaten out of their homes in the bauxite mining towns of Mackenzie and Wismar and Christianburg by gangs of Africans, by Burnham's supporters, Mahendra fell silent. A few of the refugees had drifted in to Coverton to stay with family or friends. They had all seen them. They were easy to pick out for they walked about with their eyes fixed to the earth as if they expected it to open up like a grave beneath them. They trusted nothing, not even the earth itself, and one survivor, a girl of fifteen, just sat and stared and trembled. She shook uncontrollably, and could not sleep, and if she did, if she ever fell asleep out of sheer exhaustion, she always woke up screaming. They broke over the village – her screams – they rolled over the rooftops like a storm, and no one who heard her could help but weep, and it was her screams more than anything else that had moved Vickram to act, and to apply for emigration to the United States.

'If anyone did that to my Shanti, I would have to kill them, kill them for sure,' he said, then added, 'and I don't want to live in a place that makes me think like that, to think of killing a man. You ask Krish, ask Ma what they think, Mahendra. Ask them if I should stay here with my baby girl. And as if the Wismar Massacre was not enough, look at what they did again when the *Sun Chapman* launch exploded. No, brother, I have to go.'

When Vickram brought up the bombing of the river launch, Mahendra sucked his teeth and said that the Africans had blamed them, had blamed Jagan and his party for planting the bomb that had exploded the launch that was going upriver from Georgetown to the mining towns, had exploded the launch in the Demerara River and killed all the Africans onboard, killed forty of them. 'They said that it was retaliation for Wismar, for what happened two months ago,' he said and sucked his teeth again. 'And if we did it, so what, eh? Who said that we have to sit down and take rape and murder quietly and do nothing about it, eh? Stewps!'

'Well, if it's all about revenge, about tit-for-tat, then it's alright because the same mining-town people just went out and hunted for more coolie people when the news reached them about the explosion. They went out and killed five more Indians, even a lil boy, ten-year-old Maurice Bacchus who was just trying to protect his baby sister, Deborah, from the gangs. Stewps! You stay here and play your games with people's lives but I'm going, and once I get set up, I'll put in papers so that Ma and Krish can come to America and live. This place is not safe for us any more no matter what Jagan says.'

It was then, when Vickram finished all that he had to say and their mother saw that his mind was made up that she started to cry and say how she had lost their father and now she was going to lose her son and her daughter-in-law and her baby granddaughter, too. 'It's too hard, too hard,' she said and she wept, and Vickram had to go over and put his hands around her and shush her and say that he would send for her, would send for her as soon as he got settled, but that Ma had to understand and see that it was best, that it was the only thing he could do to keep his family safe.

Vickram spoke like that until the very last day he left, said that he had to go in order to keep his family safe and give them a good life, and Krish and Mahendra did not see him again until years later when he returned for their mother's funeral. He wept bitterly then because he had not seen her in her last years, and because he was not with her at her final moments. They had been close and he had missed her; and his two daughters – the second born in America – did not know her at all, did not know their *ajee*, their father's mother, and she, too, died without ever knowing them. He said he always thought there was still time for them to visit, or for her to come to New York, but the truth was that she never wanted to go, never wanted to leave the house because, for her, it lived with their father's voice, with his laughter and footsteps and all his many tales, and she could never have left those behind. She had never even touched his clothes, had never thrown them out, and when Krish asked about it once, asked whether she should not clear out the wardrobe and drawers, she had looked at him as if he were a stranger making strange remarks, and he had never brought it up again. She had suffered and they, none of them, had ever found the right words to say to comfort her, and they prayed then, when she died, they performed all the rites and ceremonies needed to grant her soul eternal rest. They prayed when Mahendra took the flaming torch and lit her funeral pyre on the foreshore, prayed that she would attain *moksha*, that she would find the perfect union with God and that her soul would not ever have to be reborn into the world.

Krish prayed fervently for that peace for their mother and he wanted to believe that she would be reunited with their father and that, there, in the safety of heaven, she would find her voice again, her laughter again, for she had lived all those many years since his death with her silence wrapped closely around her as if that alone was all her comfort. Krish had watched her give herself over to it, surrender herself to the dreaded silence, and it was only when she drew her final breath that her face looked to be at peace again. She died of sadness and heartbreak and Krish, who had watched her live through it all, did not believe that he had such strength, the strength it took to live with the knowledge of the terror, to imagine the pain of the last blow, to only ever imagine how much, how hard, how cruel. He felt that he would surely have succumbed to madness. It was why he never married, and why he managed to laugh and wave his hand about whenever his brothers, or Aunt Parvati, or any of his friends told him about a nice girl they had seen for him, a girl so pretty that he was bound to fall in love the moment he set eyes on her. He would laugh and wave his hand, wave a dismissive hand, and he never told anyone, not anyone, that he may be tall and broad and strong, as strong as his father ever was, and that he could face a fight, could pit his strength against any Sampson who might come along to challenge him, but that he knew that he did not have the kind of strength to bear what his mother had, to lose the person who was as close to you as your own heart. He did not ever tell that to anyone, and he could not remember when everyone stopped pressing him about getting married and became accustomed to his solitariness, accepted it. 'No, Krish never got married,' he heard Uncle Rampat say to someone once, someone who had pointed him out as Billa's son, as one of Billa's boys. 'He took his father's death the hardest,' he heard Uncle Rampat say and Krish had drawn in his breath hard at the words and had wondered whether everyone saw him that way, as someone to pity, as someone broken.

He did not think so for he made sure that he went about his life, his daily work and tasks, with a face that showed no trace, no mark of the memory of that day when his father fell at his feet and died even though it was always there, the horror of it. Krish did not ever try to push it away or forget it. To do that would have been like forgetting his father for it was a part of his wholeness, the way he died, and the memory became a comfort even as the days continued to darken all around him, for it made him feel that he already knew the worst of all fates that could befall him or anyone around him, that he knew the worst and had survived, had managed to live through it. It made him more careful, he believed, as he went about his days, as he went about with his work, his father's work, for he had climbed into the cab of the truck, the red truck, the very next week after his father's death and had taken Boysie Karran's weekly load of produce to the city market and Boysie had slapped him on the back and said how sorry he was about their father, had repeated all the words he had said at their father's funeral about what a good man he was, what a brave man, and that he was the best friend he ever had.

Boysie had said all of it again when Krish arrived behind the wheel of the truck and he and all the men about the marketplace had slapped him on the back and said that he had big shoes to fill, and that his father would be proud to see him behind the wheel of the truck, and proud that he had picked up the business and not let everything slide, let everything get him beaten down. 'Life goes on,' they had said and Krish had said yes, yes, for he had already come to know that grief was a burdensome thing to those not connected to it. Everyone around them was always telling them that they had to go on, that they had to put everything behind them and move on, and Krish believed that that was why their mother had chosen to keep to her solitary silence through all of her last years: it was because she did not want to burden anyone with her grief.

She had folded herself away even from Krish and he had not disturbed her with any of the everyday details, any of the humdrum affairs of life and work, and he had also kept her from ever knowing all that Mahendra did for Jagan and the party, the work he did with bombs as the violence continued all around them. 'If they burn our houses, we'll burn theirs back, eh?' he had said, and he had even shown Krish once how they filled bottles with *channa*, with chickpeas, and with kerosene oil then pushed a bit of rag into it for a wick. 'We light it and throw it and we run!' Mahendra had said then laughed. 'And we always have our cutlasses at the ready. The Africans fear a coolie man and his cutlass,' he had said and laughed again.

Every time he visited he talked about all the young men, the young men just out of school like Krish who were joining up to the youth arm of the party to fight, but he never asked Krish to join, and Krish always thought that it was out of consideration for their mother, that Mahendra felt she had borne enough with the death of their father, and with Vickram and his family having gone away to America. Vickram and Padmini and Shanti were gone from her eyes as much as their father was, so Mahendra never pressed Krish to join what he called 'the struggle' because it would have been too much for both of them to face the dangers. And Krish never thought he would join up even if his brother asked for he was beginning to see that no amount of fighting or fighting talk was going to save Jagan. His days as prime minister were numbered because America was going to get rid of him and put their man, Burnham, in office. Everyone knew it even before the results of the nineteen sixty-four elections were announced, knew that Jagan would lose, would lose to Burnham. It was Boysie and Janak and Kishun and all the men about the market square who said it even before the day of the elections, even before the votes were counted. It was the new elections system, the new proportional representation system the British had brought in, they said, that would make sure that Burnham got in as prime minister.

'He's going to get in with a coalition with the lil Portuguese party, with Peter D'Aguiar's party,' Boysie said.

'They're cheating Jagan, man,' Janak said.

'And you watch and see how the Queen of England is going to hand Burnham independence, hand it to him like a gift,' Kishun said.

'After all the years that Jagan fought so hard for that.'

'But, wait! None of them know who they're dealing with.'

'D'Aguiar thinks he can deal with Burnham? Stewps!'

'That coalition won't last two mornings.'

'But America wants Jagan, the Commie, out.'

'And they don't care who gets raped or beaten or killed in the process.'

Jagan was to bring them to no shining world, after all, and Krish did little more than suck his teeth and feel relief that their mother knew little about what was going on around them for those turned out to be the last years of her life and even though Vickram was writing to them about sponsoring all of them to come to America as soon as he got himself enough savings, Krish knew that their mother would not go, would never leave the house, and that her heart was going to give out long before then even though he saved her from ever knowing the worst of the news. She never knew that Jagan lost the elections, or that the coalition government fell apart in less than two years and that Burnham chose then to rig every election, every election after that to keep himself in power. He kept it all from her and, in truth, she never asked anything much about the world any more and was content to live with only her memories for company. Because of that, she never knew how close Mahendra came to being shot along with Jagan's men in the nineteen seventy-three elections when Bholanath Parmanand and Jagan Ramessar were gunned down by Burnham's soldiers, were gunned down by the African army Burnham had created to keep him safe, to keep him in power. The soldiers did his every bidding and when Krish heard the news of the shootings that had happened on the eastern coast, on the Corentyne coast, all he could think was that his brother had gone there with his truck to help out with the party's work on election day, and that if there was any fight, any argument, any trouble, that Mahendra would surely be in the thick of it. It was not until he heard the names of the men who had been killed being announced on the radio that he felt relieved. But Mahendra had been right there, had been just yards away from the men who had fought with the soldiers, had fought to keep the ballot boxes from their constituency from being taken away by the army.

'I was there, right there,' Mahendra said to Krish when he came back from the Corentyne, and Krish thought he saw his brother tremble. 'I heard the guns pop and saw the men fall,' Mahendra said. 'That's how the rigging works. The soldiers take the boxes to the army base and stuff them with votes for Burnham. Anyone who stands in their way gets killed.'

That was all that his brother said before he went quiet and it was the first time that Krish noticed that the fight was gone from him. He heard it in his voice, heard how dejected he was, how disappointed, and it was after that rigged election, when Burnham gave himself a two-thirds majority, that Mahendra stopped all his talk about fighting, and about Jagan and the struggle, and it was shortly after, when their mother died and Vickram returned for the funeral, that Mahendra announced that he, too, was going to pack up and leave, was going to take his family to New York.

They were sitting in the bottom-house after the cremation ceremony, were sitting about and watching the night come in when Mahendra spoke of leaving, and talked to Vickram about the sponsorship, and asked how long it would take, and what he would need to do, and Krish watched Vickram step up immediately and say that it was the best thing that Mahendra could do for himself and his family, and that the sponsorship would not take long, would not take long at all, and that he would start getting up the papers as soon as he got back to New York.

'Krish, you have to come, too,' Vickram said. 'We can sell the house and everything, and we'll all live close to one other in Queens, in New York, and be a family again.' He said that they could not leave Krish behind to live all alone and he even laughed and said that they would find a nice girl for him in New York to marry, that he was not an old man yet, that he still had his broad chest and his good looks. But Krish told them then that he did not want to go and Mahendra sucked his teeth and became angry with him and asked him why he wanted to stay in that place that was falling apart, that was falling apart before their very eyes.

Krish heard himself say the words, say that he did not want to leave, and it was not until that moment, when his brothers spoke to him directly of packing up and moving away, that he knew that he wanted to stay, that he wanted to remain right there in the village and the house. He had never given it much thought before but when his brothers put it to him that afternoon, put it to him directly, he found that the sentiment had always been there, the feeling that it would be like leaving a task unfinished if he were to go. He still had his doubts, all his doubts about the world, and he knew that it was only there, in that place where their father had come and built a house and built a business that he would ever be able to discover the truth, the truth about all that their father had ever believed, and how he understood the world. It was that afternoon that he discovered that that was important to him and he knew that he could not move away, could not pack up and leave all his doubts, all his uncertainties behind. And he could not have taken them with him to a new life for a fresh start deserved that kind of fairness, deserved that you should leave the old life and all its misgivings behind.

'I have to see this to the end,' he said and his brothers jumped in immediately, thinking that he was talking about the politics of the place. They jumped in and waved their hands about and said that he only had to look about him to see that the country was dying, that the village itself was dying, that houses were being locked up and abandoned, and that all his friends, all the people he ever knew when he was growing up were living in New York.

'What do you have to see happen, eh? More rigged elections? More corruption?' Mahendra asked.

'Burnham has put his people on top, man. There's no place here for us, any more,' Vickram said.

'It's only party loyalty that gets you a job or any place in life, man,' Mahendra said. 'You'll stay here and become a Burnham man, eh? You'll become a party comrade, eh?'

'Come with us. There's plenty of good work in New York. I have a good job in a print shop, Padmini is working at Wal-Mart, and the children are going to good schools,' Vickram said. 'And Mahendra will settle in well, too, with Radika and the children. America has work for everybody who wants to work, man.'

Krish let them go on like that for a while before he cut into their arguments and said again, 'I have to stay. I have to see this to the end', and he did not care how they took his words, how they interpreted them, for he himself had only a vague idea of what it was he was expecting, what it was that he was hoping to discover, and it was his very vagueness that gave his brothers more reason to continue their arguments with him. And it was then that Mahendra told him, told him straight that there was no chance of change, and that Jagan was not going to fight Burnham because his hands were good and tied.

'Russia and Cuba like all of Burnham's socialism, all his nationalization policies, his taking over sugar and bauxite and all the radios and newspapers, so Jagan has no choice but to support all of it even though we see how everything just breaking down because Burnham is putting his party comrades to manage things they don't know about. Stewps! And Burnham has all the guns, too. The police force is African, and the army is African, and they'll just mow us down, man, just mow down any Indian who makes any trouble. Look at what they did to Bholanath and Jagan Ramessar, eh? I worked with those boys, worked close with them for so many years and they got shot down, shot down for trying to make sure the elections were fair. No, Jagan's days are done. And that man, Walter Rodney, that you're following, Krish – I know; I hear that you go to his meetings – well, his days are numbered, too. Burnham is going to deal with him good and proper. He's making people laugh at Burnham and all his stupidness, and Burnham is not going to stand for that. This place is nothing but a waste of time, man.'

It was when Mahendra spoke like that, spoke about Jagan and the party like that, that Krish heard it in his voice how frustrated he was, how dejected he had become at seeing his life's work, his whole life's struggle falling apart before his very eyes. He laughed, laughed out loud when he went on to tell Krish that Rodney, that that young academic, that historian who had formed his own political party to fight Burnham, was talking just like Jagan used to talk, was talking about rights and revolution, and about standing with the workers, and that Jagan had said all that before. 'And look what they did to him, eh? They shook him out of government. America did that. They gave Burnham money to make trouble for Jagan and his supporters, for us, for all of us, man. And that Rodney man will be stopped, too. He's getting too popular for Burnham's comfort, and America doesn't like all his socialist talk, anyway, so he'll get no support from them. They like Burnham. He's corrupt and corruptible. They can control him. But Rodney is too much of the idealist, eh? You see and be careful, Krish, when you go to his meetings because one day bullets will fly or a bomb will explode. You mark my words. I know what I'm talking about.'

Krish was not surprised to hear Mahendra talk like that about Rodney, to try and make out that the man had no chance Burnham. It was the party talking, Jagan's party. Mahendra could not allow that Rodney could ever outshine Jagan, could ever best him in any way. His brother would be loyal to Jagan to the end, no matter what, but Krish also knew that Mahendra was right about the danger, for he always felt it whenever he was standing in the crowd at Rodney's meetings, always felt the tension and was always looking about to see if Burnham's soldiers would appear out of nowhere to shoot or to round them up and lock them away. But there were too many of them for Rodney always drew a large crowd, drew Africans, Creoles, and Indians, Indians like himself who had become disillusioned with Jagan and his helplessness, his helplessness against Burnham. It was Rodney's main attractiveness that he stood high above them with his slight figure and his bushy Afro hair and waved his arms about and laughed, laughed with them when he called Burnham a King Kong and compared him to Hitler, then laughed again when he told them that Burnham's megalomania was different to Hitler's only because it was closer to comedy and farce. The man was fearless, and he was all the hope they had of change, of any good change.

'He wears an army general's uniform and calls himself the Comrade Leader and the *kabaka*, an African king. Yes, he makes himself out to be a king, a god, and is hoping that his army will conquer his own people!' Rodney said at the last meeting he held in the city and Krish was there in the crowd that laughed at the spectacle of Burnham that Rodney put before them and when, at the end of every meeting, Rodney shouted, 'Burnham must go!' Krish was always among those who cheered the loudest and the longest. That always made him remember those early days when he was a small boy and he used to rush about and cheer like that for Jagan, to rush about to hang a garland on the man's neck. It was Jagan who was supposed to bring them to a shining world, but after over a decade of doing battle, even Mahendra, a staunch party stalwart was giving up, and there were times when Krish was glad that their father was not there to see the hope and the promise vanish, vanish into thin air as if they had never been. It would have killed his spirit for sure had he lived to see the dark and dismal days that Burnham had brought them to, and to see Jagan become a cowed man, a man who could never bring himself to put aside his personal convictions for the sake of the people and the country, for who among his supporters was a Communist? No one in Coverton was. Nor was Uncle Rampat, or Boysie, or even Mahendra. None of them were Communists but they followed Jagan, as loyally as Burnham's people followed him, because he was their son, was one of their very own. They followed him even when he was outsmarted and outmaneuvered at every turn by the British and the Americans and by Burnham himself, and it was not until Krish heard Rodney speak that he started to believe again in the possibility of hope. He said as much to Mahendra that afternoon, that afternoon when his brother spoke of leaving, said that he felt that Rodney would find a way to defeat Burnham, because he had the people with him, Indians and Africans, everyone who was not afraid of a fight.

And it was then that Mahendra shook his head and said, 'It's false hope, Krish. Nothing will come of it,' and he sighed and said that he was tired, just tired of it all. 'Pa was never afraid of a fight and he died, and for what?'

'He saved us, saved the village,' Krish said.

'All the more reason to leave, Krish,' Vickram said. 'It's enough. It's enough, now.'

But Krish only shook his head again for he had come far since that day when their father fell, that day when he did not know how he would live, how he would ever breathe again. He had discovered that life was a forward-looking thing, that it pushed you along, carried you into every new day whether you wanted to or not. That was how he lived, how he survived, and he became accustomed to all the hardships of living in a ruined country, and even felt that it kept him alert, kept him on his toes for he was constantly looking about him for signs of danger. He would lose all that, lose all that edge if he went away, and when Mahendra continued to speak that afternoon of leaving, of going away with his family, Krish already started to feel the loss of it. But he had come to know that loss was a part of the whole, was part of life, and when Mahendra left and took Radika and their three children, all grown into their teenage years, when he took them all to safe ground in New York, the house grew very quiet.

There were no more afternoon visits, or weekend visits when he and Mahendra would sit and go over the day's news, when they would settle back in the hammocks in the bottom-house and talk about Burnham's latest moves, about the food shortages and the long lines everywhere for kerosene and gasoline, and about the water shortages and the dark nights without any electricity. They would talk like that while Radika and the children, whenever they came with him, bustled about the kitchen and the yard and filled them with happy noises of play and laughter and busy cooking sounds. And it was only after he left that Krish realized that whenever Mahendra had talked about the shortages and hardships, that he was really going over all the reasons, the many reasons why he should leave. The list had grown longer with each visit, had become endless, and Krish found that he missed that, missed his brother's voice telling him that split peas and flour and onions and garlic and even sugar were in short supply, that Burnham had made the country good and bankrupt and that there was no money to buy anything, anything at all. And Krish was missing him, was missing his political talk and his passion, the way he had thrown his energy into the party work without doubt, without question, was missing his brother's voice going on about everything in the world when he woke up one morning and heard it clearly in his head, heard Mahendra telling him that Rodney's days were numbered and that he would get shot or blown up, would get killed for sure. It was only a few months after he left that Krish woke up to his brother's voice in his head and to the news that Rodney had been assassinated, that a bomb had exploded in his car and killed him instantly. The bomb exploded and the whole country went quiet. Even those who had not followed Rodney or supported him went quiet for the warning was clear, was clear to everyone, and they all knew that they had come to the end of all hope for no one was going to do that again, was going to risk their life like that again.

For days after, Krish did not think, or feel, or talk, and he moved through the horror the only way he knew how, moved through it knowing that if he were to live, that if he were to survive, he had to push through it and get to the other side. He had done that before, had moved past the worst, and Rodney's assassination gave him back all his doubts, all his distrust and misgivings. Krish could not help but feel again that there were no gods or goodness, or *devis* who were born out of the sea to save their world. He did not believe any of it, did not trust any of it, and did not know how his father could ever have filled his head with such nonsense, such foolishness, could ever have told him such stories and made him think that faith and belief were all that were needed for a good and successful life, for Rodney was a good man and he, too, had fallen, had met with a cruel and untimely death. It took him back to his father's, to the injustice and the cruelty, and to his feeling, at the time, that the whole world had come loose, had broken away from its moorings and had descended into madness. He always remembered the confusions of that day, and he always felt that it was because he was trying so hard to make sense of everything, to find reason and explanation even out of the horror, that he had looked out and seen the *devi*, had seen her through his tears, through his inconsolable grief, had seen her standing at the very edge of the crowd that had gathered to mourn for his father.

It was her hair, hair that had flowed and curled all around her face like waves, that made him recognize her immediately for she was exactly as his father always described her whenever he told Krish about the goddess on those many mornings when they had gone to the canal to catch fish, to catch the small, jumping fish to fill his pail. He knew her by her hair and her voice which had climbed and climbed, clear and high above all the others when they sang the *bhajans* that asked God to grant his father good and eternal rest, for his father always said that, too, that when the girl sang, it was a sound like heaven itself. And when he and his brothers and Uncle Rampat and Boysie and some of the men from the temple had hoisted the *dholi*, the funeral berth on which their father was laid out, had hoisted it onto their shoulders and set off for the foreshore, he had seen her move though the crowd to dance before them, to dance to the *tapoo* drums with jumping feet all the way to the foreshore where the pyre had been built to receive the *dholi* which the men from the temple had fashioned into a grand palace of five peaks made from cloths of red, gold and white that were stretched taut over a bamboo frame and decorated with strings of golden beads and ribbons and glittering tinsel. It was a splendid thing they had done and it was then, when they had placed the *dholi* on the stacked wood and Krish had felt the weight of it slip from his shoulders, slip away forever, that he had wept, had covered his face and wept uncontrollably. He had lost sight of the *devi* then, lost sight of her when Mahendra took the torch to the pyre, and the flames had leapt and eaten into the wood, into the bone, and the *dholi* and all its grand glitter had gone up in flames. He had covered his face and wept for their father's death, for a death which they had, none of them, ever thought possible.

They had always put it away from their minds because it was difficult to think of a world without him. He had been so alive at every moment, so alive and full of spirit, and he had filled out all the days of their lives so fully that they had none of them ever thought that he, too, that their father only had his allotted time on earth. But he had spoken of it, their father, he had told them how he wanted to be cremated and have his ashes strewn into the sea so that he could be returned home to the Ganges. He had spoken of it when the English had relented and allowed the Hindus to cremate their dead as they had done for centuries. It was men like Jung Bahadur Singh who had fought for those cultural rights and Krish remembered clearly how their father had spoken about the man, had spoken about him admirably and had told Krish and his brothers that that was what a good fight was, that it was about standing firm for what you believed to be right no matter what. 'That's what makes a man – such faith, such belief. It's never about beating people over the head,' he had said, and he had laughed and said that they were to make sure and cremate him then scatter his ashes in the sea, and Krish remembered how he and Ma and his brothers had all laughed and told him not to talk like that about dying because he had many more years to live yet, many more years to talk and laugh and to drive his truck about the whole countryside. But they had been wrong; they had been so wrong for it was not even a good ten years later, when his father was still a strong man, a man not yet stooped with age or looking to sit about and rest himself, that he was cut down, cut down cruelly.

It was more than any of them could bear and when their mother had collapsed into their arms there at the foreshore as the pyre burned and threw smoke high into the air, he and his brothers had shushed her with some words of comfort, some words about heaven and how good a life their father had lived, and they had told her that he would surely attain *moksha*, would surely attain a perfect union with God and would never have to be reborn into the world. But Krish had known even as they spoke that their mother was a practical woman, a woman well rooted in the earth, and that, no matter what comfort they gave her, that she would feel the loss, would feel the physical pain, and understand only that their father was gone, was gone forever from her eyes. Life and death held no magic, no mystery for her. For her, they were matter-of-fact affairs, and she had left the mysteries of the world to their father who had seen magic everywhere, even in the air itself, and who could always pluck a story from it and make it live. It was not until he died that Krish saw how much their mother had needed him, had needed all his tales, all his myths and fabled tales to live fully, for, with him gone, the light went out of her eyes and the smile from her voice, and she even lost all her gossipy ways, all the bright talking that their father had always said was going to get her into trouble one day. She drew herself in from the world from that very day, from that very afternoon when they had returned home the flames were dying down on the foreshore. She had stayed up all night in her room and wept. Krish had heard her. He and his brothers had collapsed into the hammocks in the bottom-house, and they had fallen asleep out of sheer exhaustion, but Krish had found that he could not sleep that night, could not sleep while their mother wept, and he had stayed up and listened to her crying and had known that she would weep well into the morning hours when they would return to gather up their father's ashes and scatter them in the sea.

And it was because of that, because he was still awake and listening to the weeping of their mother, and weeping himself, and feeling such confusions in his head, feeling anger even at their father for walking into his death like that that he came to see the *devi* again, came to see her pass along right outside their gate on quiet feet, pass along like a shadow in the night and, without giving it any thought, he had got up and followed her. She had headed straight for Uncle Rampat and Aunt Parvati's house, and when she got there he had watched her go through the gate, had watched her flow through the gate much like water, much like air itself, and go up the garden path between the crotons and the hibiscus bushes. From where he was crouched low behind the fence, Krish had seen that Uncle Rampat and Aunt Parvati were still up and that Aunt Parvati was consoling Uncle Rampat who was still weeping over his friend's death, over Billa who was his own-own *jahaji bhai*, his shipmate, his only friend, his best friend in the world. His voice was pitched high and had carried through the still night air, and he was saying over and over, 'Only God knows why.' He was weeping and talking like that and Aunt Parvati had her arms around him and was shushing him like a baby, and that was how the girl found them in the dark bottom-house – crying and mourning and remembering their *jahaji bhai*.

They were sitting down like that and mourning his father when they had looked up and seen the girl, had seen her standing before them as if she had stepped right out of the air itself, and Krish had seen how they had left off their weeping immediately and had embraced her and kissed her on both cheeks and how they had sat and talked and laughed easily with her as if all the years that had passed since she went away had never been. It was as if they were prepared for it, as if they always knew that the day would come when they would see her again. Krish could not hear what the girl was saying to them for she had spoken in a low voice but he imagined that she would be telling them about all that had happened during those years when they had thought her lost, and she was probably telling them, too, how his father, how Billa had seen her that day by the sea wall, had watched her make the sea rise up and wash over the burning city. Whatever it was she had said to them, it made them smile, even laugh. Krish had never heard Aunt Parvati laugh like that in all the years he had known her, but he had seen her that night, had seen how her face had lit up like a moon, and even when the girl got up to leave, when she embraced them and kissed them both on the cheek and turned to wave goodbye, even then, Uncle Rampat and Aunt Parvati had smiled and smiled into the night as if it was enough that she had returned even if it was only to say goodbye again. She had left them and passed right by Krish, right by where he was crouched low in the shadow of the fence, but she had not looked at him, and Krish had moved out of the shadow and followed her her as she had moved steadily forward through the lane and over the bridge that led into Paradise.

He had walked quickly behind her, had even thought to catch up to her and ask her something, anything that came into his head but in all his grief and confusion he could think of nothing to say to her. He had only felt his feet stumbling about in the dark as she had glided through the night, had moved forward before him. There was no moon, and he had remembered that there were rumours that the men from Paradise were going to use the cover of darkness to attack

Coverton that night, that they were planning to come with sticks and cutlasses and bottle bombs to burn and beat and do even worse, and that everyone had drawn back into their homes and locked their doors and windows and were waiting for the night to pass and the darkness to be over.

But Krish had plunged himself into it, had rushed headlong through the night and followed the shadow of the girl, the thin wispy shadow, with no thought of any danger, and he had laughed at himself then, had laughed at the thought that he was being as foolhardy as his father had been. But there was no time to think of danger for the shadow was moving steadily forward and Krish had to hurry to stay close to it, and he had quickened his pace when they crossed the bridge into Paradise where Sampson was standing before a crowd of men. He had seen the dark giant standing tall against the night sky in middle of the main road and Krish had felt a fear then, a fear of the stick that Sampson held on his shoulder like a rifle because he knew how hard, how quick it could fall. He had felt afraid and had drawn himself into the shadow of the bridge even as he had seen the *devi* walk up to the men, walk slowly and calmly up to them. And, as she had got closer, Krish heard her singing to them, heard her singing a song of clear, high notes, a calming song like a lullaby, and she had held out her arms to Sampson, and sang to him about her baby boy who was to come into her arms and rest there forever. She had sung like that and reached out her arms to Sampson and Krish had seen then how Sampson had leaned over and put down the stick, the stick that still glistened with his father's blood, had seen him put it away then stretch out his arms to the *devi*, and Krish had heard him, had heard him say clearly through the darkness, 'Mammy!'

Krish had held his breath as the girl had taken Sampson's hand and led him to the canal, had held his breath when they waded out into the middle of the stream and when he had seen, seen clearly how the *devi* smiled at Sampson before the water had moved in to close over them. He had crouched low in the shadow of the bridge and watched until every ripple had widened and widened until they had disappeared and the water had grown still, and he had sat there and wept for his father, for the death and loss of him, had wept until he was exhausted and fell asleep for he had awoken to the warmth of the sun on his face, and when he had looked about him, had looked closely at the water of the canal, at the very spot where he remembered seeing the *devi* disappear with Sampson, all he had seen was the water's stillness, a stillness like innocence, and all his doubts, all his confusions had returned.

All the talk during the days and weeks that followed did not help for when everyone said that Sampson had disappeared, that he had run off into the interior, into the bush and into a mining camp to hide from the shame and the horror of what he had done, it only made Krish wonder more at what he had seen. He came to believe that it was a dream, an imagining in his head, and when he had looked and looked through the newspapers on the day after the riots and the fires and had found only a mere mention of a storm, of high winds that had swept in from the north and pushed the fire south to the tenement yards, to the shanty town that edged the city's southern boundary, a storm that had made the waves crash over the wall and made the waters of the Demerara climb its banks and flood the streets and houses of Tiger Bay, a riverside city slum, Krish became even more convinced that it was all an imagining that had come out of his grief and confusion. It was like a story that his father might have made up to console him, to quiet him, and Krish felt a deep sadness for his father then, felt sad that he had lived all of his life placing such store in myth and magic, and that he had missed out on the reality of the world, had missed out on its true existence.

He was reminded of it, was reminded of all the cruelties of that reality when Rodney fell, when he was assassinated, and he was glad that he knew how to embrace the worst of the world, how to embrace it as a steadiness, a surety, then move beyond it, move through it, and let the world take care of itself without benefit of any faith in it. He filled all the days that followed like that with work, and with keeping an eye on Uncle Rampat and Aunt Parvati who had grown old and looked to him as all the family they had left. With his brothers and their families gone, Krish, too, felt that they were the only people around who were close to him, and he took to dropping by in the afternoons and talking over all the day's news, telling them what he had heard about Burnham's latest moves, about how he was going to set himself up as president for life. But Krish spoke like that about the things that were going on about them in an even voice, spoke without anger or surprise, and he found that Uncle Rampat, too, would hardly make any comments about the politics of the place and preferred to tell him stories of his father and how they had crossed the *kala pani* holding on to nothing but each other and dreams, such dreams of the new world. And it was there, sitting in their bottom-house one afternoon late that Uncle Rampat and Aunt Parvati told Krish that they were going to leave their house to him.

They had already sold up their paddy fields and Auntie Parvati had long since turned down the pots and pans in her kitchen for good. They had no one else to leave it to, Uncle Rampat said, and since Krish was staying, since he was not planning to go to America, they thought that he should have the house. 'Sell it, rent it, do whatever you want with it,' Uncle Rampat said, and Krish told him not to talk like that because he had a good many years left to live, but Uncle Rampat only waved his hand and said that he had already lived too long, and that sometimes he wished that he had never lived to see the things he had, to see the world turn itself upside down like it had. The slave work of the cane fields had been bad enough, he said, and they thought they had faced the worst of it, had seen and felt the worst that the world could hand them. 'But all this,' he said and he turned his hands inside out, 'all this,' he said and he shook his head. 'It is more than a lifetime can bear,' he said, and he would often ask then about his brothers, ask how they were getting on and Krish would read them the letters that came from Mahendra and Vickram, and show them the pictures they sent of themselves and their families all bundled up in heavy coats and standing about in the snow and against trees that had lost all their leaves. The would look at the pictures and laugh and say that they would never have survived living in such a cold, cold country, and Aunt Parvati always said how she had watched them grow, grow up from babies, from small boys, and how it was the most blessed thing of all to watch your children grow into their lives, to watch them settle into their lives. She would talk like that then start to cry, so Uncle Rampat told Krish not to bring the photographs around any more. 'It's her heart,' he said. 'It lives with so many memories and I fear that it would break under the strain of too much remembering.'

Krish never felt bold enough to ask Uncle Rampat about those memories even though he guessed that they had to do with the girl they had picked up from the sea, the girl that he had heard his father and mother and even Sampson talk about, the girl who had run off, had run off like water itself, and who he had seen in a dream on the night of his father's funeral. But Krish never asked Uncle Rampat about it until Aunt Parvati died, until she left them, left him and Uncle Rampat in the bottom-house one evening late, left them with no words in particular, no words of farewell, and no goodbyes, and it was not until she left them like that with a smile and wave of the hand and Uncle Rampat came to Krish's house the next morning, well before sunrise, and said that Auntie Parvati had died, and started to weep and talk about her life that Krish felt that he could ask about the memories that had put such a strain on her heart. He made hot, sweet tea and sat with Uncle Rampat in the bottom-house and waited for the sun to come up, and Krish listened to him say over and over that he never did enough, never said enough, and now his Parvati was gone and it was too late, too late for anything, and Krish made assuring sounds then, made shushing sounds and told him that Auntie Parvati always knew how he felt, always knew how much he cared, and that he had given her a good life, the best life.

'Oh, my boy,' Uncle Rampat said. 'You don't know the pain, the heartache, the loss, how much she had to bear. I brought her here, took her away from all her family and brought her here. We ran away from things we could not bear because we were young and, perhaps, foolish, and a child, a baby girl was given to us, but then we lost her, lost her to the world. She came back to us once, that night when your father died – we saw our Neela then. She was just as we remembered her, all young and sweet, but she only came to leave again and your auntie's heart just went and broke itself all over again.'

And it was when Uncle Rampat spoke like that, when he said that the girl had visited them that Krish came to know that it had not been a dreaming in his head when he had seen the *devi* that day at his father's funeral, and had followed her that night, had followed her through the darkness, and seen her take Sampson down to the waters of the canal. The memory of it made him bold, and he asked Uncle Rampat about her, asked him everything, and even thought that it might distract him from his grief and turn his thoughts away from Aunt Parvati and her death. But Uncle Rampat did not say much. He only threw up his hands up and said that the girl was a wayward child who had wanted her own way with everything, but that they had loved her, had loved her as their own, and had indulged her with everything.

'She liked to sing in her sweet, sweet voice while she combed and combed her hair. It was a pretty golden comb she had, and she used to sit and sing to herself and comb her hair, her long, long hair, and your Aunt Parvati used to fret-up herself so about that, about what she called the girl's singing and hair-combing nonsense. It was why she wanted to get the girl married and get her feet settled properly on the earth. But then the girl just picked herself up and ran off one day and your Aunt Parvati was never the same again. Poor Parvati.' Uncle Rampat stopped then to weep and talk about his Parvati again, and all that she had borne in life. 'The girl left her comb behind, and it was your auntie's work every day to shine it up and put it back on the little dressing table in her room. And after we saw the girl that one night when she came back, your auntie lived all the rest of her days believing that her Neela left it behind because she was going to return for it one day and that when she did, she would stay for good. It kept her going all these years, that hope.' Uncle Rampat stopped to weep again, and when he spoke again, it was to remember Krish's father, his good friend Billa, and to say how he, too, had had such hope and belief in the world. 'He had that up until the very end, eh? He passed by my gate that day, that day he died, and waved to us and said that he had such news, such news for me and Parvati but then he went and met his death and we never knew, never knew all these long years what it was that he had to tell us. Do you know, son? Do you know what the news was?'

Uncle Rampat stopped and turned to Krish and Krish found that he could only shake his head, shake his head and say no, no, for he did not think that it would have been any good to say to Uncle Rampat just then that his father thought that he had seen the girl, had seen their Neela rising from the sea on a giant wave. He could not say it because he himself did not know what to believe about the girl. He did not know whether she was a wayward child like Uncle Rampat said, and his mother had always said, or whether she was indeed a *devi*, a divine being who his father saw being born out of the sea. Perhaps, she was both, Krish thought, and he shook his head and let Uncle Rampat go on with his talk about how everybody was gone, how Billa and Savo and now Parvati were all gone, and that the whole world was just dying and that he had nothing to look forward to but going on to meet them. Krish shushed him then and told him not to speak like that because he had a good many years left yet to live, and the sky lightened and the sun came up and met them like that in the bottom-house and everybody passing by in the lane saw them there, and the news spread through the village and everyone came by to tell Uncle Rampat how sorry they were, and to say what a good person Aunt Parvati was, and to ask about the funeral, and it was Krish who answered them, who told them that the cremation would take place that very afternoon on the foreshore, and that he had to get about and get everything ready.

The whole village came to pray and weep for Aunt Parvati, and after all the ceremonies were over and the flames had leapt and eaten into the pyre and into the pretty *dholi* on which Aunt Parvati was laid out, a *dholi* of white lace stretched taut over a bamboo frame, Uncle Rampat returned to sit in his bottom-house and weep and he reminded Krish that he was going to leave the house to him and that he was to do anything he wanted with it. 'Keep it, sell it, rent it,' he said and he waved a dismissive hand through the air when Krish said again that he was not to talk like that about dying, and that he might even outlive Burnham and see things get better, see them turn around. Uncle Rampat laughed at that and said that that would be the day, that that would be the day, and when Burnham did die no less than a few months later, Uncle Rampat laughed and asked Krish if he was a see-far man, asked if he was one of those people who could look into the future and see it clearly.

But Burnham died and nothing changed. His men simply took over the government, and even when they tried to make things better, even when they tried to changed policies and change direction, Krish paid little attention to them for they had voted themselves into government just as Burnham had done, and had even given themselves a bigger majority than Burnham ever had, had given themselves over eighty percent of the votes. He had little time to pay any attention to them because of all the changes that were happening around him as the people of his father's generation grew old and died. It was no sooner that Burnham passed on that Boysie Karran died as well, then Kishun and Janak followed, and it was then, too, that Uncle Rampat himself took ill and laid back in his hammock and died one day, died peacefully in his sleep. Krish came back from a morning's work in the city and got the news and found out that Uncle Rampat's good friend, the Reverend Davies, was with him at his final moment and when Krish bathed and dressed and got himself ready for the funeral, he went over to Uncle Rampat's house and shook the man's hand and told him that it was good, that it was good that Uncle Rampat was not alone during his last moments.

He had become friends with the man, had given up his vexations about the work he once did among the Hindu people to convert them to Christianity. He had picked up his vexations from his father and mother and from Aunt Parvati as well, and had grown up knowing that it was a dishonourable business and, all through the years, he never did anything more than nod or raise a hand in greeting whenever he saw the reverend around the village, or saw him even at Uncle Rampat's house. But the reverend was always leaving whenever Krish arrived so it was not until Aunt Parvati died and the reverend took to coming and spending more and more time with Uncle Rampat that Krish found that he could no longer avoid the man, and Uncle Rampat had joked about the reverend, had laughed and introduced him to Krish as the best see-far man he had ever met.

'This man here saw it all,' Uncle Rampat had said and had waved his hand about. 'He had seen it all as plain as day that it was all going to turn into a hell on earth.'

The reverend had laughed and turned to Krish and said right off, 'Your father never liked me. He thought I was doing the devil's work.' He had laughed and his frame had shook and Krish had seen how frail he was, had seen that he was nothing more than a bag of bones. The sun had turned him brown, had tanned his skin like leather and made it tough for he did little else than walk about the villages all day since his congregation had been taken over by an energetic young man who had gone abroad and studied the Bible and had come back and expanded the church and placed a grand cross on its roof. The Indian Christians in the villages flocked to hear him preach, to hear the young Reverend Edwin Seeraj, and the reverend became something old and worn, something to be tossed aside. He was forgotten by his congregation and by his people in Canada who had sent him out so many years before to gather up the souls of the Indians for Jesus.

'I would be a stranger there,' he had said to Krish that day when they first got to talking then he had laughed and said again, 'Doing the devil's work, your father said.' It was that, that he could laugh at himself, and that he was such a frail and pitiful figure that had made Krish let down his guard and give up his vexations, and he, too, had laughed and had found himself listening when the reverend continued. 'Your father was the first to fall, my boy. But he was saved from the worst. Perhaps, he was the one who was saved, saved from this hell.'

It was then that Uncle Rampat had told Krish how the reverend had foreseen all that had happened, had seen how the divide between the Indians and Africans would widen and deepen unless there was good leadership, good leadership that would know how to deal with it and hold it together.

'Yes,' Reverend Davies had said. 'But even I did not see how badly it would turn out. Even I did not foresee Burnham.'

'And what's going to happen next?' Krish had asked. 'What happens now?' he had asked, and the reverend had shaken his head and said that destruction would surely follow destruction, and that things would get much worse before they ever got better.

'It's the trials and tribulations of the world,' the reverend had said and when Krish had said that he sounded like he was talking about things from his Bible, he had said, 'No, no. I've long since given up on such beliefs. How can one bear witness to all that has happened here and still believe in heaven or hell or any redemption? The horrors wear away one's soul.'

'But his father, Krish's father – he believed to the last,' Uncle Rampat had said.

'Men who have overcome much in life do that, stay true to faith no matter what,' the reverend had said, 'because it is often their faith that has seen them through the worse.'

'Billa was such a man,' Uncle Rampat had said.

'He overcame much?' the reverend had asked.

'The *kala pani*, the crossing, the new life, the old life,' Uncle Rampat had said and Krish had remembered then all the stories that his father had told him, tales about Pondicherry and the Bay of Bengal and wrestling with the biggest *sura* in the sea, and tales about sea storms and goddesses, and had wondered, not for the first time, about the one story that his father told only to himself, the one he always threw out wide over the dark waters of the canal during their early morning fishing trips, and Krish had wondered whether it was something about that story that gave his father such faith. He would never know whether his father, had he lived, would ever have told him that story, would ever have trusted him with its secrets, and he had never asked Uncle Rampat about it, about whether he knew the story that strung together place names like Pondicherry and Tamil Nadu and Orissa. He had never asked him because he did not believe that Uncle Rampat knew it either for Uncle Rampat's stories of his father, of his *jahaji bhai,* always started at the depot in Calcutta, and they never told about the fishing boats, and the great sharks that his father had wrestled and brought down. Uncle Rampat only knew about the sea voyage and the baby that was born out of the restless sea, and about the big fight with Sampson, and he liked to talk like that in the afternoons when the reverend and Krish visited, liked to go over his life and tell them all that he knew. He liked to tell them how he had met his Parvati and how he had been bold enough to marry her in a *jaimaal* wedding, and how they had made a nice life in the new world. He talked like that and let his memory ramble on through the years and he often laughed and told them how he had planned once to buy himself a motor car, a long, sleek, silver car that he was going to drive about the countryside with his Parvati and the girl, the girl Neela, sitting up in the back like maharanis. 'Then she left, went away,' Uncle Rampat would say, 'and I never bothered with it again.' He always went quiet whenever he mentioned Neela, whenever any of his memories rambled on to meet up with her, and Krish and the reverend would let him rest his thoughts, would sit in silence and wait until he was ready to pick up the trail of a memory again. He laid out his life before them like a parting gift, like someone leaving them with the best of all that he was and all that he ever knew, and Krish and Reverend Davies always sat and listened to him in reverenced silence.

Krish was not unprepared for the news of Uncle Rampat's death for he had watched him become frailer with each passing year, each passing month, and he wondered then whether he needed to ready himself for similar news about his brothers for each of their letters in recent years had been filled with news of aches and pains and reports of illnesses. They were all getting older and Krish even thought that he himself might arrive at his final years without ever knowing the kind of faith that his father once held, for the world around him was continuing to fall apart and become more and more dismal. It inspired no trust, no hope, and his brothers never gave up writing to him about packing up and coming to New York. It was not too late, they said. But Krish knew that it was. He was too old, too set in his ways to make the adjustments that would have been necessary for a new life in a strange and distant land. He had grown accustomed to the village and the city, to the hardships of blackouts and shortages, and to all the hopelessness, and he did not believe that he could move about in any other world as easily.

And even if he were to leave then, after Uncle Rampat died, he would only have been a bother to his brothers. Vickram was ailing, and Mahendra was old and having knee pains, and he was living alone for Radika had died some years before and the children were all grown and were making their way in the world as young Americans. It was Krish who wrote to his brothers constantly and told them that they should visit, that they should come and see him, and they always wrote back and said yes, yes, but they gave him no dates, no definite times, and there were many days when Krish felt very alone. The only company he had left was the old reverend. He was about the only familiar face around him, and the man took to dropping by and sitting in the bottom-house with him, or lying back in a hammock, and they would pass the afternoons like that, would pass the afternoons in silence or in some rambling talk and wait for the night to close in, and Krish would always think that there were worse ways to pass the time than in such peace and quiet.

Krish was to remember that thought in the years and years that followed for it had no sooner passed through his mind, and he had no sooner come to like the calmness of his days, the ordinariness of his days, that the whole world changed, and he got caught up in its big excitement. He found himself laughing and talking to the reverend and to anyone who would listen of bright possibilities, of shining worlds, and of promise and hope. It all started with the fall of the Berlin wall and the death of Communism. There was no Red threat any more, no danger any more and America itself returned to make sure that the very next general elections would be free and fair. President Jimmy Carter himself came to look over the elections and Krish went out and cast his vote for Jagan. He cast his vote for the man who had promised them all the shining possibilities of the world. He was swept up in the momentum, in the merriment of the times, and he forgave Jagan for all that he had ever thought about him, forgave him his weakness and his naivety because everyone knew that Jagan was sure to win. He still had the majority Indian vote, and when he did, when Jagan won, Krish wrote long letters to his brothers and said that they should think of returning and spending their last years at home because everything was going to get better, everything was going to turn around. He told them that he would fix up Uncle Rampat and Aunt Parvati's house and that they could use both houses, that they could live between the two houses, and that all the children could come and visit, too. And after he wrote to his brothers, he went by the house to check on all that would have to be done to get it ready. He had not done much with it other than have someone go by regularly to clean it and trim the bushes and sweep the yard and keep the bottom-house tidy. But after he sent the letter off, he went and walked through the whole house for the first time to give it a proper looking-over.

He went through each room and tested the floorboards and checked the windows and doors, looked at the hinges and locks, and it was when he walked into the small room at the back of the house, a room that overlooked the garden in the backyard that still bloomed with hibiscus bushes, that he found the comb, the golden comb, lying on the small dressing table right where Uncle Rampat said it would be. It was lying there and sparkling in the light from the windows, and Krish laughed a little and picked it up and turned it about this way and that, and he saw that it was a pretty thing, a nice ornament, and he tucked it away in his shirt pocket and remembered all that Uncle Rampat had said about the girl and how she was going to return for it one day, was going to return for it then stay for good. Krish laughed again and closed up the house, and waited for his brothers' reply even as he got some carpenters together to fix the loose boards and tighten up all the hinges. The men talked and laughed as they worked and the foreman, a man from the village named Hardat, said that all the locked-up houses, all the abandoned houses were getting fixed up. 'Everybody's coming home, eh? Everything will get better now, eh?' he said and Krish said yes, yes, and laughed with him.

Everywhere that Krish went, everyone spoke like that, spoke about change and everything getting better. It was as if they had not breathed, had not truly breathed for nearly thirty years and had all suddenly been let out into fresh air. It was a heady feeling. People laughed and spoke in high voices and even the Africans settled down after they lost the elections, and Krish wanted his brothers to come home and see the world turn all bright and shining, and become the world that their father always knew was possible. But the truth was that they had grown old in a distant land and they did not have the energy to move again. They wrote to him and said that they wanted to stay close to their children and their grandchildren – Mahendra had three already – and that they both were seeing doctors and had to keep up with their checkups and medications. But they said that they were glad that everything was getting better, and that Krish would not have to suffer any hardships any more, and Mahendra said that he was glad that Jagan had his chance to shine, to shine at last, and that Pa would have been glad to see it happen because he was always a Jagan man. Krish laughed a little when he read that even though he was disappointed that his brothers were not going to return.

He had been looking forward to their company, had been

looking forward to swinging in the hammocks in the bottom-house and going over the day's news like they used to do ever since they were small boys. But the truth was that everybody had moved on with their lives and it was too much to hope that Vickram and Mahendra would leave their new life to return. And it was not too long after after their letters came that so disappointed Krish that Krish held his head in his hands and thanked god that his brothers had chosen to stay in New York, after all, had chosen to remain with their families on safe ground, for Jagan died, his heart failed him and he died just a couple years after taking office, and when he died Krish watched with horror as everything fell apart again. The promise of change, of hope – it fled, and a terror moved in, a homegrown terror that was armed with automatic rifles, an African terror, and Krish came to have fear, to have real fear of the threat that was pressing in from all sides. The Africans had had some grudging respect for Jagan, for him as an old man who had suffered much at the hands of Burnham, but with him gone, they saw an opening, a weakness in his party, and they took up arms and took their fight to the streets and to the villages, to the Indian villages all along the coast, villages like Coverton, and Krish found himself staying up with the men every night to keep watch, to sit with sticks and cutlasses and keep watch and hope that the Africans who were armed with AK-47s would not invade their village. They kept watch on the bridge over the canal that led to Paradise, kept watch on the main road for any movement, and Krish found himself thinking of the spot where his father died, found himself remembering the exact spot and how it had run with blood.

The villages sat side by side, were neighbours, but there was little movement between them any more. The dominoes games that Krish remembered from his young days were just that, a memory. No one from Coverton had reason to go over to Paradise, and the people of Paradise had no business in Coverton either and the violence that had brought his father down erupted again because Jagan had failed to secure the country by reforming the police and army, by reforming the armed forces. He had left them in the hands of the Africans and as the violence escalated and the terror beat and robbed and raped and killed Indians, Jagan's men found that they had no forces at their command, no forces that could go out and stop the terror and disarm the criminals. And when African academics and politicians moved in to give reason and justification for the terror, when they said that Africans were marginalized and discriminated against by the Indian government, Krish found himself shaking his head and wondering, wondering aloud to the reverend one afternoon about what they were hoping to gain. 'Even if they overthrew the elected government,' Krish said, 'they would not be recognized by the international community, they would not be able to form a legitimate government.'

'It's nihilism. Destruction for destruction's sake,' Reverend Davies said. 'That's reason enough.'

The old man said that then fell quiet and they stayed like that in the bottom-house until the night closed in and it was time for Krish to take down the cutlass from the crossbeams under the house's flooring and go out to help keep watch on the village. The cutlass was his father's. It had cut down sugar cane stalks, and had been used for all kinds of tasks around the yard, and when Krish picked it up and whipped it through the air he knew that his palm fitted around the handle much like his father's had. He had sharpened the blade, had rubbed it against a wet stone and had oiled its edge until it was a silver streak, and whenever he picked it up he felt his father's hand there, there on the handle with his own and that comforted him, gave him courage, even when the violence spilled over from the nights and ran through the daytime as the Africans grew more bold and invaded Indian village shops to rob and beat, and to kill, to shoot bullets into the heads of Indians, even old men like Yacoob Mohamed who was killed one day, one January day at three o'clock in the afternoon when six of the bandits robbed Dolly's Variety Store in Better Hope Village, and shot Yacoob dead as he sat on the bridge outside the shop, shot him for nothing, for nothing at all other than that he was an Indian.

Krish was among the thousands who went to the funerals, to the funerals of the Indians from the villages who were killed. They went to the funerals and wept because they all felt that it could have been them, could have been any one of them who could have taken the bullet to the head. The news of each day's attack, each day's invasion ran through the villages and brought new levels of panic and it was then, when the violence left the cover of night and ran about openly in the daytime that Krish heard a man speaking, an Indian man speaking plainly about the violence and its racial nature, speaking plainly about the failures of Jagan and his men, and about what had to be done.

'I am an Indian,' he said, the man named Ravi Dev, 'and I speak for myself and for my fellow Indians. In a society so divided, so divided by ethnicity and race, I would not presume to speak for Africans or Amerindians or any other group. We need leaders of all the various groups in our society to come together and speak to each other as equals, and I stand willing to work with such leaders. We must work together to create a government that includes everyone.'

The man spoke like that, spoke plainly about race and racism, and how it was the one issue, the most important issue that had to be tackled. He said it when everybody, when Jagan's men and Burnham's men, liked to pretend that there was no racism, no racism at all, and it was no surprise that they all turned on Dev and called him a racist, and said that it was he who was creating division in the society with his talk about racism and ethnicity, and when Krish brought up Dev's name in one of their afternoon talks, the reverend laughed and said that Dev would not last, would not last long on the political scene.

'Why? Why not, man?' Krish asked. 'He's talking the truth. He's putting it plain and straight.'

Krish heard the reverend sigh before he said, 'Truth means taking responsibility, means acting, means doing something to fix things. No one wants to do that. Jagan and Burnham lived well off the lie that there is no racism, and now their men are doing the same. Both sides gain from the lie. Whoever gets in to government, they proclaim the lie that they're the government for everyone. Everyone knows it's a lie but everyone is comfortable with it because no one has the courage to deal with the problem. It's easier to lie. No, Dev won't last long. Both sides will move in to get him.'

'Stewps! So you're being a see-far man again, eh?' Krish asked and when the old man just laughed and waved his hand about, Krish told him that he liked Dev for talking the truth. 'I'm going to support him, man. I'm going to join up with Dev's party. I like the man. He has courage and I'm going to stand with him,' he said then added, 'Look how Mahendra worked with Jagan for nearly twenty years, and it came to nothing. Stewps! Maybe it's time I take a stand, eh? My father used to say that fighting for what you know is right is the only kind of fighting that's worth anything, and I'm not too old yet to put up a good fight, eh?'

'You go and join up, son. Just know that Dev will not last,' the reverend said, and Krish sucked his teeth again and said that if everybody gave up like that then nothing would ever get done. And it was thinking like that, thinking that it was time he took a stand that made Krish go out the very next day and sign up to become a member of Ravi Dev's party.

He came to know the man up close, came to know that he had come back home from New York where he was a lawyer, had come back home like Krish had wanted his brothers to do, had returned to live at home when the Berlin Wall fell with a thought that he could help with all the rebuilding that would be needed. But Dev, like everybody else, was only to see everything fall apart again, and when the African violence started to move about freely in the Indian villages, in all the Indian neighbourhoods, Dev found that he could not stand by and watch that happen without taking a stand.

'Both sides have their security dilemmas,' Dev said at his public meetings. 'Indians were left unprotected by Burnham's government, and now by Jagan's because he failed to reform the army and police. Africans, on the other hand, feel they can never win an election because they are outnumbered in a country where voting is done, largely, along racial lines. They even justify all the rigging that Burnham did for that very reason. I say that if our country is to move forward we have to create a system of government where everyone is included and where everyone feels secure. We continue to ignore this issue at our peril.'

Krish stood up at Dev's meetings and cheered when the man talked, cheered like he once did for Jagan when he was a boy, and for Walter Rodney when Rodney took the fight to Burnham. He used his truck to fetch stages and banners and microphones for Dev's meetings all over the countryside like Mahendra once did for Jagan. Dev was going to run in the next general elections, and Krish was there with him at every village meeting, and was with him when the meetings had to move out of public spaces and into bottom-houses because Jagan's men started to burn their banners and rip down their posters, and scare the Indian villagers, scare them off from attending Dev's meetings. They told them that Dev was a *neemakaram*, a traitor, and that he was going to split the Indian vote and allow Burnham's men to regain the government. They said all that and tried to keep Indians from voting for Dev, but there were enough people like Krish, enough villagers all along the countryside, and enough of the educated Indians in the city, who saw the truth of what Dev was saying, and despite the best efforts of Jagan's men, he won a seat in parliament in the elections.

But even as Dev took up his seat, Krish feared that the reverend was right and that Dev would not last for, by then, there were rumours everywhere that Jagan's men had come up with a solution to the violence against the Indian communities. Krish heard about it first in the market square in the city, heard about the phantom force that had been created by one of the government's drug-lord friends, by one of the Indians who was big in the drug-running business that transshipped cocaine and marijuana from Colombia to the United

States. The old man had heard the rumours, as well, had heard all the talk about the phantom force as he walked about the villages, and Krish had no sooner exchanged all that he had heard with the reverend that the bodies started to fall, started to turn up dead, all riddled through with bullets. The television news and the front pages of the newspapers ran with blood as the pictures showed them, showed dozens of the criminals lying dead in ditches and trenches and by the roadside, lying dead right where they fell, and when Dev condemned the killings, when he pointed out that extra-judicial killings were not a solution, were not a long-term solution to the country's security issues, Indians all across the country turned on him, turned on him savagely and said that Jagan's men were right to call him a *neemakaram*.

Even Hardat, the foreman, even he met Krish in a village lane one day and cursed him out, cursed him out for being a Ravi Dev man, cursed him to his face and spat on the ground, and said that Jagan's men were doing the right thing. 'They're killing off all those criminals who were robbing and killing us, man. Why has Dev got a problem with that, eh? Stewps! He's not with us, man.' When Hardat pushed his face right into Krish's and spoke like that, spoke with so much anger about traitors and *neemakarams*, Krish found that he could not say anything, that he could not bring himself to argue or explain or say anything at all, and when he laid back in his hammock that afternoon and the reverend said, 'So it's over?' Krish replied, 'Yes. You were right. Dev will not win a seat again.'

'There's nothing like feeling good to make everyone forget how bad it was,' the old man said.

'It was a good fight,' Krish said.

'Your father would be proud,' the old man said.

'But we failed,' Krish said.

'No, my boy,' the old man said. 'There's no failure in standing up for what is right. Your father would be proud.'

It was then, when the reverend said again that his father would be proud, when he even made Krish out to be a hero for taking a stand, for taking a brave stand that Krish started to remember all that his father used to say to him about the way he understood the world. His father had spoken to him as someone who came from a land that had existed since ancient times. That gave a man patience and a certain way of looking at the world, gave him an understanding that time could not be hurried because there was an eternity of it, and that there were only so many events, so many possibilities that could occur in the span of a man's life. It was there that faith and hope came in, and Krish came to see then that to give up on faith and hope was to give up on life itself. It was a simple truth, a simple understanding, and Krish was surprised to find, as he lay in his hammock and listened to the old man's silence, that he had had that faith all along, that faith in the shining world and its bright possibilities. In the darkness that had settled around them for so many long years, he had seen only the doubts and uncertainties, had seen only the horrors but, that afternoon, when the reverend said to him that he had stood up, had stood up for what he believed to be right, he saw that it was faith alone that had made him stand with Walter Rodney, then stand even firmer with Ravi Dev. It was never an expectation of triumph since both men had the odds stacked against them. It was faith and the hope of a bright future, the future that his father always knew to be possible. He was his father's star, after all, he thought, and he laughed a little to himself and swung in the hammock, to and fro, and he let out a deep sigh and let go of his doubts and uncertainties, let go of them in the afternoon's silence. It was easier than he thought, for it had become second nature to him to worry and wonder and question everything even though he knew all along that his father would have never lied to him, would never have filled his head with foolishness.

His stories, all his stories of myth and magic, were as real and true as any that ever lived, and Krish wondered aloud whether his brothers remembered their father's words, and his many glorious stories, and if the memories made their last days easier for each letter came with more and more news of Vickram's failing health and Mahendra's illnesses. Krish spoke aloud about his memories and his brother's illnesses but he got no reply from the reverend for he had fallen asleep. He did that often. He fell asleep and might sleep like that until daybreak when he would shuffle off quietly after Krish made him some hot, sweet tea, would shuffle off to walk about the villages and pick up rumours and gossip.

Krish saw him sink lower and lower into his hammock as if he were disappearing by slow degrees, and knew that he did not have too many years to live. But unlike Uncle Rampat who had talked about all his life during his last days, the reverend preferred to hold with silence. He told no tales of home or family, of the people he had left behind all those many years ago in Canada, and he had little to say about all that he had seen and heard since he had come out to the colony. But Krish took to talking to him, endlessly sometimes, because he thought that it was good for the old man to stir himself and say a few words from time to time. And that was how he came to ask the reverend one afternoon late, how he came to joke with him about his great unbelief, about his giving up on the Bible and all its many miracles, and came to ask him about the girl, the girl, Neela, the *devi* who used to walk about among them, and whether he believed in any of the stories about her. There was a long silence after he asked the question, and Krish had given up on getting any reply when the reverend said, 'She's the only thing I believe in.' He thought he heard the old man chuckle then, and Krish laughed a little to himself, as well, and went upstairs to his room and tumbled through the drawers until he found the comb, the golden comb that he had put away after he had found it in Uncle Rampat and Aunt Parvati's house. He looked at the comb and saw how it sparkled, how it drew radiance from the moon and the stars in the falling evening light. He put it away in his shirt pocket and, that night, after the old man had fallen asleep, Krish went down to the bank of the canal and remembered all the days of his life, remembered the fishing jaunts with his father, and his mother's voice, her laughter, and even his father's death. He found that he could think of that moment, that he could relive the shock of it with calmness, and with a newfound composure. He had come far, he thought. He, too, had journeyed through troubled times. He, too, had had his crossing, his *kala pani* to bear, and he found that the new steadiness helped when he got the news of Vickram's death, and when, just five months later, Mahendra died as well.

When the news came, when he got the news of his brothers' deaths, first one then the other, Krish wound his white dhoti around his waist and tied the red and gold Madras kerchief over it and went to the temple to bow before the gods and goddesses and ask that their souls be given a safe and peaceful journey into heaven. He prayed as his father had taught him and he went regularly to the temple to pray and make sacrifice and to sprinkle warm blood on the goddess Mariemmen, and, in the quiet of the days that followed, he rediscovered all his books of history and literature, books that he had enjoyed reading as a boy, and he picked them up again and spent many of his evening hours reading, reading aloud at times to the old man even if he was asleep. He found his copy of the 'Bhagavad Gita' and remembered his father telling him how it was such books, such words as were written in that song of God, that had made them strong, strong enough to withstand anything, and Krish opened the book and read aloud, 'In the beginning/The Lord of beings/Created all men,/To each his duty.' He read the Gita for the sound alone, for the sound of the words and did not care that the old man was asleep or that there was no one to listen. It was enough that he could read, in the afternoon quiet, the words of Lord Krishna when he said to Arjuna as they stood on the field of battle, 'I am the birthless, the deathless,/Lord of all that breathes.'

And it was reading the Gita, reading the music of the words that gave him the idea to give over Uncle Rampat and Aunt Parvati's house to the *mandir* and the temple, the Tamil temple that he attended, and to let the pandits use it as a cultural centre to teach Hindi and Sanscrit and Tamil, and to let singers and drummers and dancers pass on all their skills to the children so that they, too, would know the history of their world, would know it through all the *bhajans*, all the hymns to the deities, through the beat of the *tabla* and *dolak* and *tapoo*, and through all the dances, through the *kathak* and *bharata natyam*, and the *kandyan*. And he did that, he presented the house to them and they named the centre for Uncle Rampat and Aunt Parvati, and whenever Krish passed by the house in the afternoon and heard how it drummed and sang and rang with the bells of the dancers' anklets, he knew that Uncle Rampat and Aunt Parvati would have been pleased with his decision.

When he did that, when he made his decision and settled the house, Krish felt that he, too, was settling in to his last years. He only worked for a few hours each day. He came and went in and out of the city but he made few new friends. He did not have the energy it took to make new attachments so he went about the world with a quick pace and easy manner that did not encourage long conversations. It was enough that the reverend came by each afternoon to lay back in a hammock and keep silence with him, or to listen to him read aloud from the newspaper or whatever book was handy. Or he would read the letters that came from his nieces and nephews, from Mahendra and Vickram's children, who wrote to him and sent him many photographs that were always full of smiling faces, faces that held traces of himself, and of his father and mother, and of his brothers. He saw it all there in the curve of a cheek, or in the sharp angle of a chin. They told him that he should get a telephone, and that he must get a computer and get on the internet so that they could send him email. They would send him photographs on the net, they said, of themselves and their children. They had some six children between them for his brothers' children were married and settled, and were all doing well and they never spoke of ever returning to their father's country. But they might visit, they said, they might visit and bring the children to see their grandparents' home. They had gone on holiday to India, they said, had taken the children to see the land of their ancestors and they had been to Mumbai and Kolkota and had seen the Taj Mahal. They had so many photographs, they said, and they told him again that he must get on the net, and Krish read the letters and laughed and thought how the only net he knew was a cast net, and when he replied to them, when he sat down to pen a letter, he told them about his life in the village, and his work, and how well the truck was running, and told them all about the old man, the reverend who came by to keep him company and how he once used to turn the Hindus away from all that they knew about themselves.

He never wrote anything about the politics of the place, never talked about Jagan's men, about their corruption and mismanagement, about the shame of it, and he found that he was glad that his brothers' children and grandchildren were far away from all of it, from all the continued devastation that came from corrupt men and their corrupt practices. But his brothers' children knew about it, knew more than even he did when the drug lord who, all the rumours said, had led the phantom force, the mercenaries who had killed the African criminals, was picked up by the US drug enforcement authorities and was brought before a New York court on drug trafficking charges. He confessed and took a plea bargain and when his lawyer was then charged and found guilty of witness tampering in the case, the entire saga, the entire story with all its horror upon horror became headline news, and Krish heard then what everyone already knew to be true. He heard about murder, about the training of criminals in the use of guns by army people, and about the hiding away of the bodies of beheaded men, of beheaded Indian cane-cutters by soldiers. It came out in the courtroom testimonies, the reports that read like some horror story. They seemed unreal except that all the names of the people involved had faces, faces that everyone knew as government ministers and army personnel and lawyers. His nieces and nephews wrote to him, wrote a flurry of letters about the damning revelations and wanted to know how he had survived, how he had survived it all, and when

Krish sat down to write a reply he found that he did not have the words that could describe how he had pushed on, how he had pushed ahead and come through to the other side. All he could say to his nieces and nephews was that he had survived because of faith and hope and prayer. He never told them about any of the hardships, or about the terror of the dark nights that had moved about with guns. He told them only about faith and belief, and when he wrote like that to them, he smiled a little to himself and remembered how his father had spoken to him, to him and his brothers like that, had spoken to them about keeping faith with the world.

When he finished the letter, Krish leaned back a little in his chair and realised that he was content with his life and all that he had done with it. He was somewhat surprised at that, surprised to find that he felt no anger about anything, felt no bitterness, and that he could think of no regrets. He did not even wonder what he might have done had he, too, gone off to New York, and, how his life might have turned out. Had he done that, had he moved away from the village and the house, the very house where he was born and where he could still hear his father's voice and listen to his mother in the kitchen, he believed that he would still have all his doubts, all his uncertainties about the world. That might have made him a bitter man, someone restless and quick to anger. There was something to be said for such a life, for such a contented life, he said aloud when he left his small desk and laid back in his hammock in the bottom-house, and listened to the reverend's silence.

He liked the old man's silence, liked that he did not come around to fill the air with questions or comments or small talk he had picked up during his day's walk about the villages. He liked to listen to the silence then go down to the canal in the early morning hours and cast a net out into the water and catch some fish, catch some small, jumping fish then sit there and wait for the sun to come up. He would lay back on the bank of the canal on moonless nights and moonfilled nights, and even believed that he had come to know that canal so well that he could feel the very pull of the full moon on the water, that he could see how high the water rose, and he would follow the length of it with his eyes to where it stretched itself out to the sea, to the Atlantic, and knew that it travelled all along the coast of the large northern continent, travelled to the cooler climes where his brothers' children had started over, had begun new lives far from their fathers' home and farther still from the home of their ancestors, from a place where the gods could span the earth in one stride and touch the very edge of the firmament. Those were grand stories, the finest that were ever told, and they were as fine as the story that he, too, had come to know, and he would push himself up to look at the spot where he had last seen the *devi*, had last seen her when she had disappeared beneath the water holding on to Sampson's hands. He would keep his eyes fixed on that spot for a long while for he was sure, as sure as he ever was of anything he had ever known, that one day the waters would part. Krish always put the golden comb into his pocket whenever he went down to the canal to pass the early morning hours, and he would take it out and turn it around and watch it sparkle in the first rays of the sun. It was a pretty thing and it had to be kept safely until the *devi* returned for it, and Krish decided that he would write down the stories that he had heard since he was a small boy and send them to Mahendra and Vickram's children so that they could fill in the story of their lives and know how their *aja,* how their grandfather had crossed the *kala pani* and become part of the history of the world.

He would tell them what a champion fighter he was, and how he had fought with the biggest *sura* with the sharpest teeth in the Bay of Bengal and had won, and how he had slain dragons and giants, and how he had been brave enough to set foot on a ship that had brought him to the new world, and he would tell them then the best story of all, the story of how their *aja* had been blessed enough to see a *devi* being born, a *devi* who used to walk among them and who was sure to return to their world to make everything right again for it was the way of the deities that, in every age, they returned to restore the world to righteousness. He would tell them then about the golden comb that the *devi* had left behind, and that it was a sure sign of her promised return, and that when she did, when she came back she would take the comb and draw it again through her long, wavy hair, and she would regain all her power, all her strength to weave her magic upon the earth. He had the comb and was keeping it safe, he would tell them, and he would tell them that he would show it to them when they came to visit, and they would see for themselves how it glittered and how pretty it was and they would know, just as he did, that the *devi* was sure to return for it one day. He would tell them the story so that they would know the whole of it, and they would tell it to their children, and Krish thought that if they were to say to him that he was a fine storyteller, as fine a storyteller as ever lived, that he would tell them that it was their grandfather, that it was their *aja* who was the finest storyteller of all the world and that it took faith, faith, such as he alone had, to make such a story live.

Krish was sure that the story would never be lost, that it would go on and be told for ages yet just as he told it to himself far into the night to the waning moon and the far spread of stars. It was as magical a tale as had ever been told and if he ever came close to losing the thread of it, of losing hold of all that it meant, he only had to look at the golden comb to see how it glistened and glittered to know for sure, as sure as his father was, how it would all turn out.

Om shanti shanti shanti
Hare om

Also from Cutting Edge Press:

A Death in the Family
Ryhaan Shah

When Mohammed Ahmad Ally dies, his family gathers for the religious rites and burial and recall the troubled relationship they had with him. He had lived by tradition and by his deeply held Islamic views, and his children, as he always said, were there to make him proud.

He had been a dominant and domineering figure in their lives, had arranged the marriage of his elder daughter, Maryam, to the son of a good friend; had sent his only boy, Khalil, off to New York to study law; and had disowned his younger daughter, Dee, for marrying a Hindu.

Even as friends and business colleagues remember Ally as kind and generous, his children and sister-in-law Hamida, his late wife's youngest sister, remember a different man, a man who had been authoritarian and bigoted.

The family open up to each other and, in the process, resolve issues that had been seething below the surface of their own relationships with each other. Ally's death becomes a transformative event that leads them to begin to renew their familial ties…